I0629708

Just Stories

by
Lawrence Chalfin

Dedication

To all those who, whether in reality or fantasy,
have touched my path
and left the memory traces that grace these stories,
I thank you with all my heart.

Acknowledgements

To Jacob Miller, my editor, words cannot express the deepest appreciation and gratitude I feel. Your steadfast support, honest critique, and encouragement have made this collection a reality. To Susan Glattstein, my special friend in life, who helped design, format and proofread these efforts and never laughed once, except at my less-than-worthy puns and jokes. To Barbara Saslow who nudged me forward as I was about to move backward. To Steve Chalfin, the most loyal brother one could have, whose editorial consultation advanced this collection. To Aaron Chalfin, the best son a father could have, who read these stories with a helpful eye. To Brittany Chalfin, my loving daughter-in-law and a future Charlotte Bronte, much gratitude for your understanding of the journey of a writer. Finally, to all my friends who tolerated my self-absorption and maintained their loyalty, a heartfelt thanks. I consider myself a fortunate person to have all of you.

Table of Contents

Taffy Family Village

Mark clutched Just-a-Dog, his soft stuffed animal and thought of his mother's smile when she'd first placed him into his arms. "He is just a dog, Markey, my sweetie little boy, but a very special one." The dog would stand guard next to him when the Dart Baggers tried to attack with their poisoned wing spears. Today, Mark also eyed Wendell, his gray and white corduroy kitten, resting on the rocking chair. He reached for kitty's ear to hold along with Just-a-Dog because something was going on. Even at four-and-a-half years, Mark knew that. He touched the soft part of his own ear with the thumb and second finger of his free hand. He wished he had the bumpy cloth diaper that he sometimes hung over his head but that was resting inside his pillowcase at the end of his bed. He settled for putting his Universe Man power ring on, hoping it would not turn his finger yucky blue like it did when he kept it on overnight.

His mother moved towards him from the kitchen. Mommy looked pretty. She was wearing a red blouse with a bow, and a black skirt. Her shoes were shiny black just like the helmet worn by the wicked Father John, King of the Dart Baggers. She must be going out later, Mark thought. Maybe Auntie Ellen was coming over and they would play "Catch me if you possibly can." Mommy's face was painted; her lips and cheeks were pink. She had things stuck on her ears that flashed. And she smelled good, like a bowl of peaches.

The telephone rang; it must have been for the one, two, three, fourth time this morning. Mark wiggled his fingers to the sound and the meaning of four in his mind. His mother's green eyes sparkled. She had just washed her brown hair this morning over the bathtub and now it was puffy, like the air underneath was blowing it up. After breakfast she had used a toothpick to clean prune bits that had gotten stuck on her front teeth. She laughed a sheep laugh each time she spoke into the phone. The sun, shining through the half-open window, put a golden light on the wood floor that already had lots of dark icky spots. Mark did not see any monster shapes or dust balls from the sun's rays and that made his tummy feel better. Later, the weather would be warm enough for the older boys upstairs to listen to their radio on the fire escape. His mother would never let him do that.

She turned to him saying this was the day Daddy was finally coming home. Mark knew Daddy was a soldier on a ship near a land called The Filerpreens, for the longest time, but now the boat was coming back to America. Daddy would have to go first, Mommy said, to Angel Island near San Francisco to get a clean uniform. Then he would fly on an airplane all the way home to New York. Mark hoped Universe Man would fly next to the airplane and protect it from the thunder guns on Father John's air whacker. There were lots of Dart Baggers in The Filerpreens, Mommy told him, but they had all been captured by General MeCarta. He trapped them with a big net and their poison spilled out onto the dirt. Some of the soldier men had hurt their arms and legs and got blinded, but not Daddy. He was a strong man and he protected himself.

What's a Daddy, again? Mark knew the answer but, still, there were moments when he was not so certain. There were pictures of his Daddy all through the house. Mark's favorite was the one of Daddy standing on a boat in a bathing suit, holding up a big fish and smiling. Daddy had a bunch of hair under his arm. Under his own arm there was nothing but a brown freckle; he had checked many times. It was confusing, thinking about Daddy. One moment he had an image in his mind of a large man with black hair and moustache, but, in a flash, it was gone. His head felt crowded today like it never had before. He nestled Just-a-Dog under his chin and whispered to Wendell, "Hello cat. Meow, little cat."

The doorbell rang. His mother breezed past him, that puffy hair of hers rising even more. Her smell was in the air; Mark could taste the bits of peach pit she sometimes forgot to remove when she served those yummies.

The door opened. From a safe distance Mark saw a tall man in a strange looking hat with a huge beak. There was something shiny in the middle of the hat above the beak. It made Mark think of that nutty bird, Woody Woodpecker, who bothered everybody with his silly laugh.

The man was wearing a uniform the color of caramel candy. There were colored ribbons hanging from the shirt, near his heart area, just like in one of the pictures that Mommy had put of him on the piano in the living room. Daddy's eyes looked wet, like he might cry, standing in the doorway. His hair was short, close to his head, but still black. Mark searched for the moustache but it was not there. Daddy must have gone to Big Al Zimmer, the barber man, just like he did. He must have gotten the monsterest red lollipop before Mr. Big Al cut his hair off. The Daddy man ran into the house; he took off his hat and threw it all the way to the couch in the back of the living room near the piano. He then began kissing Mommy on the lips.

"What, what, is going on…?" Mark muttered to himself. His mother lifted one of her black shoes, like maybe her knee hurt, but she was kissing the man called Daddy back. Yes, she was kissing the man back. Was Daddy a secret spy, and a Dart Bagger? Maybe he was using a poisoned wing spear or worse, a foot fang, so he could put Mommy to sleep and carry her away. Mark was frozen, torn by two powerful urges: to turn and run to his room, or to stand and watch.

Soon the man let his mother go and turned his eyes to him. He was smiling, an even bigger smile than in the picture where he was holding the fish. Mark saw his Daddy's eyelids open, showing large blue-gray eyes, which were round like marbles. Mark was afraid the man's eyeballs would leap out of his head and land on the floor. Daddy's lips were also cracked and had white crust-like marks on them as if they had been out in the cold too long. When that happened to Mark, his mother rubbed some creamy stuff on them which made the hurt go away fast.

"Well, who do we have here?" the man hollered. "Your Daddy's home for good. Boy have I missed you; the last time I laid eyes on ya, you were a little tyke, seven months old, crawling on all fours."

With that, the man pulled Mark up toward him firmly but gently. The man's chest was gigantic. Mark tried to imagine the hair that must be on it, and under Daddy's arms.

Mark was scared. He closed his eyes shut for as long as he could so no light could come in them. He also had to pee badly and he did not want that to come out. Mommy would have a mean look whenever she had to clean up his accidents. There was no telling what this man would do. Most of all, he did not want to cry, so when his eyes opened he next tried to hold his breath. That never, ever, worked very long. Something told him to protest, like maybe putting up his hand as the man, his Daddy, reached for him and turned him round and round in the air; something else told him not to smile. Universe Man never smiled once when he was captured by Father John and taken to his hidden palace on Sky Mountain. But he could not obey these thoughts. And besides, he was feeling dizzy.

There were new smells. This man did not smell at all like his mother. He smelled like Bonamo's Salt Water Taffy from the Atlantic Ocean. Licorice was Mark's favorite flavor even if it did get stuck on his teeth, just like the prune bits did on Mommy's. Anyway, taffy was a word he'd heard many times before. Taffy Family Village was the name of a place in lots of stories Mommy read to him at sleep time. Fritz the Bull Frog, Wanda Wanamaker Weasel and Samuel J. Snail were the elders of the village. They and the rest of the animals were always getting in and out of trouble there, but it was a happy place.

There was a weirder odor coming from the man's hairy neck and underarm area: oily, peanut-like. The caramel candy uniform shirt that Daddy had on reminded Mark of the stiff wrapping paper his mother used when she would send presents to Grandma and Grandpa. They lived on a farm in the country with cows and pigs. There was stinky pooh everywhere there.

Daddy's tie was tucked into the middle of his shirt. Mark could feel it as Daddy held him. Mark dropped Wendell. He looked down at the kitty lying on the green rug with his eyes staring up at the ceiling. He did not reach for him. Was the cat purring? Wow! Just-a-Dog was now draped around the giant man's left shoulder. Was the special dog barking a happy bark? And his mother had moved closer to him and Daddy. She was crying and laughing at the same time.

"That terrible, terrible war is finally over and now I have my two boys here, safe and sound." Tears were running down her cheeks and mixing with the pink paint.

Mommy must be right about this, Mark decided. Sometimes the way she'd say things, with her lips shaking, he knew she meant business. She got it right almost every time. She also looked a lot like Princess Verna Lee who Universe Man was going to marry after he put all the Dart Baggers in jail. Mommy's words reminded him of how the stories of Taffy Family Village ended, with everyone going to be happy for awhile.

The next day Mark asked his mother if the Daddy man could read him a story at sleep time. He felt the jumping feeling in his body he'd felt before but this time it was even more.

Daddy was on the middle of the bed. He was going to read the story of the founding of Taffy Family Village. The bed sank in the middle when Daddy sat down. His leg looked like three people put together. If he was a Dart Bagger, he might be even stronger than Father John. That was a spooky thought. If Daddy was a hero guy, though, he could sit on top of Father John and stop him from using his evil weapons. Mark sat cross-legged in front of his pillow. He pulled the blanket, rising from the cool sheet underneath, toward his tummy. Daddy kept staring at the book. His eyes were moving fast from side to side. What was he thinking about?

"Here we go sonny, the story of "The Founding of Taffy Family Village.""

Daddy cannot read the way Mommy can, Mark thought to himself. He stops a lot and keeps turning the pages of the book back and forth. He also says words funny. It takes him the longest time to say Cro-man-thing-ton, the name of the island that had the big wave come over it from the ocean that blew the roof off Samuel J. Snail's house deep under the ground and that blew Wanda Wanamaker Weasel out of her kitchen, and that smothered Fritz the Frog so much that he almost couldn't breathe. The animals were going to be drownt but they helped each other and builded Taffy Family Village.

Mark felt chilly even with the blanket covering him. He stopped listening to Daddy's up and down voice. He checked for kitchen noise. He did not hear any, which meant his mother had finished cleaning up and would be coming to him to wish him sweet dreams. She came there every single night. When the story was over Daddy leaned over and touched Mark's shoulder with the fingertips of his right hand.

"Your mother must be the best reader in the whole wide world."

"She is."

"Did she read to you a lot while I was away?"

"Every night."

"Thanks for letting me read tonight." A shadow passed by the far window. Mark hoped it was Universe Man riding through to guard the house.

Daddy reached for a paper bag he had on the floor at the side of the bed. The bag was shaped like a kooky hat. It was long and kind of curved from whatever was inside it.

"I got you something today at Macy's I thought you might like," he said, fumbling with the mysterious hat bag holding the surprise.

Daddy stood up and like magic he pulled out a…a…stuffed animal, a…elephant. He held it high to the ceiling.

"This here is Tumpy, the baby elephant with the gray mohair coat and the red leather feet and the laughing mouth. Imagine that, a laughing mouth." Mark reached under the sheet to get Just-a-Dog who was snuggling next to his feet. The stuffed animal his daddy was holding up high was huger by lots and lots. Yes, the elephant did have a smile, Daddy was right about that. This elephant might be special. Mark could introduce him to all his stuffed animals and even the animals of Taffy Family Village. He could have a big party for them and have red balloons stuck to the wall and a big layer cake with chocolate icing to lick.

"Look at this, Markey, he can sit. He can stand. He can tumble." Mark watched in amazement as the Daddy Man moved Tumpy on his bed. Just then his mother walked into the room.

"Do I see a smiling boy?"

It was possible that Just-a-Dog would move and now become the outside guard against Father John and the Dart Baggers, and against the wicked fire-breathing dragon who came up from the swamp at night, and against the ghost man shapes in the hall. The Daddy man and Tumpy might be the inside guards, closest to him, just in case something went wrong. Yes…yes. It would now be safer to fall asleep.

There was a crack of light at the bottom of the door to his room. Lying there in his bed in the midst of calm air and new fragrance Mark removed the bumpy diaper from his pillowcase.

It was made of cotton. Mommy had said many times that cotton was strong and lasted forever and ever. The diaper fell to the floor. His head now fit perfect on the soft feeling center of the pillow. He had removed the Universe Man power ring and placed it next to Tumpy. He gave the ring a push and then a pinch but it stayed hard. It was brave. It was strong and powerful. His last thought before the darkness took him was of Universe Man riding White Marsh, his silver stallion, really, really, fast through the Emerald Tree Forest. He was going to Princess Verna Lee's house. The beautiful princess would be waiting for him there near her flower garden. And she would be smiling a big smile, the way Mommy did when she talked about Daddy.

৪৩

The Home Run

Steven considered himself a lucky man. At seventy-six years of age, his wife had held her looks. The outline of a sweet figure was still there—small supple breasts, and a high waist with sublime love handles draped over it. Her legs were long, and topped by even spaced thighs that turned in at just the right angle. Steven loved caressing the hidden side of those thighs, imagining he was heading into an unknown part of a forest. He didn't mind that Sallie was shorter now and that her back was rounded and that her skin had its share of wrinkles. Her face and arms were creased, freckled, and furrowed, with birth marks that had become familiar to him. Her hair was curly, a mix of white and dark silver. In earlier years her mane was wilder, red-edged and loose-threaded, and flowed to her lower back. Doc Graves had just diagnosed Avascular Necrosis in her hip, with replacement surgery likely in the next three years. Steven worried the condition was aggravated by her past habits, but Graves told both of them to keep active. "Living tissue needs stimulation," he said.

In a month, they would be married thirty-eight years, well past four decades if their five-year courtship was included. Steven felt comfortable with the woman opposite him. There was not much he hadn't seen or experienced with her. He did his best to adjust to her habits. Sallie was often pissy, reacting to dumb things that would never bother him. If a dog was yelping, leashed next to a parking meter on the street, she'd stop and wait with the mutt, stroking and talking to it gently until the owner showed up. She would point out the symptoms of dog panic—the panting and aggressiveness, and how separation time should come in small doses and be partnered with affection. Then there was the time she told a big guy driver who'd backed his SUV into a parking space ahead of her that he must've had a small penis to pull a stunt like that. "Sweetie, you are going to get me killed one day," Steven told her.

She was into community stuff too—protesting cutbacks at the St. Anne's Branch Library, helping to delay a hi-rise condo until the builders agreed to a child care center on the ground floor, and signing a petition asking the Transit Authority to keep its buses off residential streets. She'd made a few enemies with her strong mouth. There was one protest letter, though, she had refused to sign—the one that demanded the city close the homeless shelter that opened in the middle of the night on their block. "Poor people down on their luck gotta live somewhere," she said.

Steven knew she needed nine hours sleep. Before menopause, there were a few days each month when she was touchy, cranky, and pushing him off, and he'd learned to leave her alone. Other times she'd cozy to his tone, and buy him a Brooks Brothers shirt on sale. She'd make wild puddings, mixing flavors to tantalize him and then nestle close at a movie of his choice. Her favorite colors were purple and coral.

Steven met his wife at the water fountain in the back halls of the Unitarian Church. It was not on Sundays that they graced the nave with their attendance for church ritual, but rather the mid-week evening meetings held in the fellowship hall that made them whole. The church made space for

Twelve Step groups, giving troubled souls a safe environment to confront their compulsions and re-assess their self-destructive patterns of living. Sallie attended Alcoholics Anonymous meetings, sometimes Narcotic Anonymous ones, while Steven went to Gamblers Anonymous. His first marriage ended after two fractious years when his wife discovered he'd taken her hidden stash of cash. He'd pushed her down the stairs of their house and then struck her. The violence freaked him; his sponsor helped him to put more of what he sulked about into words. The possibility of replicating such violence still weighed on him. Steven compensated with a penchant for order: no dishes left in the sink overnight, the laundry done on Saturdays and finished by noon, and income taxes posted to the IRS a month early. He'd never hit Sallie, preferring to retreat if they argued. If anything, she'd come closer to brutish behavior with her contentious nature. Time and practice was each their ally and Steven learned through years of practice the boundaries never to be crossed. He honored a higher spirit that warned never to be deliberately hurtful to each other. It was this unwritten contract that had allowed his love to prosper. Sallie offered him excitement and passion; he hoped he offered her consistency and continuity.

They'd waited months before making love, heeding the advice of the Twelve Steppers who encouraged them to consummate their friendship first. To their amazement, it had worked. Their lovemaking started out wild and frenetic, as if they'd dropped themselves into bubbling lava of a volcano. Soon it became slower, softer, with a fused appreciation of the other, and without aphrodisiacs or mind-altering enhancers.

Today she wore denim pants and a blue chambray work shirt which meant she'd garden and tend the community flower pots placed around the cul-de-sac on the dead end street near the drive adjacent to the park that was near to the boat basin on the river which gave the neighborhood its raison d'etre.

"Oh no, oh my God, oh my God, no, no, AAH…AAH… please God," she shrieked, her face flushing. She pushed the newspaper away and rose from the breakfast table as if she was gagging. She forgot about the cat who jumped from her lap, whisking to the safety of the broom closet. Sallie stared past Steven, the redness in her face vanished, replaced by a white pallor.

"What's the matter?" Steven stood and reached for his wife with hands extended from his terry cloth robe. "Honey, what's wrong?"

"Some…one died, you know, from back in my dark days," she said, trying to firm herself. She pointed her finger to the right side of the obituary page of the *New York Times*, which now lay on the black and white tiled kitchen floor. Steven retrieved the paper, his pulse quickening. What could have made her blanch out like that?

"This here…is an article about Danny Emerson, the ballplayer who spent most of his career in the minor leagues. Jesus, I remember him. He's the one that got that hit for the…is this who you mean?" Steven looked up and knew the answer. Sallie was now whimpering softly.

"You knew this guy? You never told me that?" He felt a wave of jealousy. He tried to shut down the grinding sensation in his stomach.

"I told you everything, Steven. He was just a part of…" Sallie curled her fingers making them appear arthritic. Steven made a more careful read of the obituary.

DANNY EMERSON, 70
CAREER MINOR LEAGUE BALLPLAYER
SUCCUMBS AFTER FREAK ACCIDENT.

Danny Emerson, 70, who spent twenty-one years in minor league baseball, died Friday night when a concrete slab of Goldens Bridge gave way impaling him in his pickup truck, killing him instantly. A week ago Mr. Emerson had been involved in the rescue of Carey Watson, age four, who had fallen into her family's artesian well. Mr. Emerson was among the first to reach the girl, helping to lift her to safety with ropes attached to his waist. He was honored for his heroic efforts.

Mr. Emerson had over nine thousand minor league at bats from Class D to Class AAA baseball. He is most remembered, however, for his twenty-four major league at bats and five hits, all with the New York Yankees, the last being his pinch hit bloop single in 1980, when he was forty-years of age, that clinched the pennant for the team. Emerson's lifetime minor league average was .262. After his playing career, Mr. Emerson remained in the game scouting for the Yankees. He also ran a plumbing supply business in Friendship County, New York.

There are no known survivors. Jonathan Cooke, team owner of the Yankees, announced a memorial service would be held Saturday at 11:00 AM at Marble Collegiate Church in New York City. In lieu of flowers, donations can be made to the Friendship County Little League Association where Mr. Emerson had been a longtime volunteer coach.

Glancing back at his wife, Steven realized that whatever had moved her, beyond Emerson's passing, was still in control of her. He was used to her signals of distress—the fixed gaze, the locked eyes, quivering lips, migraines, and restless left leg. Her voice could shift octaves quickly and erupt with a ferocious force. Steven's body stiffened because he knew something would be expected of him. He felt wetness under his armpits and in the small of his back. He loved his wife, though, and that made him fight his inclination to turn away.

"Sweetheart, come here," he said, moving past the breakfast table to offer her a protective cover. He walked her to the living room and stood until she seated herself on the sofa. She put one of its white pillows across her tummy. Steven pulled the hickory rocker toward her and seated himself on it. Sallie remained ashen; the whitish curls on her crown looking more stiff and angled. "The goddamned past keeps rearing its ugly head, eh? Come on, sweetie, we've been down this road before. We've had lots of practice. Remember all those sessions with Dr. Brenner?"

"Well fuck that old square-faced, asshole shrink," Sallie said, bursting from her disconsolate state. She put her head down to the pillow and gently rocked herself.

"Hey, that asshole shrink would say it's not just the cream that rises to the top but the gook has to come up with it as well."

"The gook will bury you every time" she mumbled. "I can't go through this anymore."

"Look, there's nothing you can say about the way you're feeling now that I haven't felt as well." Steven felt his eyelash flutter.

"What, now you're going to be my fucking shrink? What do you know about the price of fish?"

"I know about your drugs, the heroin, the messing around you did, and the night in the slammer in Chicago, that's what I know. And you know about my craziness."

"Yeah, I do. Anybody who has to have their toothbrush facing north and their vitamin pills laid out every night...well, he's croaking in his own way."

He wanted to throttle her at that moment, but Brenner had said to bypass the first impulse coming from your gut and listen to your head for the second one.

"So, tell me about Danny Emerson. Come on…get your head out of that pillow; you're going to hurt your neck." He knew his tone had turned assertive and that frightened him.

"It never stops," Sallie sat up. "Whenever there's a reminder, it all comes back at you. I'm not going to sleep tonight, and if I do, one of those nightmares will torture me."

"You'll sleep, baby, you will."

Steven pushed the rocker closer to her and placed his right arm on her sagging shoulder. He felt his eyes moisten over the next few minutes of silence but then, as if faithful to their relationship, or maybe to herself, Sallie began to speak.

"I met Danny Emerson once. It was in the summer, 1959 in Akron, Ohio. It was at a place called The Shady Tree Motel, and it was in Suite 1A, and it was at 1:13am. I know that sounds crazy to you, but I remember looking at my watch, just before he came into the room."

"Hey, you don't have to tell me the details if it makes you hurt. What, you had a one night stand spiked by heroin?"

Sallie motioned for him to be still and continued. "I lived in Akron maybe six months. I was traveling with Mindy then. I told you about her. She's dead many years now, poor thing. I still think about her. Well she had a boyfriend, Pete Marston, who owned a tavern, The Red Pony Bar and Grill, on a truck route in the older section of the city. When she shacked up with the guy, I decided to stay on as well. We were heavy into our habits then and Marston had a great street connection for China White."

"I never knew you'd been in Akron, the Rubber Capital of the World."

"Ha, don't make me puke. I learned the rubber guys of Akron did a lot more than rack tires. I had a room upstairs at the main house, next to the restaurant, and I could take anyone up there I wanted." Sallie paused and stared at her husband.

"I'm okay." Steven said. He remembered the story about Mindy. Had she overdosed accidentally, or was it a considered exit from her crazy life? Sallie swore Mindy would never have taken her life, but who knew what was in the mind of a deluded addict. There was a time when he'd worried about his wife's blue periods, her oversleeping, poor appetite and sullenness, and whether she might ever contemplate something like that. She placed her hand for a brief second in Steven's, before moving it back to her knee.

"There was a minor league baseball team in town, the Akron Angels. What a ridiculous name. Believe me, they were anything but angels. The town elders put those lame-brained boys on a pedestal in the downtown square every weekend, introducing them as future Hall of Famers. Half of them were overweight country bumpkins who'd dropped out of school by the eighth grade. Anyway, they were the lowest class professional team. Class A, I think?"

"Back then in the fifties the lowest minor league level was Class D."

"Oh, yes, you're right. I remember now, it was a Class C team. The C must've stood for *catastrophe* because that team never did win much." Sallie paused again. "I know you're going to hate me, Steve. Are you sure you want hear the rest of this?"

Steven sensed she might cry again and roused himself despite the hollow feeling in his gut. "Sallie, Sallie, of course I do. I didn't know anything about your time in Ohio. Please honey, get it out."

"Okay, just listen, will you. Don't judge me, like you always do."

"Nobody is going to judge you."

"Okay, okay. Where was I? Oh, well those Angel players, they'd come to The Red Pony after their games. They guzzled down the beer and wine. Marston watered down the hard drinks, though, that slimy bastard. The baseball boys played pool or darts and told foul-mouthed jokes. Saturday nights we had a talent show, with combos of blue collar yokels trying to make ends meet and off key singers and studs, crooning as if they were smooth like that cry guy fellow; what was his name… Johnnie Ray"

"Johnnie Ray? The Nabob of Sob? Nobody was cooler than him on stage, even if he was half-soused."

"Yeah, that was him. The Atomic Ray, right? We'd heard he might have been alcoholic. Well, he's six feet under now; his liver must have burst. Maybe he's lying next to Mindy. Jesus, Steve, I'm not coming out of this."

"Aw, baby, you will. You always have." Steven could not think of anything else to say. Sallie was in another place, and that made him fidgety. The masks of predictability, of routine, of certitude, and of structure were the ones he felt most comfortable with. He was stalling for time, but he didn't know why or with what purpose in mind.

"What about those Angel guys?"

"To me, most of those Angels were babies just starting out with big notions and dreams. They acted like stardom was an entitlement. There was also a mix of older guys on the team, veterans trying to hang on, feeling they'd been held back by the manager and coaches. One of the team leaders was a catcher named Willie Shortz. Everybody called him Jockey, which after awhile wasn't even funny."

"I never heard of him. Did he ever make a major league roster?"

"The majors, are you kidding? That skinhead was headed back to Palookaville to the Hall of Shame. He was small, you know, in height, but he was built like a tough shelled turtle and he had a wicked temper. Most of the boys were afraid of him. He was an enforcer, on and off the field. Well he and I had a thing. He came upstairs with me the most. I don't know why I chose him, well, maybe I do. He may have shamed me at the end but for a time he protected me like I was his virgin Momma. And he and Marston were buddies and…"

"You had an affair with this Willie Shortz guy?"

She shot an angry glance at him. "Don't whitewash this thing. Willie Shortz was my pimp, yeah, my fucking pimp."

"Well you must've been out of it, then."

"You could say that. Those baseball junkies, all they ever wanted to do was to get drunk, soar with their fantasies of stardom and then get laid at midnight. Do you want to hear more?"

"Sweetie, of course I do." Steven said. She closed her eyes for a brief second and then went on.

"Willie would set me up with townie types, locals who'd heard about what I offered. He gave me cash for putting on a happy face…I just wanted the heroin. Willie made sure I was well supplied which is why I felt safe with him. Okay, here comes the worst part. Are you…?" He inched back on his chair.

He knew she was eyeing him, noticing the front part of his foot pressing down hard on the carpet like he was stamping out a cigarette. He'd smoked in past years when he became jittery and driven, especially in football season when he made wild bets on hunches. Steven loved writing the checks and balancing the books, but Sallie let him know that she'd move everything back into her name if he started his wicked habit again. He motioned with his arm for her to continue.

"One day, Willie came up with the idea that I should, ah, fuck the starting lineup of the Angels.

"What?

"Not the pitcher, mind you. He must've had a reverence for pitchers, like they could mess up their arms or heads if they participated in a stunt like that. My god, I'm so ashamed. This is so morbid, I know." She turned away.

"Look, I didn't know you then; this is past life, honey, what's done is done. I did nasty stuff, too."

"Stuff like this is never done. Never, never, don't you understand?" Steven saw her body caving, like it had been hit by a laser from outer space. He moved closer, taking her into his arms, hoping it might block the dark images pushing up from deep inside her.

"Maybe we should, you want to stop if it's too much?"

Sallie caught his words apparently not knowing their aim. She sat up, pushed his arms away. He saw in her eyes the agitation of protest, of rebellion, and of pig-headed tenacity. His own eyeballs pushed up as if looking for a route to a different world. A clump of gray hair rose over the top of his right ear.

"I am going to tell you everything, deal with it!" she said.

"Well, if you are, did you, ah, do what Willie Shortz wanted?"

"He wanted me to fuck eight guys, one after another in a place he'd arrange. I told him he was nuts, but he kept after me, upping the amount of cash he'd have for me. Mind you, he was the fifth-place hitter on the team which meant he'd get a freebie. When he promised me fifty bucks a lay and a hundred and fifty more as a bonus if I survived, which meant not walking out, I agreed to do it. Do not ask me what was in my head. Maybe it was the five hundred bucks, more likely it was a White Lady stuffed bed waiting for me, with no men allowed."

"Wait a minute, here. What does this have to do with Danny Emerson?"

"I fucked the Angels," she said with a calm and straight tone.

"No you didn't…all of them?" Steven put his head between his legs under the rocker.

"I fucked the starting lineup of the Akron Angels, June 22, 1959. I know why I haven't told you about this before. It's not you, please believe me. This was just too much private zone and Danny Emerson had…do you really want me to go on?"

"That chicken-livered fuck. He was a moron of a ballplayer, you know. He got one lucky hit for the Yankees. I'd like to bust that coffin wide open and break his balls. And where is that guy, Shortz, now?"

"I have no idea, but would you just listen, please?"

"Sorry honey, but I hope they both hung themselves. Okay, I want to hear about Emerson, go on."

Sallie was looking directly at him. The curls in her grayish white hair were in disarray. When she pressed them out they'd be fine.

"Thank you. Well, sure enough, Willie got the team, I mean the starting team, together. He picked a Monday night when the Shady Tree Motel was the least crowded. The team was usually off on Mondays and no practices were scheduled by the coaches. Willie paid for a two-room suite at the back end of the motel. He must've bribed the desk clerk, because I didn't see anyone else around. Anyway, the Angel boys were tanked up. I could hear muted voices next door. I was buzzed too, mostly with bourbon, probably more than I'd ever taken. The shrink, Brenner, told me I was trying to numb myself— not just my…ah, my vagina, but my heart and brain. I remember it became quiet for a time, and then the door connecting the rooms opened and in came the leadoff hitter, Bones Jurgeson. He was a smallish, very thin guy, wiry, the one in the games that stole the most bases. I'm not going to tell you all the details. Half of them I don't even recall, but Bones Jurgeson I remember because he surprised me."

"Why's that?"

"This much I'll tell you. I thought, leadoff hitter, small thin guy, meant small pecker, and a quick go. Boy, I was so wrong. The man wore me out, to my bones. He had the biggest thing I had ever seen. I was already in pain, but nothing was going to stop me because I wanted that cash."

"You told this to Brenner, too?" Steven asked, afraid that she'd notice his jealousy.

"I did. You want to know what I learned from that mustached man? Among other things, I learned that it was power and control I wanted over those all American boys. I don't remember much about the middle part; I was, like, outside my body. That must've have been God's way of protecting me. Those boys had crazy nicknames; Sandman McClintock, Blue Shoes Waters, and Hondo Heyward."

"I never heard of any of them. What happened with Shortz and Danny Emerson in the room?"

"I'm coming to that. I had the most trouble with Willie. That burly caveman needed to maintain his image as team captain. He figured he was the straw that stirred the drink, that he was the stage manager of the world. He slapped me a few times to make sure I'd finish the set-up for him; he couldn't look weak to his brethren. I worried he'd take all the money after everything was over or have me mugged by one of his cronies. Nothing was too far out for that muttonhead."

"Tell me the rest, you must tell me the rest," Steven said. He heard the urgency in his voice; was it from a soul mate's unconditional love, or rather from his need to have her confessional over and done with? She gave him a weak smile.

Sallie put her head down and had her second cry. The flow of tears this time was steady and regular, like a gentle rain. Steven put both arms around her again, and held her for several minutes. She resisted him at first but then let herself be supported. She reached for Steven's handkerchief in his pant pocket, sat up and wiped her tears with it. Steven took the wet handkerchief from her to wipe a remaining one resting between two wrinkles below her right eye. Sallie continued.

"I had done it with seven of the players. We started about 10:00 PM and it was now after one in the morning. I felt dirty but I told myself one more to go and I'd have my five hundred. I felt strange, with a thumping sensation in my head. Then the door opened and the eighth-place hitter walked in. I remember telling myself to keep my thighs loose."

"It's funny, that memory thing, what you keep in and what you toss out," Steven said. "So what did this piece of lowest humanity look like?" He moved back on the rocker. He was restless, shifting his rear on the cane seat.

"You want to know my first thought when he walked in? Well, I said to myself, he could not be the team's best player if he batted in the last position. By that time I knew baseball lingo. I heard laughter in the next room. Danny Emerson was a pale-faced kid, not much more than eighteen or nineteen. He had an innocent, dimpled grin."

"Are you telling me he was just a boy?" Steven asked, his eyelids rising.

"He was a boy, alright, but such an average looking one. I was sitting on the edge of the messed up bed thinking how this boy in front of me was so garden variety, so commonplace, so ordinary, that he'd be an easy last lay. He took off his suit jacket. He had a white shirt on and a red plaid tartan tie. His hair was curly, with a red-yellow tinge. There were acne marks on his face and neck, an average amount. And he had a cap on, but not his baseball cap. It must've been one of those hats you wear on a yacht. He took it off, shook my hand, and introduced himself as Danny Emerson, the team's second baseman. His hand was broad with a bluff of cotton in the middle. 'Yes ma'am, I'm the second baseman of this here team,' he said."

"He was putting you on, eh?" Steven said. His fidgeting had ceased.

"I thought it was a joke set up by Willie just to make me beg for my money. I decided to play along; I needed a rest period. I was still feeling shaky, but the boy was like a cup of coffee for me, and brought me back to my senses. I asked him where he was from and he mentioned a coal mining town, Carbondale, in Pennsylvania. Then he started telling me about his family."

"Was it a joke, after all?"

"I didn't know for sure, but the more the boy went on, the more I was able to calm myself. 'My dad, he worked the mines most his life. Still does from time to time when extra men are needed. Them coal veins suck yer blood out, ya know. My ma, she wanted to go down the mines too, but they wouldn't let her. Ain't no place for a woman, the supervisors told her. She's still fighting the company to do it.' I thought that was weird, you know, a woman fighting to go down a coal mine," Sallie said.

"You and your women buddies would've formed a union and a picket line for that lady."

"You bet I would. I asked the boy why he wanted to be a baseball player. 'My dad, he said I had this here talent that God gave me, you know, to hit line drives and to throw bullets and run like a rabbit. He said when you got talent like that, well, you got to show it to the top side of the world where the sun shines, not in no damp, black-hearted, godforsaken place.'"

"Jesus, honey, was this guy for real? You can remember exactly what he said?"

"Like you said, it's funny what you keep in the memory box and what you throw out with the trash. It was the way he said his words; I'd never heard anyone speak like that before. I thought he was playing virgin with me and was not even a member of the Angels. I had never seen this boy before."

"You know what became of him, right?" He saw his wife could not hear him.

"I could still hear the partying through the walls. I thought maybe he was miked up or wired so when he took his bottoms off the boys next door would be able to hear everything. I asked the boy if he'd ever had sex before."

"I bet he hadn't, that was the joke, eh."

"I was waiting for that, too, but he said he'd had sex with his girlfriend back in Pennsylvania. He started to tell me about her. I wanted to stop him and have things done with, but his voice was so steady it kind of put a blanket around me. 'My honey girl, she was something special. We was planning on getting married. She got real sick, ma'am. She'd have infections most every other day. Her gums swelled up so much you could hardly see her teeth. She'd bleed a river from the littlest of cuts. Her pa thought I was sucker punching her, but I wasn't, ya know.' What was wrong with her, I asked him. Was she a hemophiliac? 'I dunno what that is, ma'am. No, she just got weaker and weaker. Couldn't do much but lay in bed, because her bones was aching fierce. Her pa took her up to the clinic in Scranton and they run a bunch of tests. They took so much blood from her arms I thought they was trying to kill her.' What was it that she had? I sat up and looked him straight in the eye. I could see he was getting a little choked up. If Shortz was trying to make me appear the fool, he was doing a good job. I placed my palms down on the bed and held them firm, just in case the door connecting the suite would burst open with Angel boys flying at me in every direction. 'She, ah, got that leukemia thing. She had the bad kind, the doctors said, the kind that runs fast and can't be fixed.' Do you mean she didn't…make it? 'Oh, yes ma'am, that's for sure. She died last year. She made it for eight more days after the docs told us what she had. Me and her pa, well, we made up and he let me sit with her in the hospital room the whole time. She wanted to go home, sleep in her own bed, but it was too late, you know. I miss sleeping in my own bed, do you sometimes? I know how to do the sex thing, though. I wanted to tell ya that.' My God, the boy did it for love; he did it for love, for his church, for his country, for his special girl, and he gave more than he would receive. Steven, at that moment in time, when he said all that to me lying there in Satan's den, I remember dissolving, my palms crumbling, rolling over, and my hitting the floor."

Steven looked crestfallen but said nothing. Brenner had said something to each of them about not attacking the other in a crisis or when secrets are exposed; wait to discuss things later and in a neutral place. "What did this boy of yours do when this happened?" His crestfallen visage was overtaken by the intense curiosity he felt; if it helped to push her confessional further, why that would be a bonus.

"The boy just stood there, awkwardly. 'Ma'am are ya all right?' He kept repeating that over and over. He must've been scared to death, like he'd be charged with killing me. I asked him to get me a glass of water from the bathroom. I managed a recovery. I kept checking the doors. I told him I was hurting, that it was a female thing. I made him promise not to tell Willie what had taken place. I still wanted the cash, but a little something inside me did change at that moment. I knew I was going to leave Akron and take my chances elsewhere, and feeling that settled me. If you survive a fire in your house, you just know you're going to live a different way. I had one last test for the boy, though."

"What was that?"

"I asked him what had made him agree to participate in this stag event. He said Willie told him it was a team ritual every year for the starting lineup and mandatory for rookies. Willie said it would be a good luck charm for him, a muscle builder that would put him in the Angels lineup every day. And the more at bats he got, the closer he'd come to moving up to the next baseball level."

"The kid bought that shit?"

"He said it with such an innocent look that you knew it was his truth. In that sheepish face with his open blue eyes I saw a mirror of forgiveness."

"And you did leave Akron after that, right?"

"I left in two weeks time. I took a bus to my cousin Betsy's in Brooklyn. She'd wanted me to come and stay with her; she knew about my addiction. I could talk to her and she never blabbed to my straight arrow parents. She got me admitted to an in-patient program at Beth Israel. I never realized the power of addiction, the hold it has on you. The follow-up stuff, going to meetings, having a sponsor, and then meeting you saved my life. I have many regrets, but allowing myself to do what I did at the Shady Tree Motel, well, that was the topper. How do you make amends for that?"

Steven reached forward and took her fisted right hand, opening it and meeting her fingers with his own. The inside of her fingers were moist as if their pores had spread wide for the tainted water droplets to find an air-driven death.

"Sallie, baby, I am so sorry. What a thing to carry for so many years. I don't know how you did it. I'm glad you told me."

"Me too…me too." For a moment she placed her head on his knee. He felt her lips kissing its cap before she righted herself.

"The kid, Danny Emerson, was not a piece of shit, after all. I just thought he was going to hurt you, bad. Did you, ah, follow his career in baseball?"

"I thought about my guardian angel for years. Remember how each spring you would talk baseball and guess how teams might do in the season? Well, I used to secretly check the newspapers for inserts of team rosters. I read articles about minor leaguers hoping to impress enough so they'd be able to move up to the top level. I never saw Emerson's name, not once. I gave up tracking him but I never forgot him."

"What about the year he played for the Yankees when they brought him up at the end of the season?"

"The first I heard about him was when he got that hit that won the pennant for them. I had no idea he was on the team. His picture was in all the papers the next day and he was interviewed on the TV news. I read, a few days later, that he'd been on the Tonight Show with Johnny Carson and that Carson had said he was a tough interview because he gave one-and two-word answers to his questions. I wished I'd seen that; he probably called Carson Sir."

"I never picked up anything from you. Nothing sticks out in my mind from that time," Steven offered.

"I'd watch you until you were asleep and then just lie there, thinking about him, that slow, polite way of relating he'd had. To me, he was God's best in an evil land. I heard people in the streets, in the grocery, or the pet store saying how it was a cheap hit he had gotten, a lucky hit, a bloop hit by an average player, and that he'd never make it back for another year."

"He never did, you know. I think he had some sort of back injury."

"So what! I mean who's to say what is carried in the moment a bat held by a human being makes contact with a slingshot fastball? Perhaps the years of hard work, patience, and practice provide a single instant that allows a wish and a dream to be realized. No, that blooper was no accidental hit. And there was nothing average about Danny Emerson, that's how I saw it. I cried often; hiding was easy for me because the shame compelled it."

"I want to get that obituary and read it again. Excuse me, babe." He gave her hand a gentle squeeze and moved to the kitchen where parts of the paper still lay on the floor.

"How much money did you say you took from that Willie guy?" He sat next to her and held her hand.

"Five hundred dollars," Sallie said, looking away.

"Do you see here in the obituary that donations can be made to the Friendship Little League Association? Well, how about if we do this, sweetie. How about if we, I mean you, donate five hundred dollars to that association. That's a lot of gloves and bats for the kids upstate."

"Do you mean it? What a great…" Sallie said, her eyelashes drifting up. She put her free hand on Steven's chest. "Wait, I want to make it a thousand dollars, no, a thousand and one dollars. Don't ask me why. We can cut back in other ways. Forget the mutual funds for once. And you can cut down on all those vitamins you take; I'll keep your body pure. Hey, look who's returned from the depths." The cat moved cautiously through the living room, stretched her reddish brown frame on the carpet, stared at Sallie, then jumped onto the sofa. She circled once and then settled in her caretaker's lap.

"I'm exhausted, aren't you" she said.

Steven checked his wife; her breathing seemed regulated. Maybe she'd be able to garden today. It would be good for her and he would have time to take in everything that happened.

It made him nervous when she was out of sorts. He depended more on her than he cared to admit. He was okay once he took the lead on matters that affected them both, but the anticipation before taking charge kept him off balance. He knew he'd have to ask his wife about the funeral service at Marble Collegiate Church; he prayed that she'd refuse to go, even if it was a chance for him to see famous Yankee ballplayers. Things could certainly get out of hand if some of the old Akron Angels were there. What if Willie Shortz was still alive? Steven put his hands over his eyes. He thought about the shrink, Brenner, and what he might've said to Sallie. He figured Brenner would probably have left it up to her, telling her that either choice, going or not, would be okay. He'd point out the opportunity for a forgiveness process, in either regard. Steven decided to bring it up after dinner. He knew his wife needed to feel safe; there was no way of getting around that. Maybe they could go to the Museum of Television and Radio and watch a tape of the Carson show. He didn't like the idea of the thousand and one dollar donation; that was more than they could afford. And he'd never give up his vitamin supplements. For a moment he thought she might be busting his balls, but he dismissed it.

"Baby, I feel blessed. Sweetie, go do your gardening for the block association; you'll feel refreshed and get your energy back. And I'm taking you out for dinner tonight. Sunshine Gardens okay with you?"

&

Hands On

I feel like that guy on TV, Mr. Wizard, who tells me why heat rises and why snow sticks on my window ledge. In two months, I make my thirteenth birthday; I plan to take full advantage of the rite of passage. I'll answer a dart throwing questioner with a missile of my own. I will not wear Pa's pin-striped tie to St. Matthew's on Sundays and I may even choose to miss the church ritual entirely. As for curfew time, well, those waters will also have to be tested. I am thinking about all this as I stand inside Milowski Brothers Meat and Poultry Shop waiting on the order for my Ma. Fat John Milowski, the older of the two butcher kin, is busy with other customers, too busy to look my way. I've gotten used to that.

It is the second Thursday of July, 1960, and the sun is high enough for its rays to slide through the dark spotted window frame in back of me. I feel moist, even a little shaky, in this refrigerated space. Milowski eyes me from behind the vanilla colored counter that spans his shop. The glass casing protecting his meat and poultry seems impenetrable. The silver hair on the fat man's crown looks stiff, as if the strands have been polished with sticky glue. He has the largest hands I have ever seen. Worst of all, he is tall, Gary Cooper tall. I hate it when he calls me "little one," or "laddie boy" and most of all, "Pedro...lito" because I'm short and have darkish skin. I wish I had the wizardry to make him invisible.

"My name is Peter," I always say in vain protest. I know he does this because my father is from the island of Madeira, the pearl of the Atlantic. Pa has the same last name, Zarco, as one of the two sea captains from Portugal who accidentally discovered the beach paradise while sailing off course from the African coast in the 1400's. Pa has just gone back there to work on a ship. Ma is deciding whether we are going to move there to be with him. I miss Pa because it's the summer and if he were here he'd be taking off from his job in construction and watching me play hardball. He's way taller and stronger than me but I'll be catching up with him soon. I'm not sure if Milowski's attempts at humiliating me mean that he hates my Ma or that he loves her.

"They got any refrigeration in Madeira, boy?" I'm waiting for this familiar line, knowing that no matter what I say to it, I'll hear the sing-song refrain come next week. I am wearing gym shorts. I push them down lower so my knees will not show and bring the white tee shirt over my waist. I'm set to do laps at the YMCA outdoor pool later.

Today, Milowski is sweating just like me. Drops of water are running down next to his barbed-wire sideburns. I'm laughing, thinking about the ground sirloin he is wrapping, how it's being greased by his sweat. I scan the half-open freezer behind the cash register to see if his brother Harry is there. He isn't. Not even Freddy, the delivery boy is there. The fat hippopotamus is by himself.

"Here's your order, Pete, fresh ribs included, like your Ma asked for." He hands me the package then shifts his eyes to Miss Sophia Mudd who is on my left. "Mudslinger" as we call her, is the Assistant Principal at my school. Her chest is huge under her purple blouse. She lives three blocks over from me in a new twelve story white-bricked building, the highest hi-rise now in the town. Some of the apartments there even have terraces. I know from experience that Miss Mudd will yell. I figure Milowski is aware of this as well.

I walk out of the shop and brace for the first burst of hot air when it hits me. PETE, Milowski called me…PETE. The butcher man did not even say PETER; he called me PETE, like a blood brother might do in a foxhole. I feel my chest swelling. I can't wait for the growth spurt everyone says I'm due to have because then I can eyeball Milowski and tell him a thing or two. It's a good feeling to carry that you are arriving, even if you don't know where you will land.

Heading south on Newton Avenue back to my Ma's with the fresh stewing meat, I decide I'm definitely going to do it. I'm going to hold Anne Franklin's hand when she comes to the movies with me on Saturday. We are set to see the matinee of "Psycho." I pray she hasn't found out that I saw the thriller last week with Willie Sanford, Robbie Marks, and Robbie's dad. That was a real tuned-in papa because he let us sit by ourselves. I told those friends of mine later I figured out the ending half way into the film. Actually, I'd wet my pants; I mean that hasn't happened since my Ma would wake me up nights when I was younger so I'd take a leak and protect her sheets.

Anne Franklin sits two rows in front of me in my seventh grade class. She has straight carrot-colored hair that flows off her shoulders as if lifted by a breeze. Her fine hairs are so glossy that you just know they have been fresh washed every day with scented soap leaving a yummy-smelling residue. They never crisscross leaving a knot. I can honestly say I have never seen any bumps in her hair at all. Sometimes she wears a ponytail and then I can see her ears. They look like the softest apricots in the preserved fruit section at Benny's Candy Shop on East Main. I want to play with those ears and run my fingers around the thin edges.

It is the same with her skin. Anne's face is smooth like the bowling ball Ma got for me. There are no freckles or birthmarks on her arms. How in the world did she get away with that? And her knees are white, no scratches or bruises that I can make out. My Ma, when I see her scrubbing the kitchen floor, she'll glance up and say to me if she has to do this forever she will suffer housemaid's knees for sure. I feel bad when that picture comes to mind, but I'm still wondering if Anne Franklin ever leaves her house because it looks to me like the sun has never touched her.

A bunch of us are hogging the top stoop of Moose Meghan's brownstone, our regular hang out. Mrs. Silverio's flower pots hover just over our heads. I toppled one recently with a wild fast ball. The Spalding slipped out of my hand. I sit with my back to the window to avoid Mrs. Silverio's murderous stare. Moose is big-limbed with bulging cheeks and rear end. His size makes him the leader of the pack, even if he's a bit of a dummy.

"If Anne Franklin had curly hair, she'd be the spitting image of Marilyn Monroe, don't you think?" I'm looking at the Moose in disbelief as he rants on about Anne as if he's onto my secret, or worse, that he has some kind of intimate knowledge of her.

"DiMaggio could do a lot worse than Princess Anne Franklin," one of the other guys replies and we all laugh. I'm scared of the Moose because he is twice my size, but I am more scared of Anne the way I would be if I were to meet the great Marilyn. I think about Monroe a lot, especially the picture of her skirt blowing up to her waist.

"Yeah, and she's got the longest legs for someone who is so short," I say weakly with my eyes half shut. I am just trying to be in the mix. Anne is one of the few girls I can stare straight at when I have the guts. I managed to hold my head firm long enough for her to tell me she wanted to see that movie, "Psycho," because everyone was talking about how scared they were crawling under their seats and all.

"Watch out for me, Pete, because I can get real nervous," she'd said to me.

"You got it," I told her, with my lowest voice, and placing two fingers on the top of her shoulder. When I remember this, I realize Anne can never go for the Moose. She has too much refinery, and he, well, he has none that I can see.

"Hey, lookee here, little Pedro is blushing. Why he's got a crush on Franklin," Moose says with a commanding tone.

"I do not, you are full of it. You have the crush," I manage to respond. My cheeks are reddening like burning ember. I want to tell the guys about the Saturday matinee just in case any of them might be there. I feel a pain in the right side of my stomach; maybe my appendix is about to burst.

Truth to tell, most of the guys are afraid of Anne. She keeps to herself, holds a high posture, and has a sweet-sounding voice. She never uses rough language. The word, "elegant," comes to mind which scares me even more because then I see her as untouchable. All I know is if a thought from Anne comes my way something is sure to burst inside me like one of those new umbrellas where you push the button and the thing opens so fast your hand might get cut off.

I am sitting with Anne in the center section of Richards Theatre. It is the town's showplace. Calvin Coolidge and Herbert Hoover spoke there when they were running for President. I would like to have seen that. It was also used to house people when the Allegheny flooded or when there was a slow-moving hurricane. There are eight hundred seats in the three-sectioned palace. Some have gashes and the fabric can rub against your skin especially if you're wearing short pants.

Roger Sanford, Willie's older brother, took Anne and me into the theatre with a couple of his friends. Roger is home from his third year at the state college. Willie says he's looking to become an actor which seems a little weird to me. Anyway, Willie arranged everything with his brother so we would not have to sit in the twelve and under section, on the right side of the theatre. There is a matron lady on duty over there, Miss Charm we call her, a huge puss of a lady with a humongous flashlight. She patrols that right wing children's range like it's a witch's acre for evil twits. She has the nastiest, loudest, and most menacing voice I have ever heard. Roger and his buddies sit behind us. I feel protected but I worry they'll see what I am going try and do with Anne and make fun of me. I also worry they might make their own pass at Anne seeing as how attractive she is. Still, anything is better than having your eyes penetrated by the poisonous x-rays of that searching flashlight from Miss Charm. I just know she's hiding in a back row waiting to use her atomic weapon on me, even if I'm sitting in the center section.

I shift my eyes right to check Anne, I don't know how many times. I can see the five fingers of her left hand lying like a starfish gracing a sandy beach on her red plaid skirt. Her fingers are so close to my blue chinos that it gets my heart pumping even if everything else in me is frozen like hard pavement. I am miserable. I hate myself with all my might. I'm a loser, a chicken-livered, belly-flopping, weaseling-wormed, cowardly fraud. My underarms are dripping, so I must smell as well.

The shower scene in the motel run by Norman Bates has long passed where Marian Crane, played by Janet Leigh, gets stabbed. Anyone who sees that shower scene coming is a cheating, lying turd. The heroine, Crane, who you just started to care about, gets knocked off in the first thirty minutes of the film? Are you kidding me? That blows my mind even in this second sitting. When Leigh is in her underwear I make sure not to shift my eyes to Anne or her five-finger wonders.

Norman Bates talks to Crane early on, soft-soaping her, telling her about how life circumstances sets up traps, making choices quite difficult. Hell, I know about that. Crane has embezzled money from her employer but now decides to give it back. She doesn't know she is headed for oblivion when she turns on that shower to wash off her dirt. I'm not thinking about that; I am thinking about Anne's hand and trying not to throw up because of my inaction. It's getting harder to follow the story again.

The audience gasps at the action. It is a perfect opportunity for me to reach for Anne's hand, to join together and unite against the terror. I do nothing, nada, nada. Her left shoulder nudges my right as she tries to mute her shriek. She covers her mouth with both hands. I'm not protecting her like I said I would. I am a moron, a lamebrain, a dud of a stud.

I am desperate and running out of time. Marian Crane is dead and everybody is searching for her; her boyfriend, her sister and a square private investigator. Anne's fingers nestle back on her red plaid. I've just got to do something or I'll wilt.

An actor named Martin Balsam plays the square, if not a little goofy private investigator, Milton Arbogast. What a name to remember, Arbogast. Well, he's walking up the stairs of Bates' mother's home looking for whatever might be important. The Hollywood camera that follows him up is the same one that's going to capture the terror on his face as he tumbles backwards from the force of a powerful, unseen assailant. I try to firm myself knowing this is my last chance. I inch my fingers to my right. I don't much care now if they're cold and clammy, it's too late. Maybe Anne will not notice their climate change because she's becoming undone herself from the horror on the screen. Her feet are off the floor; her head pushed so far down that I can't see her swan-like neck.

I sit back in the cushioned seat so I will appear taller. I don't care about the rough fabric ends trying to poke through my chinos. I start my move. I'm just about to cross the great divide, the armrest, into the forbidden zone, when it happens! Something slides itself into my hand. I am going to die for sure.

Oh my God, oh...my God, it's her hand, Anne's hand. She is holding my hand. Yes, she is too. The fit feels perfect, no alterations needed like my Ma would say when she brings home new dungarees from Carters Men's Store for me.

"I am so scared, Peter, aren't you?" Anne whispers, turning her body toward me. I smell something yummy on her neck, maybe one of those fancy perfumes from France. She squeezes my hand with hers and we both close in on any remaining air pockets that separate us.

I'm soaring high like the American Eagle even if there is nothing above me but a ceiling of theatre sky. I can only imagine what that mountain climber guy, Edmund Hillary, must have felt when he made it to the top of Everest. Whatever there was to see was below his feet not above his mountain hood.

I pump my hand twice. Am I giving Anne an opportunity to withdraw? Maybe I want the air pockets back to feel safe. No way am I gonna let go, though. Her fingers (Ma calls them digits) are soft and stretched with satin ridges and valleys. I feel a racing pulse. I have no idea where it is coming from. My hand? Her hand? My heart? Her…her…? I feel lightheaded, like I might faint. There is a powerful sensation building in my groin. A squirt might come out of my…thing, again. I don't want that to show on my pants. I feel like a firecracker shot high into the air waiting to rupture and brighten the sky for others to marvel at.

I look at Anne. The secret is out. They got Norman Bates, that creepy motel owner for the murders. I can see the relief on her face because the tension is over. Her green eyes are dewy like the wet on morning grass. They seem to want to laugh. She has her hand in mine, wow, and she's keeping it there.

I have never seen a picture of that director guy, Alfred Hitchcock. I just know he must be huge, maybe six-feet-four inches, good looking and with hairy forearms. He is probably an ex-marine or an athlete, maybe a javelin thrower in the Olympics. I hear he's supposed to be in a scene in every movie he makes. I remind myself to ask Roger Sanford about that.

"That was so spooky, Peter. I'm out of breath,' Anne looks at me intently; her cheeks appear pinkish.

"Yeah, it was," I say as we work our way through the buzzing crowd. I take a peek at our paws cupped together. I can't tell where mine ends and hers begins.

"Let's go to the movies every Saturday," she says giving my hand a gentle squeeze. "Maybe they'll have a musical next week. I want to see "Bells Are Ringing." It's just come out you know. I love Judy Holiday; she is so funny, so… kooky crazy."

"Ah, yeah…okay, that would be okay." I don't know if I am coming or going, that's another phrase my Ma uses when things get out of whack. I haven't a clue who Judy Holiday is.

I'm walking Anne to her split-level wood frame home on Grandview Road. She calls it a mother-daughter house which puzzles me because it is really her grandma who resides downstairs while Anne and her parents are up top.

"Norman Bates had the cruelest eyes, don't you think?"

"Yup, I guess he did, sort of like Bela Lugosi, eh." I am thinking about how I can make my eyes appear sweet but I've no idea how to arrange that. Maybe I'll just keep them open wide to show Anne that I'm an honest-type guy.

"Did you hear those screeching violins and the heart thumping music," she asks me.

"Screeching violins? What are you talking about?"

"You know when Marion Crane gets it in the shower? Who do you think was making that whining, siren-like music in the background? Try to picture many violinists doing it in unison, as if they had a single bow."

"Oh, I never realized about the music…ah, I forgot that you're in the orchestra class."

"Screeching comes easy to me." She laughs an easy kind of laugh. She's real comfortable with herself. I notice the dimple on her right cheek.

Our hands part as we turn onto her street. Hers is the second place across Grandview. The lights in the living room are on behind the half-open window curtain. I see the shadow of a figure move through. I can't tell if it's her ma or pa. I feel unsteady all of a sudden, like my feet might lock themselves into the pavement. I barely make it to the steps of the front porch.

"Peter Zarco, I really enjoyed today. I'm sorry I got so nervous in the theatre. I never saw a movie like that before. I hope I won't have nightmares tonight."

"You won't," I say with as much strength as I can muster. "I had a great time too." I push away the fear to meet her blue eyes with mine. The extra second that goes by feels like an hour.

She is at her door with the brass knocker that looks fresh shined. She turns and waves the sweetest goodbye. I figure saying goodbye can actually be a way of saying hello.

I'm doing love strides home. I am not going to say a word to Ma about what happened. It isn't that she would laugh at me but sometimes she has a know-it-all smile on her face that scares me. Often at the Richards Theatre before the show starts the curtain will open to its widest extension because the movie that's coming on is going to be in this new process called Cinemascope. Well, that's how my Ma's teeth look when I see that smile of hers: cinema scoped. It makes me want to bury myself under the sheets. Actually I'm planning to lie down when I get home, maybe sleep awhile. I love doing that when things go really, really well and I can think about them over and over. The image of Anne and me, our hands welded…it makes me realize I don't want to go to Madeira even if Pa says it's the pearl of the Atlantic.

∽

My Friend Harry

There he was, my friend Harry, sitting with his head bent over the *Daily Racing Form*, checking the trotters and pacers running at Freehold. He'd parked himself at a picnic bench in the back of Benson's Ice Cream and Dairy Bar. Benson's was originally a family farm that housed two thousand cows— Jerseys and Brown Swiss, because they gave a creamier type of milk. Every day must've been a captain's paradise for the bulls boarding there, eyeing the beauties coming in from the field. Teddy Benson sold off his acreage in the late sixties to a developer putting in a shopping mall. He kept a few cows and retained space for the ice cream concession; I'm glad he did because it was a great meeting place for retired guys like us.

It was early July. I could see darkening clouds competing with the sun. Loose, grayish hair pushed out from the sides of Harry's weathered black Newark Bears cap. A number two pencil was tucked behind his left ear. I knew the hothead was going to try and get me back to the racetrack. As I neared the bench Harry looked up with a crooked smile, his cheeks widening like they'd been stretched with a stick. Holy Christ, in the name of…what was the guy wearing? Bulging out from his wrinkled blue chambray work shirt was one of those English ties, an ascot. Harry's was red, the patterned silk placed wide by his tie tack. It covered much of the chambray. English gentle-men wore silk ascots to the races like in those Hitchcock movies with Cary Grant.

"What am I suppose to say to you Harry, with your new scarf rolling down your neck? Have you jumped up in class, fella?"

"The name's Bond, James Bond," he said with a pitiful accent.

"Well, if you're really 007, you can fix me up for a night with one of your ripe tomatoes in a string bikini."

"For a price, you can have anything, buddy boy."

The wooded tables at Benson's were crowded with young families and retired couples slurping the flavor of the day. Benson's was famous for its ice cream. Their scoops were said to be larger, rounder, and smoother because of the silky cream their cows produced. A billboard high above the concession stand had a tall blue-eyed Himalayan mountaineer standing erect, with two Sherpa guides behind him beaming like they'd just seen the heavens. And above them was an ice capped Himalayan peak. It reminded me of my youthful attempts at climbing Mt. Shasta and Pikes Peak. The billboard scene, like the "no air pocket" cone that Benson's advertised, seemed puncture proof. It would've been even better for me if they'd had a female sharpie on it, showing her legs and pursing her lips. If I had seen that pulling into Benson's, I'd be there every day. The feminists would have had to carry me out.

I never sucked up to those new, mixed up flavors of ice cream that the teenagers went bonkers over: Raspberry Peach Cream, Double Chocolate Mint Cookie, and Boysenberry Delight. I stuck with Vanilla Fudge. It was Tuesday. Seniors over sixty got half off the cone or cup. Harry made the age plus two years, I made it plus one.

Harry wasn't that hard to read, but he was not dumb either. He'd given me another clue as to the nature of the meet today. Whenever he got anxious or excited, his voice would speed up and he'd slur his words and that is how he sounded when he phoned me. I studied the plot lines on his ruddy face.

"So Frankie boy, what's up?" he said, without rising. He dropped the Bond stuff. His bottom half looked the same as always—grey chino pants and white tube socks held by over-worn walking shoes. Harry shaved maybe twice a week; his salt and pepper stubble was coarse and uneven. He was an ugly looking guy to most; he even had a full inch scar at the side of his right eye. With that hair hanging from the rim of his balding crown, he probably could pass for a mad scientist mixing a poisonous concoction over a Bunsen burner. That's why the ascot was so ridiculous. It was like putting beluga caviar on a Hostess Twinkie.

Harry's frame was still formidable; he was six-foot, square-shouldered, and built like a middle linebacker. His skin was craggy and wrinkled, probably from years of going in and out of the freezer at his butcher shop. As for me, I am shorter by a couple of inches, slender and wiry. My skin is worse than Harry's, pockmarked from the never quitting acne I'd had as a kid. I used to worry that it was undiagnosed smallpox. As soon as I was of age, I stopped using antibiotics and creams prescribed by wacko skin guys. I don't even use aftershave now. My attitude is, take my puss or leave it. My wife, Ruthie, who knows me best of all, says my body reminds her of Frank Sinatra's even if my puss is like an overgrown sweet potato.

"Hey, Harry, where's your maple walnut sundae?" He folded the *Daily Racing Form* and placed it on the wooden table. Next to that was *The Racing Digest*, a monthly magazine that chronicled past and present history of the Sport of Kings. I'd read it a time or two.

"I just had a sandwich. How's retirement suiting you?" Harry retired six months ago, taking his Social Security. He didn't have a retirement fund because of his gambling habit. He'd go on junkets to Vegas, but that stopped when Atlantic City got the face lift it needed to lure the flyer boys back to the east coast. He still got his meats and poultry discounted because he knew a lot of the suppliers. His kids were gone and his wife, Alice, worked at a bakery in Freehold Township.

My retirement was more recent, you could say forced. I'm a cabinet maker and I'd worked the last twenty-two years at Sam Weldon's Kitchen and Bath Cabinetry Center. I hadn't been laid off or anything; it was that back of mine that kept acting up. I had developed something called spinal stenosis. The doctor told me to picture a narrowing of a passageway like a drawbridge closing to traffic. Well, that's what was happening in my back. So I began receiving a disability retirement pension from my union.

I loved working, making things from start to finish. I never took short cuts, no matter what the project. The cabinetry at Weldon's was low-end, for working people, but I treated each piece like it was going to go to a king or queen.

My wife, Ruthie, works for the New Jersey Highway Department as a toll collector on The Garden State Parkway. Nancy, our twenty-nine year old daughter, lives with her artist boyfriend in Portland, Maine. She works for the post office there.

"Retirement sucks, man," I said.

"Yes sir…ee, it surely does. That's exactly why we have to come up with something big, Frankie, my boy."

"My back isn't so bad that I couldn't do some lifting; Sam Weldon is just afraid of a lawsuit. With me out of the way, he can pay his apprentices half my salary. Their work will be shoddy and the customers are going to complain."

I could feel anger coursing through my veins. I felt that way whenever I'd talk about Weldon getting rid of older guys so he could pad his bottom line. Many of the veteran guys freelanced getting work from regular customers on the sly. I never did that, despite the temptation. Weldon smelled it out every time. More than once in a half-sleep haze I'd picture myself slamming a rock down on his bloated head. One time in the middle of a dream I punched Ruthie, God forgive me. It was pretty scary having such a pumped up feeling, like the one I carried about Weldon. It was like when you poured a beer too fast in a stein and you could see foam rising like a coming ocean wave.

"The work you gotta do now is handicapping, brother. How's handicapping the races different from architecting a cabinet anyways?"

"Are you off your rocker? What I do with wood and metal is based on careful analysis and science, man, science. You're pleading with Lady Luck, Harry. I see you have the *Racing Form* there," I said, eying the crumpled newspaper as he looked up with a bent smile. "Are you a deaf mute, or just a moron, Harry? I told you I'm giving up the track. I have to find something else to do. I'm going back to fishing; it's cheaper and I get fresh blues for dinner."

For the last four months we'd been going twice weekly to Freehold Raceway where trotters and pacers ran during the day. We drove Wednesdays and Fridays to a shopping center near the raceway. We'd pull into a Barnes and Noble to save on parking and then walk the few blocks to the rear entrance of the track. The admission was now free because tracks were losing their live gate to Off-Track Betting. Being cheapskates, we held off for a couple of races before springing for a two dollar program, hoping that a disgruntled loser would leave one on the pavement. Still, it was fun being there. The crowds were small, mostly men of retirement age. The seats in the grandstand made creaky noises. We pooled our money like we were a syndicate.

Up until recently, I hadn't been to the track in years, but I knew a lot about harness racing, even the flats, because my pop had been a horse player. I'd go to the races with him on weekends, and when I was old enough, I'd place bets for him. When he made a big hit, he would let me carry a stack of twenties home. Pop's face would flush easily, pink as a pig in heat. He also made weird noises with his mouth and would laugh and cough at the same time. There must've been pain in the cough because later on he developed a fast moving lung cancer. He smoked more when he gambled, I guess to settle his nerves. Ma never cracked a smiled, even when we brought home the twenties. Pop always gave her one of them. She'd put it in back of the dishes in the cupboard.

First time at Freehold, me and Harry won forty dollars each after an exacta in an early race came in paying over ninety dollars. But then we began losing a few bucks here and there. Truth of the matter was that we were probably now down a few hundred apiece. And the last time at Freehold they'd disqualified our first place horse when the harness driver went wide and blocked the favorite who was charging from off the pace.

"Frankie, I cut out an article from the *Newark Star Ledger* on the Metro Challenge, being run Saturday at Freehold.

They got the probable opening odds listed. I also got *The Racing Digest* magazine here; there's a story in it you are not going to believe." He paused, searching my eyes for the go-ahead. When he saw my grimace a frown replaced his smiling demeanor. "Ruthie got you on this, didn't she? She gave you a little lecture, huh?"

"She did not," I said, with a defensive glare; "I go where I want."

"All right, all right Frankie. Look, I got information on the Metro Challenge. I want us to go Saturday. I know it's a different day than we usually go but wait till you see what I got here. You can make yourself a grand exit from harness racing and be sitting pretty on a throne of gold." Harry's mood shifted again; he laughed a Santa Claus laugh, long and deep.

"I am not going, I'm telling you. There's always some big race: The Horse's Ass Derby, or The Steroid Cup. Who gives a crap when I'm down a bundle?"

"Very funny about The Steroid Cup. I bet half those nags have been fed some special oats, you're right about that. Anyways, listen up; I got a tip from Louie the Pineapple about a trotter originally from New Zealand that they're bringing over from the Meadowlands to run in the Metro. Louie's a scum bag for sure, but he also knows the trainers and the workout boys. They're talking about…"

"Wait a minute Harry, for Christ sake; Louie the Pineapple? That midget must be eighty-five years old. He touted for my father." I laughed to myself recalling how Louie had gotten his nickname. The guy was a pipsqueak and a weird eater, some kind of vegetarian before it was fashionable. He was also a fruit cup freak, bringing several to the track. He'd watch the work-outs of the horses in the morning, clocking them himself. The problem was when he ate his fruit salads he'd toss the pine-apple, claiming it upset his stomach. The story was when his mother figured out that he had no taste for pineapple, she used it to torture him, making him finish the pineapple bits before he left the table or when he'd been out too late.

"Louie could be ninety for all I know. Anyway, would you just listen for a minute so I can tell you what I got from him?" Harry had that face on like he was the center of gravity, sitting in his living room passing out notes on the secrets of life.

"Oh, Jesus, Harry. This had better be good."

"Like I said, they're talking about a three-year-old New Zealand born trotter, Freedom Hanover. His workouts have been fantastic. He was run nine times as a two-year-old at Freehold and some of the southern tracks."

"I know, Harry, the horse never won; they held him back and now they're going to let him loose." I rolled my eyes. Harry was pissed. He stood up; his fingers were fluttering.

"Forget it; I can't talk to you. I am telling you this is real information here. You don't want in? Go home and make your wife happy You're impossible, man." He sat down and covered his face with both hands.

The guy got me because I was starting to feel guilty, like I'd put a piece of masking tape over his mouth. Even though I knew he was playing me, I resolved to be fair.

"Okay, okay, you bloodsucker." I made an attempt to laugh and did a mock submission to him raising my hands above me and putting them down in front of him, tweaking his ascot. "So, how did Freedom Hanover do as a two-year old?"

"The horse won once, Frankie. That's right, once out of nine times. Four other times he was leading but broke stride, or parked out right, and because of that the owners stopped racing him. Trotters break and go wide much more than pacers, especially when they're young and maidens. They don't have restraints on their legs like pacers. In his last six races he was a long shot. Nobody bet him because it was known he would likely break or get parked outside. He just needed more training."

"You got all this from the Pineapple man?"

"That's right. Me and Louie talk all the time."

"How long have they kept Freedom Hanover out?"

"Almost eight months. He had to run a no-bet qualifier to be able to run for purses again. He won it easy."

"What was his time? Did he break?"

"Nope, he didn't even go wide. Now this is the thing, Frankie. His time was one minute fifty-seven seconds flat. Not exactly blue-ribbon speed, right?"

"That's long shot time in big races and even terrible in claiming races." I was wondering what was coming next.

"This is where Louie comes in. He tells me they just did what was necessary to have the horse qualify. The Freedom man was in front at the three quarters pole so the driver held him tight. The last fractions, you know the last two furlongs, were down but so what, he won easily.

"Harry, this proves nothing. Have there been any more time trials? What else do you have? You've got to come up with something more than this."

"First of all, Louie knows one of the four owners, Willie Madden. Willie lets Louie come to the farm workouts. Get this; in the farm workouts, which don't get reported, Louie's got Freedom Hanover clocked three or four seconds faster than in his qualifier."

"This guy Madden lets Louie come to his farm? How did an old, emaciated, has-been tout like Louie the Pineapple get so lucky, Harry?" I pretended to be cool but my stomach was turning over.

"That I cannot tell ya, maybe Madden owes him for something, but three or four seconds faster? Man, that's unbelievable. We're talking ten, fifteen lengths here. And like I said, the horse never went off stride once. His trainer must've worked on that for months. They ran him on a five-eighth track, not just a half-mile one. They also used blinkers and maybe that's what kept him from going wide. And this is the start of summer season when trotters run their fastest. Hey man, is this the straw that stirs the drink? Is this the goose that laid the golden egg? This info puts us one step ahead of everybody."

"I got a question for you, big man. Why are they starting him in a stakes race like the Metro? Trotters in that race have been on the circuit for a year or more; it's a crapshoot when you have better breeds running in a race like the Metro. Why not drop him down in class for a smaller purse to start?"

"Louie had the same question. Willie told Louie to check the charts because most of the horses in the Metro were the same ones Freedom Hanover had run against the previous year. Turns out Madden had it right. Five of the seven other entrants had been in at least half of Freedom Hanover's early races."

"I guess a fifty thousand dollar purse is purer gold, huh." I had to admit the story was intriguing. I could feel a rush, this time moving up my chest on through my head. "What about the other horses? What were their finishing times?" I asked. Harry was sweating now, the pearl droplets on his forehead glistening like melted glass.

"I checked that real careful like. Only once in forty-eight races this year between all of them did any trotter hit a winning time of one minute and fifty-five seconds. How do ya like them apples?" He reached for a napkin from the holder on the table and wiped the sweat bubble that had formed on the edge of his nose.

"Do you know who Freedom Hanover's sire was? You always said that was important."

"Remember Sturdy Hanover? He was a top-notch trotter who won some big bucks in his career before being put out to stud," Harry said, shooing off a couple of fat pigeons with his napkin that were pecking at a buffet of crumbs on the pavement.

"How do you know all this? Hey, would you leave the damn pigeons alone; they're not bothering you."

"Christ, Frankie, what are you a secret agent for the Audubon Society? You could look it up about Sturdy Hanover. It's the information age, baby. Sturdy Hanover ran in several stakes races, mostly at Yonkers and Roosevelt. He was retired to stud at age five because of a bowed tendon. That kind of injury is painful and takes a long time to heal. Generally the nags come back to the same form."

'What's that, the rotator cuff injury for horses?"

"Not bad, my man. Yeah, I guess that's a good comparison. The syndicate that owned the horse must've made a fortune on stud fees."

"Looks pretty good to you, eh, Harry? You say you got the morning line in the paper? Who are they using to drive?" I wanted something sweet. In a minute I'd excuse myself to get my Vanilla Fudge.

"Jesus, I didn't tell you about the driver. The owners contracted with Carmine Galenta to come over from the Meadowlands and drive Freedom Hanover here for just this race."

"Carmine Galenta? You have got to be kidding me. One of the great Galentas? How many drivers do they have in that family? Five, right, including the father, what's his name, Vitello? That will certainly bring down the odds." I was guessing what the payoff would be and whether to wheel the horse for an exacta. "What about the morning line? And what the hell is Carmine Galenta doing coming here to a dump like Freehold?"

"Frankie, Frankie. A lot of drivers do double duty. You know that. They come here for the afternoon card and then move back to the Meadowlands for the evening one. Carmine Galenta isn't going to pass up a fifty thousand dollar purse. He's gotta get at least ten percent if he takes the Freedom to the circle of roses. You interested in this now?"

"Would you tell me the morning line already?"

"I got it right here, with Louie's notes." Harry pulled a folded newspaper page from the middle of the *Daily Racing Form*. "Here it is, Freedom Hanover, fifteen to one on the morning line; that would make him the sixth or seventh choice. I figure he'll be bet down to maybe seven or eight to one."

"You mean, because other guys know what you know?" I asked.

"Well, yeah, maybe a select few. But that ain't a bad price, with what we can do with exactas. Maybe we'll box a trifecta? You've got to admit, this is a steal; you got something on for Saturday?"

"You are a thorn, Harry. I'm going to the nursing home in Metuchen with Ruth to visit her mother. They're having a big party there for the old lady; she's turning ninety-one."

"Can't you go on Sunday? By then you'll be able to hire a stretch limo," Harry said, smiling.

"Ha ha. Let's get some of Teddy Benson's best; they're going to open a new bag of walnuts just for you." I started for the concession stand. Harry jumped up and ran after me, his red ascot looking more like a hangman's knot than a smiling necktie.

"After we eat, Frankie, I wanna tell ya about the story I read in *The Racing Digest*."

I liked Benson's ice cream place because it was set on a hill away from the main road. I loved staring at the kids who knew they were in a candy land without threat from fire-eating dragons and bossy parents. In this land they'd run free, unless their feet crossed, unhinging the scoops of ice cream from their cones. I saw that happen once. Teddy Benson witnessed it, too. He waved his cane at one of his workers to give the kid another cone. He did the right thing, that Teddy Benson.

Harry didn't say much after we purchased our own creamy delights. He downed his maple walnut sundae and then started on his well-sugared coffee. He said the sugar goosed him into action. A paper airplane floated by, landing at the edge of the table. A couple of kids with shorts down to their ankles were laughing at the adjacent table.

Harry was oblivious to it all. He was hunched once more checking the day's racing card at Freehold. He followed the careers of several trotters and pacers. He knew their injury histories and sires. He had a real suspicious nature. He tried to figure out if a fix was on, with drivers and owners colluding to hold back favorites from finishing in the money so they could place wagers on long shots. If Harry saw a driver take his horse back to where the tote board was in front of the grandstand to check the odds just before post time, he'd run to place a wager on the horse before the pari-mutuel windows shut down. Now he put his paper down and pointed to *The Racing Digest*.

"I saved this for you, Frankie. There's a story in here, I'm going tell you about it now; you can read it later, okay?"

"What kind of story is this? Wait, let me guess. I know, it's about an undersized horse bought for a few hundred bucks who broke his leg, and instead of being put down was rehabbed and then returned to the winner's circle, right?" Everybody knew about Sea Biscuit, the pint horse with the heart of a champion. Harry was fingering the stubble under his chin. His eyes narrowed. He picked up *The Racing Digest* and slammed it on the picnic table.

"Man, you're a tough nut to crack. You got a fucking mother lode on your back, you know that?" He took a deep breath and continued before I could protest. "Here's the deal. I'm going to tell you this story here in the *Digest* for two minutes, not one second more. You are going to keep your trap shut for those two minutes, okay? Not one sound. Then you do what you want, because after that I'm leaving."

"Harry, Harry, I'm just…"

"You wanna go Saturday, you let me know. If not, I'm going by myself. I'll meet up with Louie to do our business. I am not passing up on this info, no way, man."

"Okay, let's get this over with, Harry. Tell me the story; I can see you are just dying to do that. Do me a favor, please; would you take off that freaking ascot, you look like a lavender pussy." He didn't listen and he took more than two minutes to tell me the story, reading parts of it. I interrupted him a few times, though.

"Seems there was this kid in Long Island (the story was titled 'The Kid') in the mid-1960's who grew up loving horses, yeah, from the first time he ever laid eyes on them. He'd get off his school bus and camp out for hours at horse trails waiting for riders to come by. Eventually he got to know many of the horse hands, even a few of the owners. There were a lot of riding academies and training stables at the tip ends of the island."

"My father once took me to a horse farm in Muttontown where they had this great tack shop. Saddle fit, that's what my pop said was the most important thing for the equestrian." I liked my first interruption.

"Saddle fit? I'd rather see ladies in low rider breeches. You're distracting me, Frankie. The kid dropped out of high school once he got himself known to the local horsemen. Maybe they felt sorry for him because he never talked about any family, and he didn't seem to have friends his age. Well, he eventually got himself hired and began making good money at training farms. He ended up with Jupiter Lane Stables."

"Jupiter Lane? I've heard of them; they're still around, right?"

"You betcha." Harry paused, turned the pages of the *Digest* to continue reading from the article.

"The kid worked for them over ten years; of course he was low man on the totem pole when he started, the assistant to the assistant stable boy. He did whatever was asked of him, mucking out the stalls, helping the blacksmith with shoeing, organizing the tack shop, doing boarding and feeding and aiding in the harness supply. The top pacers and trotters got a better type feed. Did you know that, Frankie? After a time, he worked with the veterinarian who oversaw reproduction services for the farm, like the management of broodmares, artificial insemination, semen transport and foaling supervision."

"Wait a minute, Harry. Are you telling me that the elite horses get a superior oat? And semen transport? What does that mean, sending a perfumed box lunch to Stall 54?"

"Hey, you know in the days of Robin Hood, if you were a lord or a duke, your horse got proper oats, a rub down, and a manicured stable. If you were a serf, your nag got stale hay and a cold stall. Would you let me finish, already? The kid was well liked, but more importantly, he was calm with the horses who were housed in individual and group sheds. He just understood their nature. Large paddock areas were provided for exercise, rest, and rehabilitation of the colts and fillies. It was serious business. Reputation of the farms and training stables was everything. Jupiter Lane Stables was a big outfit, a holding place for individual owners and small group syndicates."

"Just like us; we're a syndicate, eh?" I broke a smile.

"You can't do any better than teaming up with me, fella. Anyway, years went by and the kid married a local girl. Soon, he had three real kids to feed. To make ends meet, he wangled a job at night doing valet parking for the Cloud Casino at Roosevelt Raceway."

"Wow, the Cloud Casino; my pop was a grandstand regular at Roosevelt but he never made it to the famous Cloud Casino. It cost extra to get into that place. Man, I remember always wanting to see that special area, but pop would never go in, saying there were too many wise guys there selling snake oil." Harry just stared at me and went on.

"The Cloud Casino was not a place where one played craps or blackjack; it was where high-stepping bettors would come for dinner and drinks while testing the fates, and waiting for the smile of Lady Luck. The kid would work at Jupiter's during the day and then be driven to Roosevelt with their horses that were running on the evening's card. He got to know a lot about fancy cars, but he also met more owners and trainers. For the most part, he was not a bettor. Occasionally, he'd place a small wager in a middle race, but he knew where his real money was coming from. He made big buck gratuities, especially if a rosy-faced winner came out looking like Alexander the Great, pumping his chest and displaying a roll of bills. Weekends were the best for tips. Remember, Frankie, Roosevelt Raceway in the 1970's and 80's drew good crowds. There was no Off Track Betting then. The grandstand was always packed when there were big stake races, like The Roosevelt International Trot, or The Messenger Stakes, which was a leg of the Triple Crown for pacers. Some of those races had huge purses, up to a half a million dollars."

"I know that. I remember those stakes races." We were in the shade now because another ominous looking cloud had moved through, just when I thought the yellow rays of the sun had spun a brilliant web to sky's end.

"Just listen to this, now. One hot weekend July night, 1982, almost six years to the day before the track closed in 1988, the kid parked a Jaguar from a hot shot finance wizard, Dino Crivens, a regular patron and a sometime horse owner. Crivens would come straight to the track from the trading floor of The New York Stock Exchange. He was always dressed to score, in Hart, Schaffner, and Marx worsted wool suits and wide angled ties with colorful handkerchiefs in the jacket breast pocket. Crivens loved the action and high stakes betting. He took a liking to the kid and gave him good money so he'd have his car ready when he needed to leave. Passing his car keys to him that night, Crivens said, 'If you can kid, bet my horse, Train….big in the ninth. Wheel him as well for the exacta. Trifecta is up to you. Wish me luck, kid.' Well, the valet parking was jammed; it was a steamy night. The kid remembered the word Train somewhere in the name but didn't get the rest as Crivens was moving fast. He forgot about it; guys gave him tips on horses all the time. Crivens was a silent investor with a number of the other regular horsemen. The kid had never seen him so excited.

After the featured and top-pursed seventh race, his pockets deep with cash from having moved so many cars, the kid figured he'd take a shot on the ninth race, the last on the card. He had to work fast because there were huge gratuities waiting from the ninth's cheerful winners who were the last to arrive at valet parking.

He decided to place his bet as soon as the eighth race was over. He'd make sure to be first up at a pari-mutuel window. He would bet twenty to win and wheel the horse for a two dollar exacta, another fourteen dollars. For twelve more dollars he would box the horse with two other random horses for a go at the trifecta; that would be a throwaway. Forty-six dollars total. It was more than he'd usually bet, but it wasn't often that a guy like Dino Crivens would go out of his way to cut him in on information.

The kid told his two assistants to cover for him for a few minutes. The valet boys had a system, protecting each other when personal bets were to be made. There would be no trouble getting into the Cloud Casino after the eighth race; everybody knew him and security was lax at that time."

"Harry, I don't know where you're headed with this story. Is that all true? There really was such a kid?"

"I swear to God on my mother's grave this is the truest story there could be. This is human interest stuff, Frankie. You couldn't make up a story like this." Harry nodded at me, winked, and returned to his read. "Anyway, it went as planned. The kid charged into the clubhouse, grabbed a program from the many on the ground tossed by disgruntled bettors, and headed toward the pari-mutuel area. He turned to the ninth race entries. He scanned the names to get the post positions. Easy Fella, Cosmos Dream, Lasting Sun, Training Station…ah, that must be it, Train…ing Station, post number four. Then he looked at the remaining posts. Festive Night, Banjo Hanover, Gambler's Baby, and DieselTrain. The kid freaked; Diesel Train, post number eight, the worst post for trotters and pacers because of the ground that had to be made up on the turns. Diesel Train, at program odds of twenty to one, and likely to go off higher because of his outside post. He checked the driver, Vitello Galenta. Now there was a veteran driver who had been doing well at Roosevelt.

The kid didn't know what to do, because this trotter's name also had the word, Train in it. He checked the owners listed in the program. He did not recognize the names listed for either Training Station or Diesel Train. His underarms dripped. He had an impulse to run but he fought it off. Stand up like a man, not a filly, he said to himself. He figured to make a good c-note in tips that night from the overflow of cars and station wagons. He moved to a vacant spot at the pari-mutuel windows. He bet

Diesel Train to win, wheeled him in the exacta and chose two random horses, as planned, for the trifecta box. He ran back to valet parking. There was a makeshift line of customers waiting for an early start home."

"Harry, Harry, slow down, your face is flushed, don't stroke out on me."

"Not in your lifetime, and not until I finish this read, baby. Jack Lee had been the caller at Roosevelt for years. His voice was distinctive, deep, and resonant, like a well trained baritone. You must remember him, Frankie, if your pop took you to Roosevelt."

"Wait a minute; didn't Lee work at Freehold after Roosevelt went belly up?"

"Way to go. Imagine that, a guy like Lee coming to our puny Jersey track; he must've needed the money. Where was I, now? Oh, the kid had run back to valet parking.

From the parking area, one could hear the fate of a trotter or pacer and still get a head start home on the Meadowbrook Parkway. The kid was moving cars like a shepherd directing his flock, when the ninth went off. He heard Lee's fast-paced call from a car window. He opened the door of a black Cadillac and felt the crunched bill put in his hand.

The quarter in twenty-seven and one, a blistering pace. That's Training Station on top, followed by Easy Fella and Banjo Hanover. Going by the stands the first time, that's Training Station opening up a four length lead.

Half in fifty-five and two. Can Patrick Stanley, driving Training Station maintain this grueling pace? Banjo Hanover moves into second position on the rail. Easy Fella is….falling back. The crowd noise was thunderous even if some of the patrons had already left. The kid was momentarily distracted when two guys waiting for their cars got into it over who was there first.

He picked up Lee again. Three quarters in one minute, twenty-six and four. They're turning for home, with Training Station leading the way. Hell, the kid said to himself, maybe I bet the wrong horse.

Lee's voice went up a notch. Training Station is OFF STRIDE, OFF STRIDE. Drivers have to go wide. One furlong to the finish. Banjo Hanover and Gambler's Baby are neck and neck. And on the way outside here comes…Diesel Train with Vitello Galenta urging him on. It's Diesel Train and Gambler's Baby now coming to the finish. It's gonna be, gonna be… Diesel Train by a nose. Diesel Train, the longest shot in the race. That trotter, ladies and gentlemen, was more than ninety-nine to one.

Gambler's Baby, a fourteen to one shot would pay a huge price for placing. Banjo Hanover at seven to one and a fourth betting choice hung on to finish third. There were sixteen winning exacta tickets; the kid had one of them. Not bad for a crowd of over twenty thousand patrons. As for the trifecta, the kid held the sole winning ticket. That payoff was over sixty-three thousand dollars. Adding the exacta and the first place payoff, two hundred and twenty-eight dollars for a two-dollar bet, the stable boy was richer by more than seventy-four thousand dollars.

The kid made sure that Crivens' car was ready as usual, but only got a glimpse of him coming out of the Cloud Casino. Crivens was disheveled, bent over, his sport jacket and tie bunched up in his left hand. He slammed his cigarette to the ground with his free hand as if it was a Spalding rubber ball. He tried to spit twice on it and then launched the half-smoked butt to a never, never land with a right-legged dropkick. It was only then that the kid realized that Crivens' trotter had been Training Station, the trotter that had gone off stride after leading most of the way. As for the valet boy struggling to make ends meet, well, he'd bet the right wrong horse, or was it the wrong right horse? He had no idea of the payoff. Crivens grabbed his car keys from the kid and with a crony at his side sped off, nearly hitting a crossing patron."

I told myself not to look at Harry. No way, was I going to give him satisfaction. My palms were wet and clammy. Now a drop of my own sweat trickled down my forehead. I felt my heart speeding, like a bobsledder's would moving down a straightway. It was my head, though, that was crashing and pulsating. I felt that way often after sex. The worst was imagining Jack Lee calling the last two furlongs because my friend Harry really cranked up that part, as if he was in contention for an Oscar. I looked down at my left hand; it was clenched. I was picturing Diesel Train pulling wide to make his gallant stretch run. It must've been stirring.

"Frankie boy, where are you?" Harry was waving his hands in front of me. I guess it was for a time because I could smell his breath. It was stale, musky, like he'd had a liverwurst sandwich before coming to Benson's. "Were you asleep? You had a strange expression on your face. You were gone man, really gone. You okay? Hey, was that fantastic or what?"

"I was a little out of it, huh. What do they call that, a senior moment?"

"More like a senior hour. Just so you're good. What do you think of that story?" His bottom teeth were yellowish, from his smoking habit.

"That was some story, I've got to admit. It's all true, eh?"

"True as truth can be. It's like what they say here at Benson's, no air pockets in our ice cream. Well, no sir, ain't no air pockets in that story." Harry extended his grin.

"What happened to the kid? Do they go into that in the article?" I asked.

"Just like you to ask me that. Well, the kid was able to keep his name out of the papers. He wasn't identified in the article. To the trainers and workout boys, though, he became a local hero. He had a high period after that night."

"What do you mean a high period?"

"Well, for starters, he never parked cars again. He joined a syndicate of owners; he certainly knew the business pretty good by then. He disappeared after a few years, though. I think he separated from his wife for awhile. You can read it at the end; they got some kind of postscript. I didn't get into that."

"Harry, that doesn't exactly sound like a high period. I mean, losing his…"

"What do ya mean? Tell me a more amazing story than this. The guy hits it big and becomes a peacock. Instead of being called 'Kid,' he's addressed like a major league stud. He probably could waltz into the Cloud Casino free of charge. Hey, he could even dress himself better than that guy, Crivens." Harry's face tightened. His lips pursed and flattened.

"How much do you think he was paid for this story?" I wasn't sure I even cared about that; I was just trying to stabilize myself; I really wanted to know where the kid was now. I wanted to see his photograph, know how he earned a living, if he saved his marriage, if he was a good father, and if horses were still part of his life. I wanted to know how he'd survived the experience without getting corrupted and losing a light touch about matters.

"I dunno, Frank. Enough to keep him warm for a time. By the way, that horse, Diesel Train? Oh, he never won another race. He was put down three months later after fracturing a fibula during a workout. Unbelievable stuff, eh?"

"Yes sir, that is about as freaky a story as I have ever heard." I said.

"Let's get outta here, my ass hurts and this seat is sticking to my rear. You'd think Teddy Benson would come up with seat cushions to make you more comfortable. He just wants you to lick your cone, suck your shake, and then leave, prompt time. I pick you up Saturday morning, okay? After that you're on your own. We can leave after The Metro if you want. I'm telling you, Freedom Hanover's gonna do it. This is the best information ever, even if it's from the Pineapple."

The pause seemed without end. A great combination, I thought to myself. Harry had the best information he's ever had, and me, I had a tough decision as to what to do on Saturday. It was like having to decide whether to go for an inside straight with a big pot on the table or to walk away from the game.

There are moments, however, when an unseen path leads you to higher ground. You need to trust that feeling. Sometimes you did the right preparation for a hike, like having your rain gear and your protein bar and enough fluid, but you could still be blindsided because you didn't know where the trail would take you. I felt that way lots of times at work. Like those cabinetry pieces I made from scratch, each different, needing a groove or a ridge further up or further down. You just adjusted and did what was needed. It came natural to us veterans who had experience. You worked with uncertainty but never with raw, primitive fear, because you kept learning stuff and putting it in your memory vault. Once you knew where point A landed, your next task was to figure where point B would likely settle. That figuring took time but it could be a fun run finding the answer. Then, that goddamned back acted up on me.

"Harry, don't be mad; I want go with my wife to the nursing home on Saturday to visit her mother. Ruthie's got cousins, nieces, and nephews coming out of the woodwork to attend her mom's birthday. We know a lot of people at the place, not just the patients. Ruthie's mom was real good to me over the years. Let me know what happens with Freedom Han…"

Harry started yelling, and cursing me. It was like watching a wound-up toy soldier that goes nuts when placed on the floor, jerking itself in different directions. He pushed himself up, tried to roll the wooden table over, and when he couldn't, he grabbed *The Racing Digest* and flung it at me. Then the number two pencil that had been pushed behind his ear whizzed past my head. Last thing I remember is him calling me a horse's ass. How do you like that; I was being entered into my own race, The Horse's Ass Derby. I tried not to laugh at my friend Harry as he hurried to his battered Chevy. I was a little sad, actually, because my eyes felt moist, real moist.

I didn't see my friend Harry much after that. I guess he was hurt, but I didn't hold any grudges. I figured he'd come back soon enough. Friendship, I've learned, is a powerful thing.

I checked the paper Sunday morning before I left to fish off the Atlantic Highlands with a group of guys I knew. They ran the Metro in record time; one minute fifty-three and two/fifth seconds. Freedom Hanover was scratched because of a cracked heel, better known as Mud Fever. It happened more to younger horses, that Mud Fever business. Harry told me that; they usually outgrew it, he said.

છ

The Betty Boop Wallet

Phillip Pierce tried hard not to think of his credit card payment due Monday, or the Grow Light waiting for him at Wilson's Lighting Accents, or the infestation of roaches in his kitchen and bath that would require a call to his irritable landlord, or the unopened mail from Ginnie lying on the mahogany coffee table that likely would describe how the time-out period from their marriage should be executed. Instead, Phillip tried to have good thoughts—reasonable ones, sensible ones, kind ones, and high-minded ones.

At thirty-eight, Phillip's body aches were beyond his years but he also tried not to think of this. He was a tall man at six-foot-two inches, and wide-framed which disguised a recent weight gain. And notwithstanding the direction of his thoughts, lower back pain was creeping under his heavy raincoat. He had recently developed a heel spur which limited his mobility. Now he pulled his cap lower on his forehead and rubbed the stubble on his puffy jaw.

For a moment he held his breath when no one was looking. As he did, he focused on the stillness of his eyelash, the hopeful slowing of his heartbeat and the momentary quiescence of his abdomen. But, in truth, the tranquility of spirit he sought was hard to achieve because Phillip felt his life was destined to be cut short. His sense of foreboding was so strong that it kept him jumpy even when he tried, as he was doing now, to remain calm.

Phillip never walked in the parks after sunset and rarely took side streets in unfamiliar neighborhoods. He felt safest working with free weights every other day in his bedroom, doing his laundry on Thursdays, and taking his shower late at night so he'd miss the crime-laden television news. Despite all these efforts, Phillip Pierce's state of mind remained one of an arthritic soul as he approached the sturdy structure of the Dorothea Dix Training School for Girls, taking no notice of the American flag at half-mast.

The past Tuesday Heather Carol told everybody in the office that on her way to work she had found a Betty Boop in Her Red Dress wallet on the steps of the subway entrance. Nobody else seemed to have noticed it despite its eye-catching color and cartoon-like appearance. She had waited there with the wallet held high next to her cheek to see if the owner might return, as frazzled straphangers went around her. But when no one responded, not wanting to be late for sign-in, she'd put the wallet into her coat pocket and headed downtown.

It was now Friday afternoon as Phillip neared the school. A lone punctured cloud crossed the sky above old St. Anthony's Church, adjacent to the school. The church bells chimed twice, tunefully. Phillip hesitated once more, leaning against the back fender of a beat-up blue Volkswagen to collect himself. Knowing the task in front of him should be quick did not assuage the mild nausea he felt in his upper stomach.

It was a busy block, the kind that he normally avoided in mid-afternoon. Parishioners and students together meant the same thing: crowds and potential rowdiness where, in a flash, anything could happen. Phillip renewed his cautious pace. The belt of his stained raincoat had fallen out of the half-torn loop. He adjusted his soft wool, angora, and silk Kangol cap, pushing it up on his crown. The air was damp and his face was drained of color, and he was suffering from searing pain under a decayed back tooth. A course of antibiotics had been prescribed by his sullen dentist. A crown would be fashioned afterwards. Think of it as a restoration project, the dentist had said; the outer shell sculpted to encase his tooth would have a perfect structure, no matter what was underneath.

Phillip Pierce kept his distance and had no part in the unraveling of the three day wallet mystery that enlivened the Medicaid Eligibility Center's eighth floor office where he worked with Heather Carol. After four years in the military, he had returned home to finish college and when the state Medicaid program expanded, he was part of the hiring surge to help administer it. The job met his pre-requisite for order and security.

Phillip never talked to his co-workers about the First Gulf War. He'd been part of the ground force that liberated Kuwait from the Iraqi invaders and his unit was among the first to reach the center of Kuwait City. The soldiers heard stories of Iraqi summary executions, confiscation of personal property, and of torture and degradation. Children wandered the streets. He recalled a boy with a soiled dishdasha half-wrapped at the waist leading a girl in more modern attire but with her headscarf covered with caked blood.

As Phillip walked toward the Dorothea Dix Training School for Girls, he thought of the eye contact he'd made with those far away children and now took pains to look only at the sidewalk. Again, he tried to purify his mind but the sound of a jackhammer at the corner startled him. How often did he shake when he heard the sound of sniper fire in Kuwait? How many times had he ducked when the shards of shrapnel flew near him?

Good thought; that was what he had to aim for, but his tooth was killing him and he felt a sense of tightness in his limbs. He worried the rumbling agitation inside them might mean it could burst. Yes, Phillip had a decent collection of pains, inflammations, and troublesome images. He avoided anything to do with veterans' rights, no matter what Ginnie said. A couple of shots of Cutty Sark when he arrived home from work did more than filling out bureaucratic forms at the Office of Veteran's Affairs for milk-toast services.

He removed the brown paper bag that held the wallet with the childlike cast from the right pocket of his raincoat. Pressing the bag, he could feel the wallet's snap closure and the softness of its contents. It was a puzzle to him how something made of imitation leather could render such a cushioned feel.

He bent over and tied his black walking shoes, each with a double knot, as he recalled the plodding detective drama that played itself out at the office over the wallet. Phillip occupied one of the four ladder-back chairs at the large oak table in the center of a large room for the Medicaid Eligibility Specialists. Over the years, he'd seen plenty of the specialists come and go; kids from college on their first job, single mothers re-entering the work force, and bureaucratic fossils who'd transfer from job to job to disguise their shoddy work habits. Three women, including Heather Carol, were assigned to the other chairs. Two private offices for supervisory staff were further back on opposite sides of the table. The three women chattered when the supervisors were out of earshot.

Documenting Medicaid eligibility meant sifting through reams of paper. It was a stultifying business. Did applicants have proof of age, citizenship or alien status, residence, income, savings, and insurance? Phillip found his share of neglect and fraud. His power to reject and send an unknown applicant back for more specific information occasionally empowered him. He likened it to being a Medical Inspector at Ellis Island in years' past, who'd spot a mother shielding her toddler with a handkerchief over his nose so he wouldn't cough or sneeze, terrified of being noticed, quarantined, and then returned to her port of origin.

It started with the mid-morning break when the two busybody women, Jane Higgins and Rosalie Sampson, reminded Heather of the wallet she'd stuffed in her parka which hugged the back of her chair.

"C'mon, Heather, maybe there's a winning lottery ticket inside," Jane said, as she rubbed cream blush onto her cheeks with a sponge.

"Hey, if you find a winning lottery ticket in there, possession is nine-tenths of the law," Rosalie added from her chair.

Phillip could not take part in their initial excitement over the wallet. Like most of their conversations, this struck him as a banal distraction. He checked the overhead clock and saw that it was time for his morning break. He fumbled for his cigarettes in his shirt pocket but did not immediately leave for the smoking area downstairs. While he was not interested in the wallet or its fate, something kept him listening, loitering beside his desk.

In the exterior zipper coin pocket, the women found thirty-five cents and an old subway token. Two worn dollar bills were inserted in the money slot. In the clear case, instead of a driver's license, there was a photograph of a young African American girl with a wide smile in a blue cap and gown. At the bottom was a four-leaf clover and, in script, The Stanton Photography Studio.

There was more. Phillip was reminded of the old circus trick of a car sitting in the center ring and having a dozen clowns emerge unscathed, to begin the show for an astounded audience.

"What are these cards, here?" Jane said, pulling several out from the corner of the back compartment where the dollar bills had been.

"This is a card from Women's Health at Montefiore Medical Center," Heather said, having taken the bunched up cards from Jane, spreading them on an empty area of the oak table. "The name on the hospital card is Kizzy Tryon."

"Hey, here's a business card from a Pediatric Social Worker," Rosalie interjected.

"Yeah, but it's from another hospital, Roosevelt; I know that place well," Jane said, as if remembering a trip to its emergency room.

Phillip went to the coat rack where his raincoat hung, fingering the cigarette that he'd removed from his pocket. He figured there would still be enough time to get downstairs; the chief problem was waiting for the elevators which were either cramped or breaking down. He was sick of walking up and down staircases that held body odors and crumbs of fast food. He'd also picked up a sweet weed-like smell more than once.

There was more: the women found a laundry slip, a discount coupon for Toys "R" Us, and a receipt for a skirt from a shop called Happy Times Fashion in Astoria, Queens.

"This young girl gets around," Rosalie laughed.

"Come on, be serious people. Can you imagine what the girl must be feeling? She's most likely poor," Heather said, reaching for the last card, opening it and reading it to the others. "This is a WIC card. See, I thought she must have money troubles. Here is another picture of her." Heather waved the card toward the neon light. "Kizzy Tryon, no cap and gown in this one, but she's still got that winning smile. Kizzy, what a name! Actually, I like it; it has a certain ring to it."

"It's from that book, Roots; remember when it was on TV for like a week or something?" Jane said, bright-eyed. "Wait, Heather, check that card, isn't there another one stuck to it?"

Heather turned the card around and realized her co-worker was right. She pulled the attached one apart revealing a second WIC picture ID.

"It looks like a three- or four-year-old boy, right? Maybe it's her brother; he's got that family smile, don't you think?" Heather said. "Oh, no, don't tell me it's the girl's son; she must have been the youngest mother in the maternity ward."

"Look, there's some script on the bottom. Can you read it?" Jane stood in the middle of the three women. She took the card from Heather. "This is a name here…um, Nathaniel Martin Tryon, am I reading it…?"

"Well, that would explain the WIC card and the other ones, too." Rosalie interrupted. "This girl probably gets food vouchers. Her kid looks anemic or underweight; he's got a really thin face."

"Listen up, guys, we have just got to return this wallet," Heather said firmly.

"Why don't you take it to the police station near where you live? They'll have a Lost and Found." Phillip was surprised by the briskness of his voice but he felt compelled to speak, like he'd broken into a women's soap opera.

"The police station? Are you kidding? They will just put it in a box and store it in an underground tomb. Would you go to the police department if you lost a wallet?" Jane Higgins' eyebrows rose, her reddened cheeks following.

Phillip had seen that cast before. Draping his raincoat over his left arm, he headed for the stairwell and his smoke, hoping it would drain the tension shooting through his mid-section.

When Phillip returned, he found out Jane had called The Stanton Photography Studio and Happy Times Fashion while Heather had contacted the Pediatric Social Worker. To his surprise, notwithstanding privacy protocols, the social worker had responded. Heather had the softest voice of the women and that must've done it. The social worker agreed to contact Kizzy, who would then call Heather to set up the return.

There was a bit of telephone tag; Phillip took the first call from the girl called Kizzy. Her voice was slow, careful and low-toned, but otherwise pleasantly melodic. Ultimately, Heather arranged to meet the girl on Friday at school's end, but on that morning was told summarily that her supervisory evaluation had been shifted and would take place that afternoon. It was a professional terror Phillip and the others had to endure every six months; he'd been through many of them. He learned quickly to remain numb and defer to the higher authorities in the bureaucratic hierarchy, even if they were all royal jackasses. Heather looked crestfallen but everybody realized she had little choice but to participate in the hastily arranged meeting.

Heather knew Phillip lived close to the Dorothea Dix School and when he'd told her of his plan to see his dentist just after lunch and then return home, she inveigled him into being the one to return the wallet. Heather was even-tempered and rational, a tiny ray of sunshine in a dust-filled office. If he could talk to anyone about the tenderness above his chest or the chronic inflammation of his right knee or the tight band he often felt around his head, it was his ever-respectful colleague.

Phillip now pulled his blue cap back down, wanting to push the images from the office away. It was time to be done with the duty at hand. His back tooth continued to ache as he reached the main doors of the school. He would fill his prescription afterwards and take the first two amoxicillin capsules when he returned home. Young girls milled about in front of the school; they were spirited, playful, laughing—no doubt because it was Friday afternoon and the rigidity of their institutional life was over for the week.

Security measures were evident inside the entrance to the school. There were walk-through metal detectors, video and intercom systems, and two-way radios to allow security personnel to communicate throughout the building. Phillip had developed osteochondritis while in the military. Surgery had removed the loose fragments of cartilage and bone from his right ankle and small drill holes were placed therein to stimulate new blood vessels and to form scar tissue. Phillip was sure that metallic residue from the drill holes would touch off the sensitive metal detectors. He'd heard stories about pacemakers doing just that at airports with the spooked victim then being subjected to a public frisking.

As Phillip walked inside he saw a heavyset security guard in a blue uniform seated at a table. Two women, probably teachers' aides, sat nearby.

"Yes, sir, can I help you?" one of the women said, looking up.

"Ah, I'm here to see, ah, a Miss Kizzy Tryon, one of your students. I have a wallet to return to her," Phillip said, feeling uncomfortable. He wondered if he blushed. At least no bells or whistles had gone off.

"A wallet? Can I see some identification, sir?" The woman looked at her co-worker. "Kizzy Tryon; didn't we just see her?"

Phillip opened his raincoat and took out his driver's license from his credit card holder in his pants pocket. He signed in as directed by the security guard, who rose to point to the open guest book at the back of the table. He was also told to stand face forward so he could be photographed by the front camera.

"Hey Cassandra, where's Kizzy at?" The co-worker yelled at one of the fifteen to twenty young women in the large room adjacent to the lobby. "Is she sitting with you guys? Go get her. There's a man here, waiting to see her, says he's got her wallet."

Several book bags lay on the tiled floor in and around the room. The girls, like a Greek chorus, began to move toward Phillip. He did not like being stared at, and felt a moistness below his cap. He resolved not take the hat off.

"Go get your wallet Kizzy. Nathaniel's going to be real happy, too," Phillip heard one of the girls say. There was a buzz of approval from her friends.

A petite girl dressed in denim overalls and a zipped purple sweat jacket walked toward him. The overalls had multiple utility and tool pockets that could carry pens and pencils, maybe a ruler, perhaps a weapon like a single-action mini-revolver or a folding knife. Phillip's jaw tightened, his puffed jowls beneath stiffening like a plaster of Paris. The woman's hair was divided into large sections and soft braids adorned with yellow beads hung freely. There was puzzlement in her eyes.

"Where's Miss Heather, the lady I talked to on the phone?" she asked. The chorus of students hushed behind her, shifting their glances to the white-faced man in front of them.

"Um, she couldn't make it. I work with her. She had to attend a meeting." Phillip sensed the solemn quietude around him. The security guard held his stiff upright pose, his mutton chop arms reaching downward as if ready to raise a weapon. The teacher's aides halted their conversation. He handed the wallet to Kizzy. "Check to see if everything is there."

Kizzy opened the prize and turned it over and over as if waking from a dream. She placed it next to her ear and shook it and then smelled its pink cover. Her smile, all the while, widened like a theatre curtain might to reveal a majestic set. She opened the returned prize to examine its contents. She held the old, unusable, token high from the zipper pocket for everyone to see.

"Yes, yes, everything is here," she shrieked, jumping up and throwing her hands in the air. There was a roar of approval from her friends; they thrust their hands upward along with their heroine. It went on for a few moments, but then, in almost perfect unison, the group began to calm itself, eyes shifting from each other to the unkempt, puzzled, stiff, uncertain-looking man in front of them.

There was a long, considered pause. Those seconds seemed like an eternity to Phillip as if what they might do next could penetrate his turtle-like shell. His left thumb started to flutter.

He felt hot and cold at the same time. He had no idea…a few of the girls began to applaud, slowly at first, and then others joined in, lifting the decibel count. They held their applause for a time. The teacher's aides rose from their chairs to acknowledge the happy ending being played out in front of them. The security guard had a perplexed expression, as if he'd seen an alien, but not of the kind that required his brawn.

Phillip's mind raced, even as his body stiffened further. He began to tremble; it was all he could do not to burst forth. He pressed down on his chest, on his heart, on his stomach, and on his toes to quell the rising panic within him. He felt he was suffocating; he could not draw a deep breath. He felt knots of pain from his shoelaces. He tried to mouth the words, 'I didn't do it, I didn't do it; it wasn't me.'

On the outskirts of Kuwait City, he'd felt the same choking feeling, the same startle, the same agitation, and the same feeling of exposure. His unit had swept through a village that suffered losses from friendly fire, rather than the ordinance of a departing Iraqi enemy. The soldiers knew the intelligence error would never be acknowledged; they just lowered their heads and hoped their uniforms would merge with the desert dust.

In a shell-ridden back alley, he'd come upon a Kuwaiti shopkeeper who lay mortally wounded, bleeding profusely. Phillip went on a knee to attempt to support the man whose half-closed eyes pushed up toward his skull. He knew that sight was the first sense to leave the dying soul. When the artillery bombardment and gunfire ebbed, the villagers opened their doors and approached their fallen friend whose blood covered Phillip's boot and pant leg. The silence, in that cratered passageway, was more deafening than the carpet bombing from a B-52. Phillip understood, looking at the Kuwaitis' eyes, their disillusionment, their protest against war, tribal hubris, and the politics of black gold, even if they were now safe to occupy their homes. Squatting there, next to the man with the smell of his ending near, Phillip's heart raced, and his mouth dried. He felt his body disengaging from itself as he tried to evade the shame that enveloped him. *'It wasn't me, I didn't do it; it's not my fault.'*

Phillip bolted, gasping for air, almost knocking over the security guard who was too stunned to react. He forgot about his recent heel spur. Part of him realized how silly he might have appeared to the gathered clan of the blithesome girls at the Dorothea Dix School, but he was in the grip of an impulse beyond his control. He needed air and an open field, a known field. He had trouble swallowing; his breathing was shallow and rapid. He tried holding his breath as he ran but that only made things worse, the panic bursting through with the force of a pulsating geyser. He had no idea what was happening to him.

He managed to stop at his local pharmacy to fill his prescription; the wait time there helped to mollify him. His breathing became full and regular only when he approached his five-story graystone, the foundation most familiar to him.

His apartment had once exuded precision and order, but now with Ginnie gone, cracks of waste appeared. A Playboy magazine lay on top of the Pembroke table near the front door. Dust balls rose up under the flaps of the table. A spider plant that hung from the ceiling next to the living room window sagged. How much the Grow Light waiting at Wilson's would help was debatable. A graveyard of cigarette ash on his computer table settled on a tray looking like stale lava lining a mountain slope. Next to it was a half-empty bottle of Cutty Sark. A stale corn flake lay at the table's edge trying not to fall and papers were strewn about.

Phillip tossed his raincoat and raced to the bathroom to take the amoxicillin, with lots of water. His back tooth shot pellets of pain. Ginnie would never take antibiotics for toothaches; she'd rub herbs like clove oil, cow parsnip tincture, or bark of white willow on the area to reduce inflammation. He returned to the living room to recline on his brown leather chair adjacent to the sofa, unaware of its loosening walnut base. He poured a Cutty Sark and reached into his shirt pocket for his cigarettes. He could still smell Ginnie's spicy and aromatic fragrance which had penetrated the sofa, and the leather chair she had ceded to him, and the Tree of Life drapery behind him with its shorn tiebacks.

He nursed his drink and took a long, cool drag on his cigarette, staring through the hanging spider leaf. He now felt steady, strong, but in a way he had not experienced before. Kizzy Tryon was no more than seventeen-years old. Her son had to be younger than five; otherwise he would not have qualified for the WIC program with its grants of infant formula and iron fortified cereal. Heather was right; Kizzy must've endured plenty of hardships in her life. Perhaps she'd been abused, even raped, or abandoned. Her environment was, no doubt, a raw one. She probably wore second-hand clothes, sought out dollar stores for bargains, never attended movies or concerts, or traveled. All she had was a drive to improve her life and that engaging smile.

Phillip began to embrace more fully the meaning of returning her wallet, as shabby, inexpensive, and as used as it appeared to be. In the midst of Kizzy's harsh life, Heather had given her a gift of unconditional kindness. The girl could store it as a memory and return to it during the inevitable times when she'd face a world that likely would remain unloving, and unfair.

Phillip put out his cigarette. He poured another shot of Cutty Sark, which he sipped slowly. He reclined several more minutes in his favorite chair, in the continued reverie about the vicissitudes of the day. An ease came over him, as if his body had been swallowed by a descending light sent to warm and protect him. Oddly, he felt good about himself for a moment and the feeling slightly startled him. He was able to dismiss the pain from his decayed tooth. He picked himself up, his body in step with itself, and started toward the bedroom. In the hallway mirror, he caught sight of himself and was surprised to note the small depression from the single dimple on his left cheek, and that he was smiling. In the bedroom, he retrieved the metal tool box and returned with it to his chair.

He opened the box and there it was, shining in front of him, the magnificent icon with its golden cover. Its appearance was distinctive with a massive frame and slide. The Desert Eagle with the powerful .50 Action Express cartridge was the most handsome of handguns—powerful, agile, with excellent accuracy and limited recoil. He had tested it many times at the Rod and Gun Club in Yonkers. It was cleaned and its six parts were now fully assembled. Hollywood knew this beauty was something special because it signified that revolvers and single-shot pistols were dated. They had first used the Desert Eagle in 1984 in *The Year of the Dragon*, with Mickey Rourke. More recently, it was onscreen in two Arnold Schwarzenegger movies, *The Last Action Hero* and *Eraser*.

Like most people he knew, Ginnie was terrified of guns. "I do not want any accidents in this house; I'm not going near you when I see that thing, lock it up!" She'd added this to her usual complaints about his lack of spontaneity and intimacy. "Take a different route to work, surprise yourself, then maybe you'll surprise me," she'd say to him when she was pissed. "Why don't you ever come home with a dozen roses? If you can't manage that, well, get me tulips. I like tulips."

He'd been impervious and narrow; she was right about that. Then there was her wish to have children, which he'd resisted. She'd come from a large family in Vermont and was now back in a suburb of Montpelier doing substitute teaching where her older sister lived. He couldn't imagine himself a parent; he was a good soldier doing his duty, not a commander formulating policy. How could he spread his genetic load when it was so hollow and compromised?

He looked at the Cutty Sark but did not reach for the near-empty bottle. Neither did he press his shirt pocket to get a read on how many cigarettes he had left. He no longer thought about his cheerless dentist with his promises of perfection. He no longer pondered about Heather Carol or the two boobs who worked with her. He no longer cared how he might have looked to the beatific schoolgirls at the Dorothea Dix Training School for Girls from whom he had fled.

Kizzy Tryon was the last to distance from his mind. He knew if she was with him now she'd wave goodbye, and broaden her winning smile. She would tell him that she'd continue to think of him from time to time because he had been the one to return her wallet.

He removed the Desert Eagle from the otherwise empty tool box. He made sure that his finger draped full over the hair trigger. He stared for a moment into empty space and reminded himself of the good thoughts Kizzy Tryon had inspired. He pointed the gun at his right temple and after several seconds of holding his breath he pulled the trigger. There was a burst of celestial light and in that light Phillip Pierce's collection of invisible hurts and inflammations were sucked into a patch of golden earth, and he dropped the gun to the floor.

∞

Reverse Tide

Last night, despite the rainstorm, I visited Wally and Karin in West Orange, New Jersey. Wally, standing a half foot taller than me and with broad shoulders, was my fraternity brother and we remained close after college. He'd met Karin, an attractive, petite woman with an easy demeanor, in his senior year and by graduation he was engaged. I was an usher at their wedding, ten months later. Now, after a dozen years of marriage there were two children—Mark, age six, and Jamie, age four. Mark was lanky and had curly brown hair. His blue and red Spiderman pajamas were chocolate stained. Jamie was stockier and had his father's build with puffed cheeks that had a reddish hue. His pajama top had "dino tracks," dinosaurs with footprints in a myriad of colors. I knew growth spurts were forming in each, even though they were too young to realize it.

During my visit the kids were fascinated with their latest book, King Wacky, and asked me to read it to them on the living room sofa, as their father sat opposite us on the wing chair just in case I messed up. I felt honored and put my best effort into the reading, knowing they'd probably heard the story fifty times before. Mark allowed himself to nestle close to me, curling two fingers on my forearm. He stared up at me with a wide smile that could not fracture his smooth, young skin. Jamie placed his head on his brother's shoulder, with his eyelids at half-mast.

In the Kingdom of Woosey, so the fable went, there was a happy event; a Prince was born, Prince Wacky. One day, the Prince would become King Wacky, the ruler of Woosey. The only problem was that he had been born with his head on backwards. I laughed as I read the book, eager to see what would come next. Wacky did everything backward, like brushing his teeth before a meal and washing his hands afterward. He said, "Good Morning," at night and "Good Night," in the morning.

After becoming King of Woosey, Wacky looked to take a Queen. An arrangement was made for him to marry Princess Honey, from a neighboring land. When Wacky met the beautiful princess, he fell in love instantly and said to her, "Princess Honey, you are the ugliest thing I've ever seen." Because of this remark, there was almost a war between the two kingdoms, but it all ended happily as Wacky and the Princess secured their love and their two lands remained at peace.

"And, and, and, you are the most horriblest Daddy in New Jersey and the whole wide world," Jamie, the four-year-old, said to his father, checking for affirmation from his older brother. "And…ah, you smell, you smell stinky, like a gorilla," he added for good measure. He was braving tough waters here; a gutsy little kid, I thought. His father, who'd been stone-faced, leaned forward.

"Jamie, my boy, you are the dumbest son a father could ever have. Your brain is the size of a pea. And as for you, Marky, when the stork came I wanted a little girl named Malvina; instead, he dropped off the most ridiculous boy on Mommy and Daddy's bed." Wally sighed, threw his hands in the air as if to say a father had to take whatever was given to him.

The two boys huddled together, trying to remain serious, whispering in consultation for their next move.

"Daddy, me and Jamie, we think…" Mark exploded with laughter followed by Jamie who slid from the sofa onto the plush carpet.

"Yes, my two simple-minded kids, do you have something to say to your father?"

I realized the scene in front of me was less about King Wacky's dilemma, and more about private language. It reminded me of the high-pitched whistle my recent girlfriend, Candy, and I used at department stores and street fairs when we lost each other in the maze of sections. I guess an off tune, oscillating refrain to "Here Comes the Bride" from pursed lips, can count as private language, too. When we argued, we had an arrangement that either could shout out, "full moon setting" which was our signal for an hour's timeout. A "half-moon" meant thirty minutes. I once asked for an "eighth-moon" which cracked her up so much she forgot what she was pissed about.

At thirty-two, Candy remained fresh-faced in my memory, with long black hair that reached below her shoulders. Sometimes she wore her hair in a ponytail held together by bright-colored silk scarves. She rarely applied makeup. Her ears tucked close to the sides of her head. Her green eyes were open and searching, with luscious centers of emerald, and her eyebrows curved up and away. Then there were Candy's breasts. Cupcake Left and Cupcake Right, I called them. They were small, round, and centered in the most exquisite way, like a blossomed rosebush. She liked having them held and caressed, saying she could cum from just that alone. I'd make up stories about Cupcake Left and Cupcake

Right as if they were two rivalrous but loving sisters. I allowed myself to imagine that I was the prize they sought, especially when Candy would place my hand on the edge of her nipple. "Come closer, honey," she'd whisper. Those words sealed the contract which advanced our connection. Candy was far away now, in Seattle.

Back in New Jersey, I watched Mark and Jamie, their shoulders hunched with hands over their mouths, as they tried for a last jab at their dad.

"Um, Daddy, you're the stupidest Daddy, cause…cause you go out in your underwear in the winter," Mark said.

"Yeah, you do Daddy. I saw you do that and you pee peed in the snow, three times," Jamie chirped, as he positioned himself back on the sofa.

"Me and Jamie know you are the worst Daddy, ever. Want to know why?"

"I sure do, my two strange yellow-bellied sapsuckers."
I nodded at Wally for his crafty response, one that kept the game going.

"You're the worst Daddy, cause you never take us anywhere. No play dates, no movies, no baseball games. You keep us locked in the basement, without food or water." Mark stood like a confident prosecutor and pushed up on his toes to squeeze the delight from his coup de grace.

Just then Karin appeared wiping her hands with a dish towel. "Wally, it's getting late. You better get your buddy down to the stop, you never know about the DeCamp buses."

"Okay, honey, you put these nincompoops to bed."

"I agree with Daddy," she said looking at her boys. "We have two of the naughtiest boys parents could have." As I stood up to get my coat I thought, again, how Wally had made a good choice for a mate.

At the bus shelter at Northfield and Gregory Avenues, an older lady was there with a rain hat pulled over a pair of narrow eyes that looked like silver-plated knives. With her trench coat's collar standing up to her chin, she resembled a spy in one of those 1940's espionage movies; a Nazi, of course.

"The bus is sure to be late on a night like this," said an arriving, youthful-looking woman wearing a purple and red Gore-Tex windbreaker. She pulled down its hood to reveal wild flowing hair that crested on her shoulders. Aside from being young, she seemed fresh in a good way, as if nothing was a big deal with her. And she smelled like an evergreen.

"Yup, I guess you're likely right about that," I mumbled with effort, glancing back at my presumed Nazi spy.

Ten minutes went by when a car pulled up at the light. The passenger-side window rolled down and an old guy leaned out, "If you're waiting for the DeCamp bus, it was in an accident a few blocks back, just so you know you'll be waiting awhile."

I knew the next bus, the last, was more than an hour away and as I was trying to decide whether to call Wally back, the young woman spoke, "I'm going back to work; anyone want to come with me and dry off?"

"Back to work? You're kidding me, aren't you? Nobody goes back to work after leaving for the day."

"Oh, it's no problem. I work at Wyeth's Chemists around the corner. It's our turn to be on call for the town, so today we're open twenty-four hours. I'll catch the last bus; I know the schedule by heart."

"What are you going to do back at work?" I asked, realizing I didn't want this daisy of a woman to leave. I felt the pull of my blue suspenders on my mid-section and noticed the rain was holding steady with a thickening mist. There was sure to be a fog in the early morning.

"I'm a Pharmacy Aide. I'll stock the late day deliveries; we're always behind on that. We're near Valley General. Their emergency room patients will be coming to us tonight. Listen, I'm not standing here getting a slow soaking; anybody coming?"

She left, moving up Northfield with an airy bounce like she could weave enough between the raindrops to stay warm. When a rain pellet dropped on my lower lip, I decided to follow her. I saw the Nazi move deeper into the shelter, waving her hand to let me know she'd remain there.

"Wait up, Miss, I'm coming." When we were side by side, I realized she was carrying books and asked her if she was a student.

"Yes, I'm working at the pharmacy to put myself through Rutgers."

"Good for you. That must be hard—working while going to school."

"It's not too hard; I like my job and I love being a student."

"What are you studying?"

"I'm majoring in education; I want to become a Special Ed teacher."

She was easy to talk to—attractive, sunny, with a wide smile that showed pinkish gums which looked like tiny pillows cushioning pedestals of ivory. Most of all, she seemed enthusiastic about life. I didn't know anybody who loved being a student.

"Anything special taking you into Manhattan tonight?"

"Well, if the bus ever comes, I'm going to my mother's in Brooklyn to be there for a christening tomorrow." At that point we arrived Wyeth's and, once inside, she waved me towards a chair. "Here, you can sit in Mr. Willington's task chair. It swivels 360 degrees, so you can see whatever there is to see."

"Hey, I'll be fine. I'm just grateful for a dry place to sit."

Somehow we got to the subject of her boyfriend and she blushed when I asked if she hoped to be married. Then, I felt intrusive and left her alone. I hadn't even bothered to ask her name or offer mine. After she sauntered off to the back of the pharmacy, I could see her working on the shelves stocked with medicines. There were two narrow aisles in front for patrons. I was sitting in a small room off one of them.

Testing the chair with the full swivel in the middle of the room, I went straight into a reverie about my trip to Canada with Candy a year ago, a few months before she took off for Seattle. It was in late spring and we toured the Bay of Fundy in New Brunswick Province. The Bay has the highest tides in the world and when they meet at the starting point of the Saint John River, the flow of the river reverses its natural current.

We were in Moncton, a city in the province, on the Petitcodiac River, which also attached itself to the Bay of Fundy. They had something there called a Tidal Bore. Twice a day, a wave of water advanced up river, pushed by a rapid rise of the tide at its mouth, boring its way through narrow channels and against the natural flow. Late afternoon, tourists gathered at the tapered riverbed, dry during the day, to wait for the gush of water forcing its way upstream. There was an exact timetable to herald its arrival.

"Hey, sweetie, what if one day the reverse flow didn't come or if it gushed a minute late?," I said to Candy. I remembered holding her left hand with my right and using my left to check my watch. I wanted to reverse the reverse, hoping it would give me a feeling of being on top of matters.

"What are you talking about? Stick to things you can change." She tickled the inside of my palm with her finger.

"No, really, what if I had the power to disrupt this time-table; suppose I had a dam put up downstream?" Candy had a playful spirit, loved a good joke, but she caught my childlike craziness. I really wanted to get her back to the hotel room to see what we could do with our own tidal flows.

"Grow up, big boy" she said, with a knowing smile.

The reverse tide came on time, with energy and a forceful grace. There was a muted buzz from the tourists. As for me, well, the predictability was actually soothing and I had a feeling of calm.

"Hey, sir," the young Pharmacy Aide said, removing her white coat with the Wyeth's Chemists printed on the lapel, "We'd better get to the bus stop. How'd you like the famous task chair?" I didn't like her calling me sir; it made me feel ancient.

The bus to Port Authority was overcrowded because of the earlier mishap and I was forced to stand, another turnabout of form. The Nazi was nowhere to be seen. I couldn't get next to my protector to catch any further wisdom she might offer. She'd taken a seat in a back row and her quiet "goodbye" was lost in the chatter of disgruntled passengers. Also, her fresh evergreen smell was overtaken by the dank environs of the weather-beaten bus.

Port Authority on a late Saturday night is ripe for pick-pockets and scam artists. I did a quickstep to the west side subway and felt relieved when I arrived home. I spotted Candy's unopened letter lying on my night table. A dust ball sat on the envelope under the two cancelled Forever stamps. The letter came Thursday, two days earlier. Make that three since it was now past midnight. I liked opening mail on Sundays; there was no one I had to answer to, at least right away.

I opened the letter and read it, cracking a smile when I saw how she'd signed it. The first two paragraphs tickled my funny bone but they also made me a little mad.

Hey Mister,

If you happen to be reading this with a cutie at your side, could you at least warn her of the sharp daggers that protrude from your menacing toes? That's a pre-existing condition, you know, never manicuring your toenails. You never took care of them for me. These are not the words of an aggressive female, but rather an informed representation from someone who cares about you and wishes the best for you.

So, how are you, my friend? Here is the news from this end of the world, an area you figured would be the ass-end of civilization. The first thing I can repeat to you is, well, I really continue to like it here.

Anyway, I'm writing because I'll be taking a few days off at the end of the semester, in mid-June, and I'd love it if you'd come to Seattle for a visit. There's lots to do and the sun will be back out for the summer.

Let me know what you think. Give me a call when you can; I know it's your nature to mull things over for awhile.

Full Moon Sometimes Blue.

Love,
Candy

I wished I could take the best meaning out of her words, and out of circumstances in general. Candy was so good at doing that. She's a Curriculum Guidance Specialist in the Department of Education at the University of Washington, a tenure track position. She moved to Seattle last August to join her best friend from college, Emma Worthington. Emma is a budding playwright who'd won a grant from the National Endowment for the Humanities. When she came east to visit Candy, I did my best disappearing act.

So after four years together, and despite our best efforts, Candy and I have gone our separate ways, agreeing to remain friends, whatever that means. I have never been to the city of the Space Needle and Pikes Place Market. I felt numb after reading the letter a second time. I decided to take a shower, hoping I could sleep late.

Most times I don't remember my dreams, but that night maybe because of feeling out of whack, I had one that stayed with me—every detail. I dreamt my apartment was transformed into a home in the country. The people and furniture were scaled to a miniature, like a Lilliputian village. In the dream, I was normal-sized, sitting on my bed in tight-fitting pajamas, leaning over in confused amazement watching the scene unfold beneath me.

There was a flurry of activity and movement as two women, one older with grayish hair, probably the mother of the other, washed and stacked dishes in the kitchen. Their conversation was spirited. Meantime, in the living room, a group of children sat around a Monopoly board. I could see two green houses on Park Place and a red hotel on Boardwalk, the best properties to own. Game money was strewn about. A young boy pointed to the television, which was playing a cartoon. His playmates looked up and roared with laughter. A cocker spaniel, dozing on its paw near a sun splattered window, lifted its winsome face and barked twice.

In the bedroom, a pile of laundry was neatly stacked on a white canopied poster bed. A bald, clean-shaven man dressed in brown khakis and green polo shirt practiced his golf swing with a short iron from a set of clubs positioned next to the dresser bureau. And there was a second bedroom, freshly painted in a soft yellow tone. The hardwood floor was buffed bright and looked like a glazed peach. Two hard hat construction men were testing the grooves at corners to ensure that the room's foundation was solid. It was otherwise empty.

Outside the living room window an older man, tanned, in a blush mesh hat, worked in a small garden, weeding and planting. The sun inched across a pristine sky and suggested the noon hour. A pruning hook lay on the grass near an overgrown cranberry bush and a row of sunflowers in bud stage prepared to turn west to follow the moving sun. The man lifted the brim of his hat and wiped his forehead with a red bandana handkerchief as a woman arrived with a tray of food, acknowledging his efforts on the sculptured garden.

Despite my giant status, I felt uncertain about the cheerful life movement in front of me because it had no pause and that frightened me. I decided to snuff it all out. I put my right foot down on the Monopoly board and the laughing boys and turned it hard like a man putting out his finished cigarette. Funny thing was, when I lifted my foot back up, the boys and the surrounding furniture, at first flattened, just snapped back into place.

I did it three times, once even jumping high and landing with both feet, stomping on the garden. Each time there was a snap back to function much like one of those candles that can't be blown out after it has been lit.

I woke up lightheaded with a racing pulse and a damp pajama top. It was before seven, early for me on a Sunday. So much for sleeping till noon. I had no idea as to the significance of the dream. Did it suggest chaos or did it suggest order? I was more for the chaos theory. But, if it was chaos, how come the people and everything around them snapped back to size and shape?

I checked the clock again on my bedside table hoping I was wrong about the time, and that I'd fallen back to sleep. I noticed Candy's letter sitting there, where I'd left it hours before, and re-read it. "Full Moon Sometimes Blue. Love, Candy" was how she'd ended it, in handsome looking script.

I didn't know how Candy did it or why, but she found the centermost spot of my being. I missed her naked body draping over me, her arm and long fingers settling on my mid-section. I missed those fingers when they were active, spreading delight and arousing my genitalia, coiled and ready to spring to its partnered task. But the folds of skin and the nerve endings in my lower region that expanded in its pleasure also pushed upward to another center in me, the one that housed the deepest regard for another. It was the place where envy and jealousy were dismantled through the exchange of ideas and the discovery of common values. Why did she have to move three thousand miles away?

I consider myself a secular humanist which to me means enjoy things while you can, and maybe do a few good deeds along the way. When something is dead to me, however, it lays dead and dormant forever. So, when I closed the door after Candy left, I meant it to be shut. Now I'm left to wonder if this was just my angry spirit at work and that maybe what I was feeling could not remain buried under the turning leaves of that day last summer when Candy got into her car to drive cross-country to Seattle.

I used to smoke, and sometimes I feel the familiar cravings and the desire for the "feel good" sensation that would arrive within seconds of a puff. I settled for getting some sweetened cereal and bringing it back to my bed.

There is a question I've had for years about the rules of multiplication. I could never quite figure out why a minus two multiplied by a minus two equaled a plus four. How could two minuses result in a plus? Two plus numbers multiplied never yielded a minus result. Something about that seemed out of sync to me even though I accepted the rule. So, could two people who were in debt join together and come out ahead? Now there was a reversal of fortune, a downside that became an upside. I was thinking again about that King Wacky guy. He didn't do too badly for himself. He got his Princess Honey and became the benevolent ruler of his land. Humpty Dumpty should have been so lucky.

I must've dozed off as at one in the afternoon I woke, still holding Candy's letter. I opened the wide-slatted Venetian blind, avoiding the black soot on the edges as much as possible. The window sill was wet from last night's rain, but the fog that I'd expected was nowhere to be seen. A high sun had broken through the puffed grey cotton clouds. Through an alleyway, I could see the outline of a horse chestnut beginning to flower in Central Park, a block east.

I dressed and grabbed my day pack and headed to Barnes and Nobles on Broadway. I went there lots of Sundays, picked an aisle and section for myself and used my pack for a cushion against a wall. I liked reading travel books, but today after having a coffee with extra sugar at the second floor café near the Children's Book Section, I went to the aisle that carried the paperbacks on self-improvement. I loved reading the bios of the authors on the back flaps, trying to decide which ones might be authentic. I had paper and a Manila envelope in my pack; a pen was in my pocket, just in case there was anything memorable enough to note. I checked my wallet to make sure I had postage stamps. I laughed at the notion that I might be mailing something on a Sunday.

It went well at the bookstore and I headed to Belvedere Castle in Central Park. The turret of the castle was the highest point in the park. Perhaps I'd be lifted on a bed of leaves supported by an even wind, to circle the park's treasures: Bethesda Fountain, Lasker Rink and Pool, Duke Ellington Circle, The Dairy and Chess and Checkers House, and The Reservoir with its surrounding horse trails. I'd see children at play near the statue of Hans Christian Anderson. I would return through the Great Lawn knowing that I'd have crossed a field of joy, a field where the highest kite might have grazed the bluest sky.

I found a park bench that appeared to be splinter free. I pulled out the writing paper from my backpack. I laughed, this time out loud, not caring if anyone saw my flushed face. I wrote Candy that I was surprised and saddened to hear from her, and that I'd been able to keep her out of my mind since her move to Seattle. I told her that memories of good times together were few and far between while the rocky ones loomed large and insurmountable. It was my view that the quality time we shared together was minimal and more of the flesh than the spirit. Yes, for me, it was nothing more than a below the belt relationship with no sustaining feelings, and so I was therefore refusing her offer of a visit to Seattle as well as the suggestion that we talk on the phone. There simply was nothing to discuss as far as I was concerned. I felt relieved as I put this on the writing paper, and the words came with an easy flow.

The Manila envelope was full and ready to be placed in a mailbox. I wished there was a Sunday pickup; it was enough to know that the Post Office was considering dropping the Saturday one. The wind was calm and still. The sun was beginning to set and its final rays would cast a wide glow over the park. It was almost five in the evening. The rest of the night would provide a warm solace from the afterlife of the events that started with my visit to Wally and Karin's. I suggested, in the first paragraph, that Candy read the enclosed book, "King Wacky," before finishing my letter.

⁂

Dances of Life

The waiting was the worst part, loitering beside the hospital bed his doctor arranged for him at home. The prospect of having to sit with my father still held the usual terror. It was his face I recalled most, the raising of his bushy eyelashes, the saliva cresting at the corner of his lip, and the sweat dripping from his sideburns.

"The chemotherapy is sapping your father's strength and no longer doing its job," my mother had told me in her weekly call. "He is going to have home hospice care and he's asked for you to come."

So I flew to Philadelphia and the east coast humidity of late summer from Idaho where I'd been working for three years as a Conservation Coordinator at a Forest Training Center, a job my father frowned at. My father was always demanding; he was a high school history teacher who didn't suffer fools lightly, but he could be sweet and even gregarious when it suited his needs. Worst for me were his periods of silence when I had no idea what was floating through his mind. I knew he was the man who thought women wearing slacks were "Lesbos." I knew he was the man who left vegetables on his plate in favor of a second slice of sirloin. I knew he was the man who told me fascism was coming to America because presidents acted like generals with absolute power. The feeling of not wanting to be like him haunted me and made me think I was partnering with the devil.

"Be a good boy, get me some water, no ice," he said to me when I entered the antiseptic-smelling room on my second day with him. His frame, once spectacular with broad shoulders, a sculpted chest, powerful legs, and extra wide feet that required special order shoes, was now withered and frail. I closed my eyes when I saw bony strictures pushing out from his skin. He was less than six feet now. The white boxer shorts, cuffed slacks, and pima cotton shirts with stays were long gone. I started to imagine him as a human skeleton. Today, he lay under a starched white linen sheet.

"Remember, no ice," he said, again, as I moved to the bathroom with his cup. I saw his prison, the hospital bed with its head and foot-boards looking like balsa wood bookends holding an archaic fossil. I spotted the controls for the raising and lowering of the bed's height. The mattress was supple but I knew my father would never rise from it, and that he would rust, weaken further, and turn to ash.

"Here's your water, Dad, just the way you like it," I smiled. His eyes were open, but appeared to be focused on images far away. After he drank some water, he coughed, spit into a tissue and then broke his silence with a voice that contained more strength than I expected.

"There is something I have wanted to show you, all these years." He reached for a metal toolbox on the night table to his right. "Do you remember Thomas Milton? He died in a car accident when you were about twelve or thirteen."

"I do. Wasn't he the man that played chess with me?"

"He was a hell of a chess player. Well, when I was twenty-seven years old, like you now, and just two years shy of meeting your mother, I accompanied Thomas and his wife on a weekend to visit their seven-year-old son Frankie. I was kind of a godfather to him. It was the kid's first venture at sleep away camp."

"Is this the same son that went to, uh…?"

"Oxford, that's right. He's still living in London. Anyway, the campgrounds were in the Pocono Mountains adjacent to a lake. After some organized activities, the kids had two hours to spend with their parents. Frankie wanted to show us a fort in the woods and then walk along the lake's edge to try and skip rocks across the surface. The fort turned out to be more like a holding area, maybe a sentry post from an earlier time. It was about fifty yards from the water, enclosed except for a back entrance. The layered rocks were substantial, and reached my chest when I stood inside. I decided to remain at the fort while my friends went to the lake with their son. The rocks were uneven, as if the assemblers had left them purposely spiked to discourage anyone from sitting against them too long. As I tried to nestle into a comfortable position, I felt movement in the rock at the small of my back. I turned, and to my surprise I was able to manipulate this rock from side to side. I squatted and looked through the tiny space, only to see two more rocks behind the one I had been able to wiggle. Then, I noticed that between the second and third rock, sat a beige-colored cloth pushed deep into a crevice. I couldn't reach it with my hands and a stick didn't help but I continued jiggling the rocks until I was able to nudge them enough so that the cloth wrapping dislodged itself, falling to the narrow side. Now the stick that hadn't worked before helped push the cloth toward me. Finally, I had it. It was a piece of lace, sturdy with dirt and twigs on it. The lace was the covering for a crisp-feeling paper rolled up inside, like a map. Perhaps a map that would take me to a stash of forgotten riches, perhaps a scroll from tribal nomads or an Indian tribe that had lodged in the area, perhaps a letter from a lover never collected, or perhaps nothing more than specifications of a county water line. Those were my thoughts, but I unfurled what turned out to be the most exquisite writing paper, in excellent condition, with a watermark embossed at the bottom."

"Dad, what's this about? Why are you telling me this now? A watermark?"

"Wait, I'll explain and you'll see for yourself. The script on it was from an ink that, because of its viscosity, had maintained a perfectly clear legibility. I realized that this was a well thought out placement I had come upon."

I was hooked at this point and even more so when he opened the toolbox and removed the writing paper, still furled, with a makeshift ribbon around its middle. It looked weathered to me.

"Here, take it downstairs to read. Dry your hands first; there are perspiration stains everywhere. I am a little tired, now. I'm going to take a nap."

So I carried the document down the staircase and this is what I read as I sat, cross-legged, on the carpet in front of my father's wing chair.

On This Twenty-Third Day of June, 1870

Thank you so much parents and townspeople for coming today. You have become my dear, dear confidants. I am proud and indeed fortunate to be standing here to address you as the School Master of the first graduating class at the Big Springs School, our one-room schoolhouse in Douglas County, Kansas.

It is amazing to me how thirty-two pupils, grades one to eight, have managed to learn so well in such a small room. The twelve eighth graders that graduated at last Sunday's ceremony will enter an uncertain world. I trust that their instruction here will stand them in good stead. Perhaps one of them will even choose to further his education and complete an advanced certificate in normal school training so he might teach in a schoolhouse such as ours. I thank Miss Elsa Standwell and Mr. Elmer Higgins, our Art and Music teachers, who come to us monthly to offer students an appreciation of culture. Big Springs School has been used for church services, election polling, tax collection, pot luck suppers, and quilting bees. Oh, and of course, the children have had their spelling bees here.

If you would allow an aside for a more personal story today, I would like to confess to you the reason I feel so fortunate to be standing here as the teacher at the school. It is the reason I have asked for this unusual meeting, just a week after the children's graduation festivities.

As you are aware, we have come out of a great war, although it may be a misrepresentation to claim that any war is great. One might argue that the nation's recent struggles resulting in so much anguish and loss have come from a necessary conflict. Perhaps those struggles will assure a continued unity and growth of our country. History will judge if that is so.

I participated in this war. I was raised in the East and after the enemy triumphed at the second Battle of Bull Run, I joined the Pennsylvania Militia that organized on September 11th of 1862 and mustered some twelve days later. I served with the First Regiment, Company H, under Colonel Henry McCormick. From the moment the thousands of us answered the call to arms, our lives changed. The goal of remaining alive superseded all other thoughts, even though at times we felt that we were laboring in the service of a righteous cause. Doing one's duty was predicated on honor and dignity, but we soldiers also knew it was the fear of exposure, exposure of our terrors to our commanders and brothers, that kept us in line.

There came a time in our military expeditions when we gathered in a wide field near a homestead. The autumnal mornings kept our toes numb and the afternoon sun sapped us dry. We were too tuckered out from maneuvers to move to the high ground. The enemy loomed above a ridge and soon they opened fire. It was the first time, my friends, that I was to join the battle and if there was a jolt of fear, why there was a rush of excitement as well.

There was bedlam on the field with Blue and Gray volunteers engaging like worker ants asserting themselves against an intruder. I wondered about the terror those in the homestead might be experiencing as they huddled in their cellar wondering which side would arrive at their door first, and with what demands.

I saw one of our officers fall. It was Captain William H. Hawkins, one of the older company leaders. Captain Hawkins was a hard case–a huffy man, always jawing at us privates, denying privileges, and demanding that we lace our boots properly and take exceptional care of our muskets. He would have us stand erect even at the end of a day's walk while he strutted about like a peacock lecturing us on the stratagems of war, referencing Alexander the Great, Genghis Khan, and Napoleon. The men despised him and called him pock-faced because the fissures on his cheeks would redden as he grew more inflammatory in his speech.

There had been a day in the recent past when, as we rested in a clearing, I was ordered to gather firewood. As I was completing the task I spotted a lone figure with his back to me, sitting hunched over on a rock, head bowed. He wore our uniform, so I approached. I saw that it was the pock-faced Captain Hawkins. The big bug looked small sitting there. He was crying softly, his hands over his eyes. There was a letter lying on the ground to his right with a patch of dirt over part of it. He remained in this pose for several minutes. The wind picked up and I thought the letter would blow away. The fear he might see me overtook any further curiosity I had but my eyes were moist at witnessing the Captain's assuredly bad personal news. I turned to light out.

"Who's there?" he bellowed, dropping his hands and turning in my direction. I let my load slide from my arms and

I bolted from the woods. I was terrified I had been recognized so I moved like the jackrabbit being chased by the fox. I could only imagine the shape and magnitude of the vengeance he would wreak on me, though none ever came.

Now let me return to the bedlam on the field of battle. Captain Hawkins was on the forward part of the ridge bleeding profusely. I then did a not very smart thing. I crossed the plain to where he had planted himself on his right knee. His pants were red-stained and they surely would need a proper burial.

"It's you," he said, looking up with a stricken expression. "What are you doing here? Toe the mark, boy, get back to your duty."

"Get up, sir, we need you," I sang out. The sounds from the muskets were deafening. I helped him to his feet and we somehow made it to a more protected area at the back of our lines. I had no explanation for what I had done. It seemed quite foreign from any previous sense I had of myself.

If you would like, my dear people, to know the fate of Captain Hawkins, I can report to you that he survived, and without need for old sawbones to perform his ghastly task. I heard three years later he took part in General William T. Sherman's campaign in the south against Generals Joseph Johnston and Pierre G.T. Beauregard at the Battle of Bentonville in 1865, one of the enemy's last major offensives. Anyways, I was told I would receive a promotion for my action, in addition to The Civil War Campaign Medal given to all who served.

As it happened, a few weeks later we were scattered deep in a vast forest in the Pennsylvania woods. There had been intermittent engagements with the enemy. One day after traversing many miles, our Company came upon a lake. The calm water and the untouched landscape made it seem like we had found a passageway to the heavens. We could not help but let our guards down. We bathed, shaved and cavorted, pretending it was a future time. We talked of loved ones, sang with the flitting sparrows and hoped to hear the penetrating sound, not of a musket, but rather of a woodpecker boring holes to ready a home for mating.

It was at this moment of wishful fantasy that we were attacked by a well-closeted enemy. Some of our men remained to engage in hand-to-hand fighting, while others...well, I did another not very smart thing. I ran. I ran with the clearest sense that I was already mustered out but just had not experienced the drumming as yet. I imagined a secesher gazing at my stiff corpse and whispering with a cold heart, "There lies somebody's darling." Those of us that skedaddled were on our own hook; we were no longer brothers in arms. We melted into the black oaks, slippery elms, and chokecherries that had begun to shed their leaves in anticipation of the first frost.

I moved along the edge of the forest as close to the water as possible. I had only the duds on my back and my Bowie knife. I shivered as the autumn sun began to set. I felt cowardly, shamefaced, and wicked from my slithering away. I was wholly undeserving of a promotion and resolved to refuse it if offered. As for the Campaign Medal, I would place it under the first stack of rubble I came upon.

I had moved a considerable distance when I came upon an abandoned lookout post close to the lake. It was a powerful structure—round, with many rocks. A corsage of leaves and forest matter had been placed over the rocks to allow it to blend naturally with the landscape. If the lake was the conduit to the heavens, well, this observation post was a place which portended violence.

At first I decided to remain there, but a better judgment came when I realized I did not know whether the post was constructed by friend or foe. I decided to hide by fashioning a bed of leaves nearby. There, I would be able to hear any group of men that approached to bivouac.

I was played out and dozed for a time. I dreamed of my mother tending her garden, growing vegetables and telling me the tomatoes were ready to be picked, and then I was awakened by the sounds of men. There were maybe five or six of them who had taken refuge at the post. My heart started to beat wildly; was I to be rescued or rather captured and sent to one those prison camps that I had heard about? I quickly realized from the men's chatter and accents and references to battles with the Armies of the Shenandoah and to anecdotes about General Benjamin Bragg, whom they disdained, that it was an enemy attachment.

The men conversed most of the night. I was able to identify the names and voices of some, a Billy Boler from a farm at Chickamuga, Tennessee, and a soldier named Roddy who wanted to get back to blacksmithing after war's end. None of them sounded like highbrows to me. Most of all, the group roared as they teased an apparent fresh fish, a young man with a tongue twister of a name: Wallace Walter Langston McGhee. They wanted him to lose two of his names because of the extra time it took officers to address him. There was something about this man's uniform not fitting well because of his lanky build. Another said his jawbone, and the arrow-like scar on it, pointed to the ground just the way that no good orangutan in the White House, Abe Lincoln's did. The man, McGhee, must have been a shy kind, a pie eater, because I could not hear if he responded to his mates. It all seemed in good jest with bark juice passed to each, which made my own thirst grow. Eventually they settled down and traded songs which led to waterworks, in all.

Tho, to the homes we never may return,
Ne'er press again our lov'd ones in our arms,
O'er our lone graves their faithful hearts will mourn,
Then cheer, boys, cheer! Such death hath no alarms!

Still, the fear of discovery paralyzed me. One of the men came close to my nest to relieve himself. I was afraid my trembling would stir the leaves and make them rise. I lay awake hours fearing if I made an unforest like sound, a snore, a cough or a grunt, it would lead to my capture. I must have surrendered to the need for sleep in the early morning hours.

I awakened with a start. I put my hand over my nose and mouth; both were cold to the touch. The sun was high, like it might be close to the noon hour. Other than the sounds of grasshopper sparrows perched above, it was quiet. I listened for the chatter of the homesick men. There was none, nor was there an aroma of venison or a trail of smoke from a dying campfire.

I stood up, brushed the leaves from my tattered pants, and checked for movement in every direction. It felt like a Sunday morning before church service. I moved toward the outpost hoping the men might have stored some hardtack or goobers, or better yet, a jug of water.

As I neared, a lone man rose from the rear entranceway. His slouch hat lay on a back rock. He must have been left to picket the area, to monitor his enemy's gatherings on the lake. He was cleaning his single-shot muzzle-loading percussion musket. It looked like a Springfield, much like the one I used. If it was, he had probably taken it off a Blue soldier, because the Confederate boys used the British Enfield. I recall having a fleeting sense of outrage, as if I would have to right that wrong.

The man had a terror-stricken, ashen countenance. He was tall, thin, emaciated looking, even if he was but a youth. One suspender hung down his baggy gray pants. His boot-laces were untied and he wore no socks. His hair was long, unkempt, covering eyes that sunk deep. His jaw was dark and angular with a…oh my God, the arrow-like scar pointing downwards. It was that quiet man, Wallace Walter Langston McGhee. When he realized he could not make use of his musket, he managed to remove his Arkansas Toothpick from a tattered sheath at his waist. I had pulled out my Bowie from its scabbard. I was no more than several paces from him, separated only by half-barren trees whose fallen leaves covered the ground making for a colorful tapestry. Whoever entered that middle ground between us might be undone by a prickly rock that lay underneath that autumn carpet. Perhaps the Johnny Reb had the same thought, because neither of us moved nor made a sound.

I felt like I was looking at myself. It's not that I was a youth or thin or emaciated. Now, as you can see, I am broad-shouldered with a decent bread basket. It was his eyes, the weariness of them, the tiredness and fatigue in them that mirrored how I imagined mine to be. We continued to stare at each other, measuring ourselves and what measure of man we thought the other to be.

I do not remember who moved first. One of us took a half step backward and the other followed. Then, there was a full step backward, as if a dance had begun. Perhaps this was just a bluff on his part, or maybe my own. But soon each of us began to sense that in this moment of mortal fear, a step to the rear would serve us equally so we might secure the remains of the day. There was not a smile, not a wave of an arm, a nod, or any acknowledgement of our unwritten contract, but just a slow-motion skedaddle. I am trying to recall if I mouthed his name…, Wall…ace Walter Lang…ston McGhee, and if he responded. I cannot say that he did, though his eyes seemed to narrow further, with a quizzical visage. Our retreat from each other was cadenced despite its lack of rehearsal. The dance of life allowed me to merge back into the forest like a gopher scurrying to its subterranean chamber. I moved on for another day, across uncertain terrain, checking for shadows of Blue or Gray figures and surviving on end-of-season berries and water from inland streams, not caring a whit if either made me sick. I made it back to my regiment at nightfall.

I was gnawed, no tortured, by self-doubt. Had I done another not so bright thing? Was this a case of abandonment of duty and a theft from the government that called me to arms? Had I dishonored my uniform through acts of cowardice and pusillanimity? Had I turned from the noble causes of the epic struggle to be nothing more than a Sunday Soldier? I had only questions, no answers.

Dear parents and fellow teachers, I know not the meaning of this story. I only know I must place it at each of your doorsteps. Perhaps this is a normal happenstance of war. Perhaps it is a kind of recurrent bellyache that I am experiencing and, in truth, does not even rise to any level of import at all. However, I would like my students to know as they make their way out into the world that their old teacher was anything but a hero. If my history lessons have been of any worth, I hope it be that none of them have to rush off to war but are lucky enough to lead quiet lives with enough time to read a book or two.

After the war, I completed my teacher training and taught for three years at a school in the Hudson Valley before coming to the wonderful state of Kansas, and to Douglas County, and to the inaugural year of Big Springs School. I have often wondered about the young man called Wallace Walter Langston McGhee who stood transfixed at the sentry post. Did he survive the war? Did he return to a farm to plow his fields? Was there a lady in waiting who wrote to him and prayed for his safe return? Did he have brothers and sisters or parents or a community like this with whom he could gather and feel cherished?

I shall be vacationing this summer in the east and will bring my fiancée here after that, if you will still have me. I will search public records again for military units of the enemy that engaged with the Pennsylvania Militia of 1862. Oh how I hanker to know these things and to meet soldier McGhee so that we can clasp hands in a bond of forgiveness and common purpose. Life is such that this gift will not likely be given to me, but I shall continue in this quest.

Now you know why I feel so fortunate to be standing here, in this wonderful community, as no more than a humble, flawed servant of God.

> Thaddeus J. Pickering, School Master
> On This Twenty-Third Day of June, 1870
> Big Springs Schoolhouse, Douglas County
> The Honorable State of Kansas
> The United States of America

"Hey, Mom, did you know about this letter? Is it real?" She'd come into the living room to water her plants. I rose from my haunches and sat myself in the wing chair.

"Your Dad told me about it two years ago when he was diagnosed with his leukemia. I don't know how he hid it from me so long."

"This family is good at keeping secrets, you know that."

"I was angry he pushed me aside but he said the letter was his lucky charm." She watered the elephant ear and moved to the two potted aloes on the plant stand beneath the window. Her hand was shaking.

"What do you mean his lucky charm?"

"He told me he used to read the letter in secret when he needed spiritual guidance, or when he had to make a decision about a life matter. It certainly is a unique document, don't you think?"

"Does he think he's a reincarnated form of the soldier and this is evidence of some kind of past life regression?"

"No, no, he just said he found the sensibilities expressed by that Mr. Pickering to be soothing. Your father being a history teacher, well, that's one thing the two of them had in common." She winked at me, moved to the sofa and placed the watering can on the coffee table. Her eyes moistened up as if she felt remorse at her lighthearted comment, and perhaps her reference to feeling pushed aside.

"Come on, Mom, what is this, a folie a deux?" I was back to doubting the authenticity of the letter, but I moved to the sofa and placed my hand on her shoulder. "Did you ever try to research this?"

"Yes we did, last year. I was going to let your father tell you, but he has other things to share with you." She pulled a Kleenex from her pant pocket to dab her left eye.

"So, what did you find out?" I let the remark about 'other things' slide.

"Here's the postscript. There was a One Room School House Project throughout the state of Kansas and there was a school named Big Springs in Douglas County, although we could never locate the actual township. The school opened in 1869 and operated until 1965."

"What, 1965? It's true, then? What about the first Headmaster, was it Pickering?"

"The Schoolmaster's name was not publicly recorded; it was listed as unknown, so it certainly could have been Mr. Pickering."

"We are looking at a piece of history. I have to read this again. Wait a minute, so Pickering came East and placed it back in…my God, this is a confessional. Was any other Pickering listed, male or female, in the public records you examined?'

"No, I've told you everything. We never looked into a family line of the Confederate soldier; we didn't know where the young man came from."

"You mean, McGhee? That still could be done." Despite my interest, any sense of exhilaration I felt was muted by the notion that more revelations would be thrust upon me. "Uh, what more does Dad want to talk about with me?"

"Your father wants to tell you about his Army experience."

"Now there is the family secret of all time." I took my hand off her shoulder.

"I can tell you he had his reasons for…"

"So Mom that *is* something you knew about." I said nothing more but a flash of temper lit through me. The flash carried the yearnings of a boy who needed to know the sum of the man he called his father. I recalled the half-answers at the dinner table when matters of personal history, like his Army service, were brought up. I recalled the apprehensive expressions of guests who were shushed by the man who raised his index finger to his lips to affirm a child was present and adult discussion was best left for later. When I had the guts to make my own inquiries, I was met with silence or distraction or with the response that I was too young to understand concerns of ethics and conscience. I was left to wonder if my father had done something shameful, something cowardly or cruel. If so, did that make me cruel as well? I learned to put my curiosity aside, to store it in a deep pit with molten rock swirling in place, so that it would never rise. And now the rules of the game were changing, and I felt a grumbling inside.

I missed most of what my mother was saying. We were weighed down with the anticipation of grief but it was like we sat in different pews. We were going to disagree about an open casket.

"I'll be outside for awhile; I will speak to Dad, later."

On the following day, I was back at my father's bedside when he brought up his military service. It was after I promised to deliver the letter with Thaddeus Pickering's post graduation remarks to the Douglas County Historical Society. He loved my suggestion of a rigorous search for soldier McGhee.

"Could you raise this goddamned bed, or do you want me to sleep forever?"

"Is that better, Dad?"

"It'll have to do. Well, when I was twenty-seven years of age and made my incredible find in those rocks, I was five years out of the army. Half the draftees who made it through their physical were sent to Vietnam. I was a member of a unit near the Cambodian border. I was a grunt."

"What's that?

"If you weren't selected and trained as an Armor Crewman, or a Mechanized Infantryman, then you were a grunt. A grunt spent his time swatting flies, wiping his brow from the oppressive humidity, and cleaning his M-14 rifle. A grunt prayed for deliverance from malaria and dengue fever, from food and water-borne diseases like hepatitis and typhoid fever, from poisonous snakes, lizards, crocodiles, stingrays, jellyfish, scorpions, plants with thorns, bacteria from parasitic worms."

"My God, this reminds me of Grandpa and his survival stories in the Philippine jungle."

"That wasn't even the half of it. I thought I would lose my hearing because of the noise, night and day."

"What, from the guns and artillery?"

"Yeah, the guns and howitzers had enormous ranges and there were Air Artillery Units that had rockets mounted on helicopters. Most of us didn't have earplugs. Anyway, I shot at the Cong more than once. Those bastards took over villages and annihilated the locals to ensure their food supply. I'm ashamed to admit it, but protecting those rice farmers filled me with pride. So much for having started out as a peacenik."

"You see, everything has a function in the natural order…"

He shifted his head to face me. "Let's see if you still think that after I tell you…wait, I need to catch my breath here."

"Are you okay? Did you take your pain medication? I'll call Mom."

"No, I want to finish this. I saw a young Vietnamese girl murdered by one of our snipers because she was carrying a backpack and moving towards us, confused by our orders to halt. It was a sack of personal belongings she was trying to transport to safer ground after we had napalmed her village."

"Oh, that's so awful."

"I wanted to yell out, "Stop! Stop!" at our marksman but I obeyed protocol that required I protect his position at all times. The girl was twelve, maybe thirteen. She took a direct hit and you could see her brains splattered on her still moving limbs."

"I'm sorry to hear a story like that. Vietnam pulled all of us down."

"Soon villagers came out from the brush in the opposite direction. There was a woman in olive pants and a white tee shirt with an ace of spades on it."

"The playing card?"

"Yup, widows wore it all the time; it signified death to the enemy. The little woman stood there motionless, like a figure at a wax museum. It must've been the girl's mother because she began to yelp as if the pain piercing her heart had arrived in her brain. I felt mummified, like my organs ceased functioning." At this point my father became silent.

I had no words to match the images, the blood, horror, dislocation, and the finality of parental loss he was sharing with me. But the silence felt like the one of partners as we each attempted to reconcile those images with the persons we were and hoped to be. He was ahead of me, leading me, and mentoring me, perhaps for the first time. I saw tears, not sweat, moving down his cheeks. I searched the linen sheet to place my right hand over the area that covered his left one, until he continued.

"In the days ahead, I saw the effects of jellied gasoline, its 2000 degree wall of fire that removed leaves from trees and plants, and the hideous scars left on the surviving villagers. They made lepers look like handsome princes."

"Dad, I'm glad you're telling me all this." I squeezed his covered hand.

"There's much more. One day I decided not to participate in these atrocities any longer. You might say I had an epiphany."

"I believe in epiphanies."

"I told my Captain I would refuse to participate in further military missions. I stood my ground despite his passionate plea I return to my squad. He told me it was hard to make a case for pacifism in the midst of a ring of fire. He was right; I was threatened with a court-martial and I became a pariah to the soldiers who continued to do their duty."

"What you did came from conscience, Dad."

"I was never sure. Maybe I was just surviving the way Pickering did, doing a dance of life."

"Well, Pickering had a conscience. Besides, you can't disconnect the wish to survive from anything, especially in wartime."

"The worst was my discharge; the lawyers worked it out though." He paused and eyed me carefully. I realized it didn't matter what he told me next, as a pride was surging through my veins. "It was only a general one, but under honorable conditions, even if my mates told me I had an impure heart." He shifted his head away, again, as if trying to avoid the eyes of the executors of his shame. He lay motionless, like the Vietnamese mother who stood as her heart was pierced. My father's heart was on fire, not from the ravages of age and illness, but from the thought of regretful action. I had known of his service in Vietnam but he'd never before told me the specifics and the circumstances of his discharge.

"Purity of the heart is reserved for angels, it's confusion and paralysis for the rest of us," I heard myself reply. I had no idea where this came from. Now I was the one to guide, but this time with my father's wish, even as he understood it would take me far ahead of him.

He pushed his fingers up from underneath the sheet to massage the underside of my thumb. "I survived, completed my graduate studies, and became a teacher of history. I worked in my last school twenty-four years. I may have done a few 'not so smart things' like Pickering, but I raised a few questions in my time," he said as he turned and faced me with a settled look, like ice had soothed the burn in his heart.

The day after my father came clean about his own war experience, he passed away in his sleep. What I said at the beginning of this remembrance was true—the waiting was the worst part, waiting for my father to die, though it no longer felt like loitering. But he did go peacefully in the end. Perhaps that was because he played out a codicil to his way of being that made things whole with me. I have a lightness of step now, as I search for my place in the world. And today, Pickering's letter rests in a glass enclosed case at the Douglas County Historical Society, to comfort future generations as it comforted my father.

&

An Offense of No Consequence

Gotham Hall, New York City, Spring, 2010.
Location: Grand Ballroom—with a ten foot tall brass
door, a 120 foot ceiling, and a stained-glass skylight.

Speaker: Homicide Detective Charles Mahon, retired,
with thinning white hair, an ample belly, and leaning on a cane.

(Polite Applause.)

Thank you ladies and gentlemen. It's an honor to be here
in this landmark structure. And it's a privilege to be on this
platform with such a distinguished panel: two attorneys, one
a prosecutor, and the other a guardian for defendant's rights;
a criminal court judge; a prison warden; and a minister, all of
whom will be sharing their most unusual cases with you.

I am a retired New York City homicide detective and *my*
most unusual case, strangely enough, occurred during my first
few weeks on the job.

It was the Fall of 1969, just weeks after the New York
Mets did the improbable, beating the heavily favored Baltimore
Orioles to claim their first World Series. Earlier in that year,
at Super Bowl III, Joe Namath and his New York Jets defeated
the Baltimore Colts, making it a *bad* year for the Crab Cake
Capital of the World. But it was also the year bad guys acted
out lunacy, with the Manson murders, and James Earl Ray
pleading guilty to the assassination of Martin Luther King. It
was the year we learned that supposed good guys maybe did

bad things, with the tragedies at Chappaquiddick and My Lai. Renewal came, though, as Neil Armstrong took man's first steps on the moon.

I want to pose a question to you; is it possible to commit an offense from which there might be no consequence, shall we say a perfect offense? I am speaking of an offense that is criminal, is clear, and is transparent. A pre-emptive strike, if you will. Those of us in the Criminal Justice system are familiar with the defense of Imminent Danger where there must be a threat of death or serious physical harm. However, can a murder committed in the light of day, before a crowd of witnesses, in which the perpetrator is apprehended, go unpunished? The case I encountered in 1969 challenged everything I had learned at John Jay College.

I had just arrived home that Monday night, November 3rd, eager to catch President Nixon's speech to the nation about his policies in Vietnam, when Tony, our dispatcher, called to tell me there had been a shooting at the Town Club. For those of you who do not know, the Town Club was a private haven for the wealthy off Fifth Avenue. Its members traded business secrets, swam in an indoor pool, and played competitive bridge. Anyway, I was told that a James Manchester, Sr. had entered the facility and approached the card table where his son, James Jr. sat, and pulled a gun and summarily executed him with a single shot to the face. He then calmly placed the weapon on the far end of the table and sat down on the nearest chair to await the arrival of the police.

My partner and I were to secure the father's home on West End Avenue, as others went to the son's residence on the eastside. By the way, that partner of mine, Billy Jensen, who worked many years with me, is in the audience tonight; he does not use a cane. (*Laughter with gentle applause.*)

It was one of those pre-war buildings on West End Avenue near Riverside Park that we arrived at, though I've never been sure which war it preceded. (*A few chuckles.*) The senior Manchester resided alone in a penthouse apartment. We learned from the super that his wife died two years prior in a ski lift accident in Switzerland; ah, the vagaries of the rich. We did not need the key, as the entrance door was ajar, like maybe we were expected.

Let me set the scene we encountered. Immediately in front of us was a long foyer with rows of lithographs and hand-colored prints on each side. A grandfather clock stood majestically at the end, next to an arched entry to the living room. Placed in the middle of the foyer was a ladder-back chair. On its cane seat was what turned out to be an Old Westerner Weathered Journal with a strap case holding it. While Billy opened it, I walked into the main room. There were built-in bookcases with rows of old texts neatly stacked without space for a new arrival. It reminded me of a room at the Morgan Library. Opposite them was a humpback sofa with end tables on each side with ornate lamps that looked like gargoyles on a temple's face. In the middle were two leather wing chairs. Near the passageway to the bedrooms was a marble inlaid wall panel depicting Japanese women in traditional dress. This décor was clearly a woman's invention.

There were two bedrooms in the rear; the first must have been reserved for guests. It was exquisitely furnished with a canopy bed, a cedar chest, and a rocking chair. The master bedroom was more forbidding with an armoire, a roll top desk and a Victorian style bed. Newspapers were stacked on a nightstand. An empty tissue box lay on the floor and a worn black sock poked out from under the bed. On top of the bed was a typewriter with paper around it. A bath towel lay near the bathroom door. It was a dark-toned room and one that suggested distress. Still, if this apartment had been designed like a railroad flat, well, it must have been the one designed for the owner of the railroad.

"Charlie, get over here. Get a load of this," Billy said, interrupting my forward observing. "This is a diary; this guy is confessing to the murder. Check this out."

Indeed, it was a journal with entries dating back six months or so. The last entry was that very day, probably just before the elder Manchester left for the Town Club. Let me read it to you.

> Monday, November 3, 1969 to the Police
>
> Gentlemen,
>
> By the time this is read, my son will have left this earth. It is my hope that he will be forgiven for the sins he authored during his pathetic life. I have no forgiveness in my heart. The deed will have been from my hand and my hand alone. I shall have waited for capture. I care not what happens to me. Other than my unkempt bed, everything is in order in the apartment; there are no drugs, medications, or potions that have corrupted my mind. All that is needed to send me to where you think I must go is contained in this journal.

This was handwritten, but done without so much as a smudge or an error in spelling, as if the words had been rehearsed for a time. But underneath it, in ink-stained, less perfect script, Manchester's innards exposed themselves.

> *The weasel-wormed, blood-sucking, parasitic ingrate, philander-*
> *ing his way, breaking the membrane of the innocent, and fucking*
> *the Almighty. Well, the Lord of Darkness shall have him now.*

This was a man bursting with rage. Billy and I sat there and read the journal as we waited for the on duty detectives to arrive. Indeed, the journal did as advertised. I am going to read just a few of the many entries, word for word, which gives insight into this madman's state of mind. Here is the first:

Thursday, May 12, 1969

> *The board would not listen. Half of them were hand-picked*
> *after Jimmy became CEO, all insiders that he manipulated*
> *with perks for years. I am an emeritus now, an honorary piece*
> *of shit. The entries were altered, and the embezzlement hidden*
> *in the name of expansion. George Arnold lied to save his ass,*
> *another one of Jimmy's boys. Two Shores, my pride and joy, is*
> *blown away like a feather in the wind. No primogeniture here,*
> *especially if I find a way to cut my boy's air supply.*

Two Shores referred to the shores of Long Island and to the company Manchester founded in 1932, which offered property and casualty insurance to homeowners. As I was to learn later, Manchester was a dreamer but he also had business acumen. Highways, like the Southern and Northern State and the Long Island Expressway were in the planning stages so he knew home expansion was inevitable. Two Shores first had to survive the Great Depression and the ensuing war but it was clear sailing afterwards. The 50's and 60's were boom years, with affordable housing expanding on the island. When light industry expanded there as well, Manchester's company was bought by a conglomerate, Universal Protection

Insurance Company which sold policies through independent agencies shaped under Universal's bylaws. Manchester was assured a prominent role in policy management and, in fact, was named the first President of the Board of Directors. By this time, however, his son was a force in the business and an advocate of modernization and rapid expansion, at any cost.

Over the years, the father's power was slowly usurped by the son. Fire-control techniques improved in the twentieth century and the company was fortunate enough not to have a significant event like The Great Chicago Fire of 1871 or the San Francisco Earthquake Fire of 1906 where hundreds of properties were destroyed. As a result, profits at Universal soared even as their underwriting standards tightened. There was embezzlement and backroom dealing going on which allowed the son to be a prolific spender. He was a high-class roller in Las Vegas and had an antique car collection that was museum worthy. In 1963 he moved his wife, Elizabeth, and two year old daughter, Annie, into one of the first luxury buildings on the east side of Manhattan, what you all know now as the Silk Stocking District.

So, picture over time an ember lit inside the old man as his power and influence recede, an ember that burns steadily. In that picture, one can imagine the inner turbulence of the elder Manchester; he's steamed that the business he's built from nothing is being trashed and pre-empted by his kid. Here is another excerpt:

Thursday, July 24, 1969

I have decided to kill him, I will do this. Elizabeth cancelled the dinner with me, again. She is in hiding, nailed to the cross, meeting James' abuse with silence, deference, and feigned loyalty. She uses a cosmetic sponge to apply the flesh colored powder under her eye, but

I see the black hole underneath. I see the despair in her eyes, the fluttering of its lash, the reddening of her ear, the foam forming at the side of her lip. The sweet creature with the misery in her heart and the torment in her soul must tolerate her husband's hammer to protect her daughter. Little Annie, my little poetess, my innocent child, birthed from the virgin spring, my reason for being, remaining, breathing. Elizabeth is not able to protect her child who is defiled by the monster. She is a servant to his needs, an ornament in his collection. So, it must be done. His blood is no longer thick, matching mine, but diluted from potions that have bedeviled his mind, a mind that is inflated and stretched to madness.

Elizabeth was likely abused by Manchester, Jr. She was tall, considered attractive and elegant, but she was sheltered, and had a voice just above a whisper. James was known for his charm and had the sociopath's touch of putting others at ease before manipulating them. But he also had a quick temper, not above throwing a punch at a perceived adversary. How often Elizabeth must have demurred to James, asking his permission on matters of importance and offering sweet phrases of surrender, "You're right, dear," or "Whatever you say." Any fear of his physical strike must have been buried in an unseen place.

She was from old money, raised in Bryn Mawr, on The Main Line outside of Philadelphia, by parents who had rigid standards of morality and who controlled every aspect of her environment. She was a debutante, a homespun girl, who attended the town college. Domestic abuse was only beginning to gain notoriety in the 60's. Still, our docs told us Elizabeth had signs of it. She was belittled and degraded by James and often was beset with headaches, stomach pains, and complained of an inability to breathe. She cloistered herself for long periods

at home. But I am getting ahead of myself, sharing the after-
math with you.

Anyway, Billy and I were sequestered in the father's
apartment, awaiting relief so we could return to our homes,
when we read the following:

Tuesday, August 12, 1969

*Annie is mute with me, still wets her bed, and cannot sleep. She
clings to her mother's leg as if it is a pillar of strength. And she limps
without apparent cause. Did he touch her south mouth? Please, God
in Heaven, make that an impossibility. If he could do that…there is
nothing left, not a layer of humanity. Annie, my lovechild, my fragrant
wind, my ballerina, has he chained you, too? Has he violated your
trust, your safe house, and drawn your sweet juice?*

As you can see, this entry alluded to Annie, Manchester,
Sr.'s young granddaughter and his belief that his son was
molesting her. If the business machinations steamed him, well,
you can imagine how this belief might have pressurized that
steam, coiled it, and readied it for release. We were never able
to verify the reality of any sexual misconduct, as the girl was
protected by counsel and never interviewed by us. She was
distanced from any legal proceeding. It certainly was possible
that little Annie's father might have been guilty of inappropriate
behavior, either undue kissing, touching, or fondling of her, or
perhaps worse. But we also had to consider the possibility that
the eldest Manchester might have been so delusional with rage
and paranoia, that it fueled his fantasy that he must protect
her. It was a tough call for the professionals.

Let me, ladies and gentlemen, present the following situation
to you as a way of helping you to understand the confusion we

experienced. Picture two older men, who do not know each other, sitting opposite each other on a city transport bus. Near them is a young girl seven or eight years of age, much like young Annie, who is interacting with her mother in a spirited manner. The first man has a broad smile, with flushed cheeks, as he observes the girl's playful antics. The second man, meanwhile, has been eying the first as a boxer might his adversary in the ring. And, as that second man departs the bus he looks back at his rival and says "You dirty old man, you should be ashamed of yourself," and spits at him. Now, which of the two might be a predator? The second man's accusatory behavior could be a deflection of his own internal conflict, but it is also possible that he has sensed a potential predator's heart beating wildly and he performs a public service by exposing him. Or, are they both free and clear, one man enjoying the playful antics of a child, and the second misreading the other's behavior in front of him. Take a moment to reflect on this. (*A low-toned hum.*) But back to the diary. Here is another entry:

Tuesday, October 13, 1969

The bloodsucker was here yesterday. He needed papers signed. Papers signed? Transferring of monies; is he mad? Doesn't he know that I know about it all? I told him where he is going, he'll not need a financial advisor. I told him I knew what he did with Annie. He said I was a crazy, demented old man. He grabbed me and shoved me into the bathroom and said if I came out he would break every bone in my body. I heard him rummaging through the apartment, ravaging my books, throwing them against the wall. Then, there was a period of silence and, finally, a hideous laugh as the door slammed shut. I shall provide him with a final silence.

This was the only entry that referenced a face-to-face meeting between the father and son. Despite his determination, the elderly man must have been terrified by his son's agitated behavior and reputation for violence. Perhaps in the dark caverns of his mind he might have imagined his son was going to kill him to further his business goals. And here we have come full circle to the defense of Imminent Danger, have we not? Here is a last entry that we found of interest.

Wednesday, October 15, 1969

I have disassembled it as best I can; all the parts are laid out to be cleaned. I have the kit, the solvent, the oil, the cleaning rod, the cloth patches, the rags, and a tooth brush to run back and forth and up and down to clear the dirt and fouling. I'll use my middle finger to spread the slide grease to remove signs of wear. When it is done I shall load the weapon for the explosion that must come. It will be done on Monday, November 3rd at the club, at the bridge tournament he is so desperate to win. As he falls from grace, he can only look up at the honeysuckle that guards the golden gate and it will be beyond his grasp.

The disassembly, cleaning, and loading of the weapon all speak to premeditation. Manchester applied considered rationality to his problem and drew no conclusion other than the need to willfully cause the death of his son. The only strange thing in his premeditation was that it did not include a wish to evade capture; it was enough for him to feel like a martyr. As for me, well, I remember feeling dazed and my fingers being numb when I finished my read of the diary. Billy and I were just not prepared for what we encountered that night. I had seen my share of blood and gore, beginning as a patrolman. You never quite get used to it but what I was used to was disorder, chaos, heat of passion and intrigue. To have everything so clear and certain disarmed me.

Billy and I rambled on about the father and the son, both monsters to us, and which one might be the most heinous. Perhaps the father had an undiagnosed brain tumor or was in a diabetic stupor. Perhaps the son was bipolar, a fashionable term these days. In any case, both seemed to qualify as sociopaths. I wondered what the old guy looked like, if his eyes were dry or clouded, or maybe red with inflammation and if his skin had thinned and paled and lost its elasticity from the bleeding under it.

We barely heard the front door open as the two detectives entered. Billy cautioned them against running into the ladder back chair, still at the center of the foyer. I knew the guys; they were veterans—older, seasoned and that calmed me. We began to fill them in on the prized piece of evidence gifted to us and the ease with which this case could be brought to a close. I felt a belated burst of energy.

There was puzzlement on their faces, eyes stretched, bringing out the wrinkles under their crowns. A guy named Henderson picked up the journal/diary and leafed through it and passed it to his partner.

"What does this aristocratic maniac look like?" I asked Henderson. "Wait, let me guess; he's tall, thin, bald, impeccably dressed but with a sun-wrinkled face like an old prune. The guy must have been lonely as a stranded crab at low tide to pull off a stunt like this. What is he, about 75–80 years of age?"

"The victim? Yeah, he was ancient looking all right, but you're wrong about his height and weight. He was short and pudgy. The fucking guy's head was blown off, so I couldn't tell you if he was bald."

"What are you talking about, the victim? I'm asking you about the pops, not his dirt bag son," I said.

"I'm telling you about him, man. The Town Club had formal pictures of him. He looked like a straight shooter to me." Henderson said, grinning and elbowing his partner who was scanning the diary next to him.

"Is that supposed to be funny? He's in custody, right, not giving you any trouble, just like he said in his diary, eh? Has his daughter-in law been contacted? What about his granddaughter?"

"Jesus, Charlie," he said to me, "Have you lost your mind, the guy's in the morgue in so many places he's probably taking up two rooms."

"Wait a minute, here, who died?"

"You don't know; they didn't tell ya? The sonny boy, when his father came into the room, got up from his bridge table, in the middle of a hand, and went up to him and shot him face up with a 38. He just sat down and waited for us. He was another squat guy, but much stockier than his old man."

"What? Are you guys playing me? The father had the gun, and it wasn't a 38, it was…"

"How'd you know the father had a gun? Oh, from the diary? Well, he did have a gun, an old Luger in his jacket pocket. He'd probably had it since the war but it was oiled and loaded and ready to go."

"There's an entry here about how he cleaned it," I said, surfing the pages and feeling the blood rushing from my cheeks. "Manchester was there to kill his son, today; it's all written here, planned as if he was an assassin on a mission from God.

Me and Billy were dispatched here to…holy shit, either Tony got the information wrong when he called me or I misheard what he said; I still don't believe this."

Ladies and gentlemen, pardon the language, but that's what I said to my comrades as I did my imitation of a white-sheeted ghost. And, that's when Billy piped in with his famous last sentence.

"What we have here, boys, is a perfect offense, an offense from which there will be no consequence." It was a sentence, a phrase, and a verdict that I repeated over and over to myself as I headed home. (*A sustained buzz from the audience, straining to see the man named Billy Jensen.*)

I hear the buzz from this audience and that buzz still cuts through me after all these years. This case had it all, with the execution of evil, the patricide, and the family dysfunction. Nonetheless, with the greatest of respect, let me ask you; did some of you feel manipulated by me? Did you feel cheated, angered, and confused by the misdirection that I purposely placed upon you? Perhaps there are some of you who figured a twist was coming and now feel affirmed and endorsed. Alas, I was not so fortunate. There were many questions I posed to myself, some of which had answers, while many did not. So, in the context of this case, and the moments it had breath, can you try and place yourself in my shoes as I have tried to place myself in yours? Either way, I suggest it invites the possibility of a challenge to our normally held notions of justice.

We like to think for every murder victim there is a defendant who gets put away. But, does so-called justice cover every possible permutation of murder? When I started on this job I thought so, but now, all these years later, I'm not so sure.

We all know that if a man attacks you with a weapon, a knife or a gun or even with his fist and you are fortunate enough to wrest the weapon from him and stab, shoot, or beat him to death, it is considered self-defense. But, what of Manchester, Jr.'s pre-emptive strike? Could it be argued successfully that as he approached his father in the card room of the Town Club, he was in imminent danger? Keep in mind that had a few more minutes gone by at that club it would have been the son lying dead among the bridge masters.

James Manchester, Jr. was indicted, but not immediately, which points to a certain amount of ambivalence on the part of the District Attorney. The murder was well publicized with the cheaper tabloids extending it out as long as they could. The family members were all but disrobed in public. The DA's office really had no choice but to pursue a legal resolution to the matter; social and political reality mandated it. Now I imagine you want to know the outcome of the trial or if there was a plea bargain. Unfortunately, I cannot give that to you because a month after his indictment, while on bail, Manchester murdered Universal's Chief of Security. He thought the guy, who had done many a foul deed for him, was stealing from him and making advances toward his wife. This deed was done with blunt force trauma but from behind, rather than face up. The weapon of choice was a sportsman's axe. The paranoid gene ran deep in the chromosomes of the Manchester family. Manchester was convicted of that killing and sentenced to prison for life. He died 12 years ago from a rotten, fast-moving cancer.

The question as to whether the son was aware of his father's diary and plot to kill him remains an interesting one. Might the father have evidenced soft signs of dementia and made a gaffe at a party, or a family function when he witnessed his son's abusive behavior? Those of us designated as senior citizens know the difficulty with memory. In any case, James Manchester, Sr. exhibited much more than memory impairment. He had lost much of his pudginess to poor nutrition and hygiene. Club members had observed changes in his appearance, pants not pressed, dribble on his jackets, and a tendency to mumble to himself. Certainly, we can posit that his judgment was compromised. Over the years there must have been some salty interchanges between father and son. In that regard, go back to that late journal entry, the one written just after the visit by the son. It was a visit marked by physical menace and terror. Is it possible the son knew of the existence of the journal and was trying to secure it? There was that reference to the rummaging of the books in the living room. What better place to hide a journal than behind books and in the recesses of the shelves holding them. This would have been a point of contention had there been a court trial. And could a court trial, with all this ambiguity, have produced a unanimous verdict in either direction? Probably not.

As an afterward, I can tell you a bit about the wife, Elizabeth, and her daughter, Annie. Well, what does a shy, held-in, abused wife do when her world is exposed? Where can she go to heal, to rejuvenate, to ask the questions and find the answers that will help her to feel safe? In the external world, that place turned out to be the city of Sunderland, in

North East England, a place damp in climate but sunny in convention and with lots of churches. Elizabeth had a woman friend from college, an exchange student, who came to Bryn Mawr from Sunderland. This friend encouraged the wounded Elizabeth to visit her in Sunderland to begin her healing process. It seemed to have worked and the two women, ultimately, joined forces to run a bed and breakfast there, aptly called The Sunny Nest Guest House. As far as I know, she continues to be a member of the Sunderland community. Folks, I imagine Elizabeth must feel secure knowing any houseguests she serves can never be permanent ones.

The daughter, Annie, now resides in San Francisco. She had first come to the Big Apple as a university student to complete her studies in photography, attending NYU's Tisch School. She's a well-established photographer in the Bay area. Her specialty is taking photographs of people at their jobs, but peculiar ones, like odor judges, coffee tasters, port-a-potty servicemen, and earthworm farmers. She is married and has two children, a girl and a boy. I met her once ten years ago; she agreed to the meet when she learned about my connection to her father's case. I found her to be a delight, much like that imagined girl on the city bus who was so lively and playful with her mother. Her engaging affect did not suggest to me a person traumatized by sexual abuse, but, then again, you never know. I have always wondered if there was a mechanism she discovered in childhood that severed the cruelties she might have witnessed from her consciousness. Some would say that's what old homicide detectives do to sleep well at night. Well, perhaps the grown-up Annie has been able to carry the best of each parent while splitting off from her being the monster in her father and the fragility of her mother. She had a sweetness central to her spirit and she found the ways to have that sweetness express itself, in her work and with her family. Renewal is the best aphrodisiac, and the best peace maker, don't you think? So, I say, hail to Neil Armstrong who made it to the moon in 1969 and hail to the Justice System and its continuing refinement.

Thank you, ladies and gentlemen. I'll turn it back over to our moderator who will introduce the next speaker.

(Sustained applause with chatter.)

෮Ⴣ

My Catch With...Babe Ruth

It's the middle of summer now and even if the city is cleared out it provides little relief from the sultry air. I check my right pocket again to make sure I have the keys to leave with the super at 110 Riverside Drive. They are for the new owners of 12C, the six-room beauty that has been in my family over sixty years. The orange brick pre-war building at west 83rd Street is majestic and covers a city block adjacent to Riverside Park. It is a fortress against the biting wind from the drive. The lobby is huge, with art deco decor. The apartment rooms are square with high ceilings and detailed moldings and fixtures. It is a shame the plumbing is breaking down. Water pressure is low and there are stains from leaky pipes everywhere, some of them resembling a Jackson Pollock canvas.

I remember dad pulling his silver Oldsmobile up to the front of the palatial structure in the winter of 1946 and beaming at me and Stevie, my three-year-old brother. Stevie's a year younger than me, almost to the day.

"Boys, this is the place I've been telling you about. Mom is up in the apartment waiting for us. Get your stuff together. Be careful of that hydrant as you get out."

I remember being hit by an icy blast of air on my cheeks as I pushed out of the car onto the frozen sidewalk. I had seen big buildings before, but standing on that tundra with chilled toes and a dry throat I felt I was being measured by a giant with hundreds of glass eyes. The fast moving clouds made it appear the building was traveling with the wind. So it was a place of magic, of wizardry, that I was coming to.

As I approach 110 now, it strikes me this might be the last time I will walk the block. It's the block that hosted my childhood. Its sidewalk carried every dream, every ecstasy, every victory, every rue and regret. It's the block where I dropped the thin-sliced loaf of seeded rye from Cake Masters, too scared to pick it up because mom would see the crime in my eyes. It's the block where I threw a touchdown pass with my new, big-size football—a spiral beauty like Charlie Connerly and Y. A. Tittle threw for the New York Giants—to a kid named Johnny who ran off with it. It's the block that saw my explosion of tears that came as I walked home from Wally Zankle's apartment (he had this new thing called television) after Bobby Thompson hit the home run to beat the Brooklyn Dodgers. Perhaps I still feel like one of "dem bums" from Brooklyn, needing to shelter dreams for the winter to wait for spring's rebirth where all things are possible.

I am almost there, to the old homestead. I spot Lady Beatrice's flower beds wilting from the stifling heat on the foot of her brownstone. The eccentric lady with her over-rouged cheeks and foot fungus surrounding her red painted toenails hanging out from her sandals must be over ninety. I am sure she is bald because her hair changes color and style every month. But it's me I am thinking about now, not Lady Beatrice. Am I to be finally relieved from duty and obligation to others? Is this a rite of passage through which my aging body must pass?

My mom died six months ago from a galloping pneumonia; she'd lived 12 more years after dad passed. He was smart enough to have purchased the apartment when 110 Riverside went co-op some 30 years ago. It was a rare, sweet decision for him considering he'd been a compulsive gambler since his first game of craps as a wise-ass kid on the dank streets of Brooklyn. His parents wanted him to be a classical pianist but he had other plans. When he became a doctor, he knew he'd laid himself a golden egg because the local banks considered him creditworthy and offered sweet advances of cash, assuming it was for modernizing his office practice. He had his fifth and last heart attack watching the sixth race at Belmont Park. Belmont, Aqueduct, Yonkers, and Roosevelt Raceways; these were his true homes. He loved betting long shots, even if they most often skunked him.

He'd once bet on a long-mane filly running against older geldings in a stakes race. The sweet mare dropped dead after leading handily at the three-eighths pole. Dad's only comment was that the nag should have waited until passing the finishing line before deciding to croak. I placed bets for him when he'd take me along, on Saturdays. I always felt funny standing on line at the fifty-dollar pari-mutuel window, waiting for someone to ask me for an ID card or if I had started to shave yet.

Dad never did appreciate how mom kept our home so neat and organized. She dusted twice a week and was first in the basement laundry on Monday morning. My favorite place was the linen closet where even a candlewick had its own designated space. I would take an extra-long breath and let it out in slow motion whenever I opened that closet because mom had sweet smelling potpourris in large bowls on the first and fifth shelves. The aromas were straightforward then; Rose, Vanilla, or Peach. These days the odors are more fancy and complicated; Lavender Lace, Pumpkin Surprise, and Autumn Foliage. It sure made toweling off lots more fun. Mom had a tough job dealing with all of us because beneath dad's white lab coat, well, he was pretty much an out-of-control teenager.

Me and Stevie fixed up the apartment so it could be sold after mom's passing. We painted the rooms, upgraded the electrical capacity for air conditioners, and buffed up the oak wood floors so they shined with the morning sun. We put new fixtures in the two baths and added a built-in microwave for the kitchen. The high bidder for the place was a banker kid who had a pleasant smile and a pregnant wife. He probably inherited the money to make such a fine investment. The guy was just too young to have earned this entitlement on his own.

Now I am sitting on a cracked park bench across the street on Riverside Drive. When I'd passed by the building entrance a moment ago, I just couldn't go in. I half expected to see either doorman Pete or Tom who'd been there since I was a tadpole. I loved taking Tom's beaked hat with the 110 on it and putting it on the floor of the east elevator and pressing the Penthouse button. Boy was that guy mad then; his face would turn beet red. I knew I'd gone too far, but I loved those palace guards. They held their smile when I came in after school with my shoulders hunched after a run-in with a teacher. Their smiles meant a lot to me, like I belonged to a special club where only members with a pass could enter. Pete and Tom and the others have been gone many years now, replaced by less caring guards, but I have learned that a flaky moustache, a double chin, or a cauliflower ear on those who care about you can never corrode with time.

I shift, trying to collect myself. Across the street two pre-adolescents in silky blue gym shorts down to their ankles come out of their four-story brownstone. They are right in front of the bus stop where the Number 5 comes every 12 minutes, so I can see them pretty well. One is a little taller than the other. They're rosy-faced, Scottish looking boys, each with long reddish hair. The older kid's hangs in a ponytail. I am more accepting now of trends like tattoos, nose rings, and foul language tee shirts. I figure these boys are brothers, maybe having returned from a month in overnight camp. They've got their baseball mitts and begin to throw a Rawlings hard ball to each other. I can see they're good. The younger kid is left-handed. They laugh and I hear one of them talk about his slider. One throw finally gets past the younger kid and rolls back to 82nd street, almost going into the sewer drain. I smile a layered smile, an ancient smile, because I know that sewer from my own overthrows.

Down the block on my right coming towards me is a lady with a dog, a goldendoodle. She pauses to pooper scoop. Goldendoodles have friendly and gentle natures. They are low shedding and hypoallergenic which makes them more alluring. I hope she will take hers close enough to let me pet him. I sense movement on my left as well. I turn to see a nanny, a young Asian woman, pushing an empty stroller with her left hand, and holding the fingers of a three- or four-year old boy with her right. It is late afternoon and they both look played out. The boy's tan shorts hang low and he has a wet bandanna tucked round his neck. His sneaker laces are untied. He has curly brown hair that holds firm despite the long day under a burning sun. His cheeks are red and he's waving a yellow Wiffle Ball bat. I can feel my eyes smiling as I watch the boy with the fatigued gait. Maybe he's hit a T-Ball home run, and is playing it back in his mind. Maybe he's playing imaginary grounders to himself, being both hitter and batter and an all-star at both. The lady with the dog is in front of me now. The little tyke is there, too. He moves past the goldendoodle as if unaware of the lick that could be his. I am back in open space following the boy's path. Sure enough, after a pace or two he drops his nanny's hand. He turns full circle and spots the bow wow that has just passed him.

"Hello dog," he says, wiggling the fingers of his left hand. The nanny pauses to wait for her charge.

"You said hello to the dog. That was very nice, Oliver," she affirms in a soft voice. The boy turns forward, and in doing so our eyes meet for the briefest of seconds. His have a glimmer. I must look old and weary to him. Maybe he knows I haven't been sleeping well. Somehow in those few seconds the boy decides to offer me his smile. His considered spontaneity moves me. He is an angel floating through space, my space. I manage a brief nod in return, to let him know I liked the greeting he'd given to me and the dog. He begins to skip down the street in a new burst of energy. He uses his bat as a magic sword to dispatch any feared invaders who might dare to interrupt his pleasure. I worry about his sneaker laces flapping up and down; I don't want him to trip and fall.

I look across the street. The Scottish lads are having a bullpen session. I remember all the catches I had in front of my building, the fastballs that pushed my own youthful dreams of stardom. I see the boys pause to let an older man pushing a shopping cart go by.

In the Spring of 1948 me and Stevie were talking about things:

"Stevie, remember last Saturday when we had a catch?"

"Yeah, I do."

"'Member that big man smiling at us, standing next to doorman Pete?"

"Oh, the man who threw the ball to us? He threw one over my head into the sewer."

"That was Pete that did that, Stevie, not the man. Well, Daddy told me that this man is the most great baseball player of all time and his name is…"

"What? That man was old. He was stinky looking. I saw doorman Pete helping him walk to his car."

"Me too, Stevie. I saw that, too. The man walked like he hurted all over. Did you see the white wiggly hairs on his face? He forgot to shave. But Daddy said that when he was young, he played baseball for the New York Yankees."

"But that man's too old to play baseball, ever."

"No, listen Stevie, 'member when Daddy took us to Yankee Stadium last year? He said that Yankee Stadium was the stadium Ruth built. He meant Babe Ruth; didn't you hear him say that?"

"Who is Babe Ruth?"

"That was him, the man, you know the man outside the building."

"How could that man have builded Yankee Stadium all by himself?"

"I don't know about that but Daddy said he hit the longest home runs ever hit in baseball."

"Really? Daddy said that? Well I am going to hit a home run if Daddy shows me how to. He never goes to the park with us."

"Yeah, I know Stevie. Daddy is too busy with his friends."

"He's in the bathroom making poops. He stays in there forever; that's what Mommy says. She doesn't like it cause she can't put her make-up on."

"Ha, ha, very funny. But, hey listen, that giant man who was playing catch with us? Well, Stevie, that was Babe Ruth, it was too."

"You're crazy and stupid. Daddy is tricking you... It's true, for real? That old guy was large. He had a ghost face. I couldn't see the Spalding ball when he threw it cause his hand was monster big."

"Remember Stevie, when we moved to this house before Christmas time? Well, Daddy said there were lots of famous star people who live here."

"Does that mean we are famous, too?"

I am north of 65 years old now, collecting Social Security and feeding off memories to mollify the slowing down process that stalks me. I am set to drop off the keys for the banker kid. I wonder when his wife is due. I picture her bringing her infant home and cooing to him about his new home. Anyway, this is how the episode in the spring of 1948 returns to me:

It's Saturday and I'm having a catch in front of my building with my five-year old brother. Stevie is small, scrawny, thin-boned, and not real developed. He is pigeon-toed so bad that my doctor dad ponders arranging corrective surgery. I am a year older and two inches taller than Stevie. I can throw harder, run faster and catch better than he can. He needs more sleep than me. He gets the hand-me-down clothes while I get most of the new stuff. When we wrestle I usually end up on top. I feel guilty about winning but I am terrified of losing. I wonder if this feeling will ever change.

As I throw the rubber pink Spalding back to Stevie, I notice the huge, round-shouldered man a few feet behind him smiling at me. He can't keep his eyes off me. I feel a chill run down my spine. I am thinking maybe my fly is unzipped or maybe there is strawberry jam on my face from breakfast or that I just look plain weird. I am also terrified this man is reading my mind.

I know Stevie is wondering why I'm not catching his return throws and why I hold the ball so long. I make a lame excuse to him that I'm going to throw him the curveball that Wally Zankle's been teaching me. I am trying to get up enough nerve to take a fuller look at the man in the circle of gray shadows standing next to Pete, our daytime doorman.

The man's face is a mix of white, black, and gray. It looks like cigarette ash. I remember when dad played gin rummy with his cronies; he'd place his Chesterfield down on the glass ashtray when it was his turn to shuffle the deck. I would watch the ash form and shape itself with the burning orange coal underneath. I'd try to guess how long it would take to break off into littler pieces from its burden of weight. Well, that is how the man's face appears to me, burdened. It is also a fragile face. Even at my distance I can make out crack lines that run across his forehead. There are dark pouches under his eyes and the jowl hangs under his jaw.

It's his eyes, though, that help me feel more at ease. They are round, full, clear, and have a twinkle as if heaven's light is pausing for a rest on the ball and lid. Maybe it's just the sun breaking through a cloud but I swear I can see the twinkle's full liveliness, moving from bright to brighter and gleam to gleamier. And the twinkle, the gleam, the brightness, are focusing on me. I turn around to check to see if there is someone else this man is staring at, but no one else is there. The attention is powerful and I feel important and vulnerable at the same moment.

The man motions for me to throw the Spalding to him. He does it again even as I remain flat-footed. I am thinking how his glow outweighs the ash that must be underneath. Stevie looks at me and turns his head. Stevie sees the man with death on his face. I know now that the salt-and pepper-faced man was The Great Bambino, The Sultan of Swat, The Colossus of Clout, Babe Ruth. He had his throat cancer then. I have read about the Babe being a womanizer, a party man, a food junkie, a drinker, and that he was never home at night which likely broke up his first marriage. The kids, though, lined up to see him wherever he went, not caring a whit about his nighttime antics. They'd caught the measure of a connection in the Babe's twinkle, like I did. It was saying to kids that he'd been where they were and he knew what they were going through. My dad would have called the Babe a pure-bred because he was natural, easy-going, and without airs.

I am a cancer survivor now. I know about metabolic profiles, bone scans, CAT scans, and MRI's. I know how it feels to be poked in places reserved for a loved one. I know what it's like to be in my oncologist's waiting room watching others being prepped for chemotherapy, as I wait for the results of my blood chemistry. I am learning to experience the joy of living each day in full bloom, because that is what I caught in that moment with the oldest man I'd ever seen as his grin widened his jaw.

I throw a high blooper over Stevie's head. I wonder to this day if I did that on purpose. It bounces in front of the man who has been eyeing me. He steadies himself with his right hand on the building wall and leans down to pick up the bouncing Spalding with his left. Doorman Pete starts to help him but the man waves him off. Then the man motions to Stevie to join me down the block.

For the next few minutes he throws an assortment of floaters to each of us. They're high flies, cans of corn, not the two-or four-seam fastballs, cutters, or splitters the professionals throw now. He is a lefty which is new to me. His arm motion is fluid, graceful, and easy. His tosses are with an economy of effort. They are tailored to the breadth of a six-year old.

Stevie goes back, back, back…pushing into my space but he makes a one-handed catch. I am impressed. "Nice catch, young fella," the man says to Stevie, whose feet start doing an Irish Jig even if he keeps the Spalding raised high. He provides his own narration to the event. "A great catch to save the game. The New York Yankees are the best team ever." Finally, he gives me the ball to throw back to the unsteady, but twinkled-eyed man. My return throws begin to hit the target the man sets for me in the middle of his chest.

"Atta boy," he says, winking at me. "You're gonna make a fine looking pitcher one day." His voice is hoarse and raspy. The lining of his throat must look like a dried up riverbed. I am wondering about the pain he is in and how his eyes can continue to sparkle if his body hurts him so much. His chest is huge. The curved shoulders cannot disguise the man's wide frame. I see his shirt hangs easily over his pants and I wonder if he's wearing a belt. His legs are spindly and they shake. His shoes are gigantic; I bet I can put half my arm into one of them. It is the feet that steady him and keep him upright. An imperial car pulls up, a blue Nash Ambassador.

"Gotta go boys, my car is here," he says to me and Stevie. "Keep playing and have fun. There is nothing like the game of baseball." This time the man lets doorman Pete assist him, holding his left arm. He makes a weird sound, arrhhh, leaning down to slide into the back seat of the shiny blue car with the canopy top. He waves at us as the car moves down the block to the red light at Riverside Drive. He holds his smile, just the way doorman Pete and doorman Tom do. I notice it is a sunny day peering across the park. There are no clouds but just a honey blue sky.

"That guy is really weird." Stevie looks up at me and tries to grab the Spalding which I am rotating in my hand.

"I don't think so, Stevie boy." I probably did not say this to my best buddy brother but I just know that's what I was feeling and what I was thinking. It is what I would say to Stevie now if he were here but he is still working. He is due to retire next year. He will have more time, like me, to savor memories. I check across the street and see the building's super chatting with one of the porters. I rise from the cracked park bench, taking the keys into my sweaty palm. I'm ready to touch the closure I had so carefully arranged.

It's done. I'm done. The exchange with the super is cordial, professional; if he is aware of the peculiarity of the moment he doesn't show it. He is likely more aware of the pregnant lady and the stiff-suited banker coming to the building the following week.

After I drop off the keys, I decide to return to the 79th Street subway on Broadway by way of Riverside Drive. I am betting that the red-haired laddie boys who look like they have just come home from the Edinburgh Festival will still be there, warming up. I figure this to be a sure bet. I've learned now that long shots rarely make it to the winner's circle unless they really work hard for a time; it is even and steady that wins most races. Cal Ripken is my baseball hero. Ripken was never the top runner, thrower, fielder, or hitter but his skills meshed to produce an effect greater than any individual one of them. That is baseball-style synergy.

I turn the corner and am back on the Drive. The boys are still demonstrating their considerable skills. The older kid is further away. He is crouched in his best Yogi Berra squat. I can see his ponytail has loosened from the heat. He is letting the younger boy, who is nearer to me, be the pitcher. The rookie is a natural lefty, a young Whitey Ford or a Sandy Koufax. He kicks his right leg high off an imagined rubber and lets the Rawlings ball fly from his left hand. I see a bullet breaking through a resistive wind. I hear that familiar crackle of the ball hitting firmly into the leather mitt.

I still have my first baseball glove. It is frayed, prickly to the touch, and beyond re-webbing. I keep it in an old gym bag in a drawer under my captain's bed. I will not put any potpourris down there; sometimes it is better to experience natural aromas, and even the ones of worn leather. I check my watch pretending I am waiting for someone so I can remain a fan of these two a moment longer. I always liked extra-inning ballgames.

I walk by slowly. The pony-tailed kid rises from his catcher's squat. His forehead glistens with beads of sweat. My eyeballs hurt from shifting them to take in the action. The younger kid is aware of me as I now stroll past him. He is twirling the Rawlings in his left hand, which is baseball sign language that there is a temporary halt in play. He is going to let me pass, even if I'd rather delay the privilege.

I am just about by them when I hear the pitcher kid say to his older buddy, "Tell me if this is a slider and not a curve, okay?"

"Jared, you are too young to try that pitch; you'll bust your arm," the presumed brother replies.

I am almost to 82nd Street. An errant throw, the slider perhaps, nudges the side of my right foot and travels toward the curb and down to the last parked car on the block.

"Sorry mister, sorry," the older boy says, coming towards me.

"Hey that's okay, I'll get it for you," I say, turning and waving my hand for him to stop. His face is like a rose in full bud. I move toward the curb where the ball is resting near the back right tire of a beat up station wagon.

I've got the Rawlings in the palm of my hand and the friction from it feels good. I straighten myself and shake the street dust from the yellow polo I am wearing. I check the ball again, rotating my fingers around the seams the way Tom Seaver might have done. I feel the two pair of eyes on me up the block waiting for the return of their object of joy. I move back to the middle part of the sidewalk and back up a few steps.

I kick my left leg just a notch so nothing will hurt too much and let the fastball fly off my right fingers. She's a beauty, from what I can see. It reaches its intended target, the young red-headed kid called Jared, who is now standing in front of his brother in their make-shift field of dreams. The ball hits the mitt that is held in front of his solar plexus, the place where wishful thoughts thrive.

"Have a good day. There is nothing like the game of baseball," I say, as I start to move forward. I cannot feel the soles of my feet; I am soaring over the Drive, over Riverside

Park, over the monkey bars I climbed in my youth, over the tree we designated as third base, like a bird that has been fitted with eternal wings.

"The old guy has a good arm," I hear the younger kid say in a high-pitched voice.

I do my best to keep moving forward.

☙

Crossing The Frontier

"Ma, where are you going? Come back here."

"Stephanie, I'm tired, that's all. Leave me alone."

"Don't tell me you're going to take a nap again?"

"What do you mean by that?"

"I know you are worried; you should see the frown on your face, Ma. Is it Alex? He's making a presentation to traders after the markets close and…"

"Alex? Why should I worry about him, he's your Prince Harry."

"What's wrong with you, Ma? You're acting so strange lately."

Stephanie Richards watched her elderly mother push herself up from the blue velvet loveseat. She noticed the woman's hesitant movement making sure her feet were planted on the carpet before standing. Her mother's green eyes lowered to the bottoms of their sockets which seemed to drag her entire facial plane down. She paused to straighten her pleated plaid skirt, and then began to shuffle down the foyer to her bedroom.

"I know what you are doing, Ma, you can't fool me. I'm too smart for your shenanigans." Stephanie felt a surge of agitation in her right leg which crossed her left as she sank deeper into the living room sofa.

"What are you talking about, Stephanie? You always talk such nonsense."

"Ha! I am not and you know it. You're still miffed about tomorrow's appointment. Don't try to deny it." Stephanie's lips trembled. She looked for her cigarettes, knowing she probably left them on the night stand in the bedroom.

Her mother's nature was to embrace silence, indecision, and deference to others in the face of life problems. But now there was something new about her—a surety, a steadiness, devoid of the uncertainty Stephanie had otherwise seen. It had been quite different with her father, who was temper-ridden and critical. His bouts of drinking only exacerbated those tendencies. She adapted though, finding her voice could be as biting and persuasive as his. Certitude was Stephanie's organizing principle and her father's death a year ago did nothing to undermine that raison d'être. With Alex, regrettably, it was more of the same. She didn't like his staying out late with his fellow options traders, which was happening too often now. She'd give him something to think about when he came home tonight. Now she watched her mother turn back to face her.

"Look Stephanie, you keep telling me I am getting older and that I should take better care of myself. Well, shouldn't afternoon siestas be part of a get-well plan?"

"You know, Ma, I've never heard you talk so much about sleep as you have recently. That's a sign of a mental disorder if you sleep too much, did you know that? Maybe I should take you to Doc Waters; would that be fun?" Stephanie yielded to her throbbing agitation, jumping from the sofa in a single movement and moving to the foyer and half-open bedroom door. Her mother looked back at her approaching daughter, but stood resolute, with a hand on the crystal door knob.

"Fun? Your father used to say you can't have too much fun." She glanced upwards, toward the ceiling. "God knows that man had his fun. Well, you'd be surprised girlie at how much you can work out in a sleep."

Stephanie pushed the door into a more open position and took a step into the room. A blue brassiere hanging from the over-the-door hook fell to the floor. "Ma, what in the world is going on?"

"What can I say? I go to sleep in one life and wake up in another. It's like having a makeover or writing your own Grimm fairy tale." Her mother waved toward the bookshelf on the left side of the bedroom.

"What? What…?"

"Anyway, I want to do my reading and if I doze, so much the better. Go take care of yourself instead of looking to bother me. Can you give me a few inches of breathing space here, please?"

"Ma, what in the name of God are you talking about? Sleep rewards, makeovers, different lives, and fairy tales? I just don't get you anymore."

– 2 –

I know you are in another place, Mama, but I still need your help. Stephanie cannot hear us even if she is smoking one of her Capri's outside the door. She thinks their slim shape enhances her sexual lure. Such rubbish I've never heard. She listens on the other phone whenever I talk to Cousin Alice.

I am eighty-three years old now and bone weary. I'm lying here tossing and turning in my blue undies, the combed cotton ones. You always said cotton that's been brushed is the most durable. When I'm asleep, even then I can feel the elastic pulling on my middle as I shift position. Has that ever happened to you, Mama, knowing you are asleep but also awake at the same moment? Sleep time is the best time to talk to you to press the wrinkles out of the things that hurt. You are my best friend, Mama. I can confide in you without feeling the cramps inside.

This is how I imagine you must look in your lofty space. You are wearing the lemon chiffon dress that hangs softly over your middle. It's the dress you wore to my wedding, the dress you have never worn again.

Mama, your hair is curly brown with shiny silver edges even if your face is creased and your skin is puffed and cracked. Your ankles are inflated with edema, so much so that it's hard to see the low-spiked shoes that grace your feet. You used to be five-foot plus but now the force of gravity has pulled you under that bar, though your true worth can never be measured by the inch.

Mama, Stephanie wants me to move to an assisted living facility. Yes, your grandbaby Stephanie who you always said had the smile of a marigold at the first light of sun. Well, darkness is the cover of my life now. I touch the darkness every day, and smell its stink. I feel its shadow running down my body.

I have regrets, Mama. I regret having been quiet instead of noisy and opinionated like everyone else around me. I regret thinking about others and never myself. I regret not having worked so I could feel loose change at the bottom of my purse. I regret never having seen a prima ballerina dance with precision as if she's on a bed of leaves. I regret I am such a fraidy-cat. What do you do, Mama, when you have regrets?

We are going to visit Wellington Gardens, the hospitality home for the elderly, tomorrow. Stephanie arranged everything. I've passed that place often on my morning walks in Tompkins Square Park. I've peered into the ground floor window and watched the aides placing white linen cloths on the tables in the dining area. I've seen residents, three or four to a table, eating lunch. I've seen their hesitant gestures in that institutional air: bony fingers reaching for a napkin that had fallen, an adjusting of a denture and a head hung down for an early slumber. The steady hum there reminded me of a church service before the liturgy started. It was the hum of structured living, of eating humble pie, I heard from that place, not the one of bustling life.

Mama, what am I to do? I lost my Charlie a year and a half ago from that lymphoma. It was in remission for a time but then it returned strong, outfoxing all those chemicals the doctors put into his body. It was hard on me because even when he was sick, he still wanted things his way. Mama, when a man gets sick you would think he'd soften and be more agreeable. Not my Charlie. When he lay in bed like a vegetable, he wanted his hamburgers made from fresh sirloin and cooked well-done or he wouldn't touch them. I had to double-mash his potatoes until they were perfectly smooth.

Sometimes though, when I stared at Charlie dozing in his hospital bed, so thin and frail with his bones threatening to cut through his skin, he reminded me of Papa. You remember, Mama, how Papa with his ruptured heart could still complain? It seems I was destined to take care of every man that crossed my path, to hand press their shirts and to cut their toenails. I read about a tribe in South America where women had equal standing with men. I would sail to that place on a whim.

When you got your sickness, Mama, you held firm to the end. We still talked about the problems of the day and made sure the house ran right. Even when I had to clean and change you, we'd talk about old lady Parson's fall and how we would get supplies to her. And remember when the kitchen wall at the Rumsey School collapsed and how we fed the workers after they rescued the trapped children?

I could never talk to Charlie, Mama, not from the first day of our marriage. So I just read books and had discussions with the characters in them. My favorite author was Charles Dickens because every character he created had a place in a grand puzzle.

I think you pretty much knew about my marriage woes; we just made a silent agreement not to fuss about it. You helped me with the trips to the library and the book club there. Then, there were the free lectures at the Y and at City College. I was too afraid to ask a question, fearful of that microphone, and that a blush would explode on my face if I dared to talk into it. My mind opened up, though, listening to the passion of words and ideas. You always said a book is a find because it will triple the mind. You were so silly, Mama, but you were so right.

Mama, you are gone now but there is a wonderful book by a Scotsman, Alexander McCall Smith, which tells about a jolly, full-figured lady who decides to start the first female private detective agency in Botswana. She uses patience and wisdom to help ordinary people in family matters and affairs of the heart. Imagine, a lady doing that in an African country where men have the final say. It felt so real and gave me a silent hope I could make my own plans one day.

Charlie was mule-headed like Papa. Once he had an idea fixed in his head, you could never budge him. There was one time I let him have it which just about separated me from my mind. It was Thanksgiving Day, two years before Charlie passed, and he'd been bothering me all day. Stephanie and Alex were over with Michelle who was in her last year of college. You would be proud of your great grandbaby, Mama. She knew I yielded to her Grandpa but we got on well. She was going to apply to medical school. How about that, a lady doctor in our family? Well, Charlie was watching the football game on television while I was slaving like an event planner arranging a wedding. I'd even made my own cranberry sauce. So Charlie tells me to go out to Meade's Deli to get fresh coleslaw and more Stella Artois, and that if Meade's was out of the Artois to go to the Associated Supermarket three blocks away and purchase it there. He was in love with that Belgian beer.

I can't really explain to you what happened next. Remember, Mama, when little Johnnie Weston had his epileptic seizure in front of us? Remember how glassy-eyed he looked just before his convulsions came on? I must have looked like that because I felt a rumbling in me, a rumbling I couldn't control. It was as if a balloon was swelling in my gut, fueled by a steady flame. I remember gagging and my breath smelling nasty. Well, whatever was down there shot upward through my throat and mouth. I thought I was going to vomit. But it was words, half-phrases, vile, insane words that were coming out, not my breakfast food. God spare me, Mama, from telling you the particulars of what I said; my face must've had nine layers of magenta with pin-pricked embers popping underneath.

Mama, I gave voice to all the injustices I had endured, like when Charley forgot to pick me up at the airport. And it was the only time I ever took a plane! Then I went into the kitchen, where just before I had removed my turkey from the oven. I cradled that turkey in my arms, took it to the open living room window, and in front of Charlie and everybody else, flung it out as far as I could. There was a Japanese garden down below my fourth floor window, a showpiece for the building owners. It never occurred to me I could kill someone who might be tending the shrubs there.

It may sound strange to you, Mama, but an ease came over me as if a river's flow had softened to a trickle. I was never a religious sort, but I knew a higher spirit would let me have this one moment of triumph. I peeked out the window; my bird was laying splattered in-between two rocks. I checked Charlie. The man was sitting in his king-size chair, his mouth open so wide that a fly could have had a field day.

Mama, Stephanie was good to me after her father died. She would taxi down from her co-op on the East Side and we'd shop, go to lunch, and take in a movie. She has it rough with her Alex. It's not that he's brutal or anything but he is so preoccupied with business. Stephanie says Alex cares more about the stock and option traders than he does about her. I think Papa was something like that with his business. You used to say all those cleaning fluids at his shop seeped into his head and poisoned his brain. You called him loopy in your little girl voice when he'd open his shop on Sunday to do jobs on what was supposed to be his day of rest. He said he did it for his family. I always knew you didn't believe that, Mama.

Six months ago Stephanie convinced me to move in with her and Alex. I'd been in my brownstone for twenty-six years and I had to admit I was getting tired walking up three flights of stairs with piles of groceries. Living with Stephanie was good for a time. I tried hard. I thought of my room as a garret in Paris. I would retire there by nine o'clock every night to give the kids time for themselves. I wouldn't show my face in the morning until Alex left for work.

Mama, I was terrified I would hear them doing it in the bedroom. I hope you don't mind my talking about such matters. I never made a peep when Charlie wanted his time. Even if I reached the end, which was not often, I would just look at him and smile. And when I forced myself to say thank you, his cheeks would swell like bubble gum. He loved when he rose up from on top of me thinking he was Captain of the Santa Maria.

Stephanie has a big mouth and uses it. Maybe things go in opposite directions with succeeding generations, although you and I are alike in personality. Michelle doesn't have a temper, but she's strong and persistent. Most of all, when she has a goal like medical school, she sticks to it.

I knew Charlie and Stephanie would butt heads from the beginning. They had drawn-out fights when she was an adolescent, yelling and cursing each other. Charlie's veins would bulge from his neck. My knees shook and I'd cover my ears watching the two of them go at it. I felt like a passenger on a propeller plane about to crash into a mountain. I wanted to tell the pilot to push higher up on his joystick but my vocal cords were frozen. Stephanie skipped school, smoked, and abused any curfew we put on her. Then Charlie would get mad and make pronouncements.

"You're turfed in the house for a week, young lady; can't you see what you're doing to your mother?" I hated that line of his. I admit some of the stuff Stephanie pulled was bad, but when she'd refuse to give up a friend Charlie didn't approve of, well, I could understand her point of view.

Mama, your little grandbaby was out of the house by the time she was seventeen. Her first marriage was a disaster.

The courtship was what, six weeks? Out of the burning hell of her home and into a heaven spiced pot she never realized was a different kind of pressure cooker. Cousin Alice calls these quick unions 'below the belt' arrangements. She says since the dawn of the universe it's been about below the belt. The man finds his image in the woman who crosses his path and then tries to mold her even further. She's right about that. Anyway, I think Stephanie just wanted to create her own space.

Mama, what would you do if you were me? About that assisted living thing? Wait, I hear Papa coming and I can be a little girl again.

– 3 –

Me: Hello, Papa, you have your army uniform on. But where are your socks, Papa? Your feet are going to catch cold. Wait here, I'll bring them to you.

Papa: Get my solid black ones, my sweet bunny girl.

Me: Here, Papa, I have unrolled them for you. I brought your newspaper, also. Why are you wearing your uniform? You never ever wear it.

Papa: Why today is a special day. It's a remembrance day for The Great War. The men at the fraternity lodge dress up today.

Me: Everybody gets into their uniform? Why, Papa?

Papa: It is a day we celebrate the people who served in the Armed Forces in the Great War to protect our country.

Me: America is not at war anymore, Papa, is it?

Papa: No, sweetheart, we won The Great War and I can guarantee you there will never be another war, ever. America is very, very strong.

Me: You mean we are safe, Papa. No dragons will catch us and swallow us? Peter and the wolf was a really scary story. The music was icky, by that man Perk...ee...v.

Papa: Sergei Prokofiev was his name. He came from Russia and could turn sounds of animals and people and things we feel into great music. Anyway, you are as safe as can be, my garden princess. Your job is to find a handsome prince and live happily ever after. Will you do that, for me?

Me: I will, Papa, I really will. Hey, what is that big color thing on your uniform?

Papa: Why that is called a citation.

Me: What is a citation?

Papa: Well, it is kind of like doing a good deed, an honorable act which gets noticed by others, and they give you praise for it.

Me: You mean someone gives you a gold star with lots of people watching?

Papa: Something like that, sweetie.

Me: What did you do, Papa, to get your citation? Tell me, Papa, what did you do?

Papa: It was nothing, why nothing at all. I just helped a man who hurt his leg get back to a place where the doctors could take care of him.

Me: Was that in The Great War? Did the man have a bullet in his leg?

Papa: He had pieces of metal called shrapnel in his leg. Metal had been flying in the air and one hit him high in the left leg and he could not move.

Me: That man must have been bleeding, lots. I bet you used more than a hundred band aids.

Papa: It was more like one large one, honey. It's called a tourniquet. Every soldier carries one.

Me: If that man could not walk anymore, how did you get him to the hospital, Papa?

Papa: First, I put the big band aid on his injured leg and wrapped it around tight so it would not bleed further.

Me: What happened next, Papa, to the hurt man?

Papa: Why then I did the fireman's carry.

Me: The fireman's carry; what is that?

Papa: It's a method that lets you carry a large person by yourself. Firemen use it to carry people who pass out because of breathing in too much smoke during a fire.

Me: How did you carry the hurt man, Papa, like a fireman would?

Papa: Well, it's kind of hard to explain. I took hold of his wrist and wrapped his arm behind my neck. Then I reached between his legs to grab his thigh, pulling him up over both my shoulders. I tried to be careful of his injured leg.

Me: Wow, did that hurt you?

Papa: Oh no. I stood up and shifted him so his weight was evenly distributed, which made it easier for me. Then I walked back to where the other soldiers were camping out. The doctors were there to greet us; someone ran ahead to tell them we were coming.

Me: Show me the fireman's carry, Papa, show me.

Papa: Come here and I'll demonstrate it on you, but let's be careful.

Me: Oh, goodie, goodie. What do I do, Papa?

Papa: Make believe your left leg is injured. Now put your arm behind my neck. No, not like that, bunny girl. Here, let me show you. Now I am going to lift you high, hold on... *Hey...ee, what a big girl you are!*

Me: Hee...hee, whee...that tickles, Papa.

Papa: And that's how I would carry you until we were both safe from harm.

Me: Put me down, Papa, put me down. I'm dizzy.

Papa: Here we go big girl, plant that foot on the ground. We wouldn't want anything to happen to you.

Me: You are so strong, Papa. Did the man yell and scream all the way home? Did the tuni...cat hurt so much he cried tears? What was his name? Was he a soldier like you?

Papa: The tourniquet reduced the man's pain. Actually, he fell into a deep sleep which made it easier for me to carry him. Private First Class Jack Brown was his name. He was a brave soldier.

Me: Oh, Papa, did Private First Class Jack die? I hope not.

Papa: No, no, sweetie, he didn't die. The doctors gave him some fresh blood, food and water, and before you knew it he was up and about.

Me: Did you ever see Private First Class Jack again?

Papa: Oh, I saw him twice in the Army hospital after that. I wanted to see how he was doing and wish him well. When the war was over he told me he was going to get on a train and go back to his home.

Me: Where was that?

Papa: He was a farmer from Alabama; think of all the fruits and vegetables he went back to grow. And that, my little dumpling, is the end of the story.

Me: I loved that story, Papa. Tell it to me again.

Papa: Well, maybe next year when we again honor the winning of the Great War.

Me: What a great idea, Papa. I want to do an honor, I mean an honor…thing so I can get a citation just like you, Papa. You know what? I am going to get your shoes from the closet. And if they are not shined, I am going to clean them so you will look perfect for the Great War celebration.

Papa: Make sure to get me my army ones, not the ones with wing tips.

Me: I am going to help all the soldiers in the world my whole life because they go to the war place and fight to protect America, America the Beautiful.

— 4 —

Alex had to admit that lately he didn't feel his best. His jet black hair kept vivid by the coloring agent his hair stylist used had thinned, and his five-foot-ten-inch frame hollowed as his shoulders rounded, and he'd gained weight. Now his doctor told him he had dry eyes and drops would be needed daily to lubricate them. He exited the elevator and ambled slowly to his tenth floor corner apartment. It was past nine o'clock. He was hoping for a smooth entry into the apartment because he was tired and wanted to shower.

"Hey babe, what's up?" Alex spotted his wife seated at the end of the sofa; she was holding the TV remote in her right hand and her foot was twitching. He ignored the red flag and removed the brass stays from the collar points of his Pima cotton shirt. He hated when he forgot to do that because they would weld themselves to their slots after laundering and then poke into his neck. He took off his pinstriped charcoal jacket and placed it over his left arm and headed for the foyer.

"Where are you going, Mister? No kiss for the wife?" His wife's brown eyes narrowed when she was pissed. The woman was barely five-foot tall, but she had the longest legs. It was wondrous when she wrapped them around him but she was not above a quick leg butt to make a point.

"You got me, wonder woman; I'm coming over for my share." Alex moved to the sofa and gave his wife a short kiss on the lips.

"Is that the best you can do fella? Hey, you smell weird, like stale lavender. Where'd you eat tonight? There's leftover chicken in the kitchen if you're still hungry."

"Nah, I'm stuffed. After the seminar, a bunch of us went to a new French place in SoHo, Cuisine de Provence. Hey, Provence, isn't that where that smelly shrub, lavender, is grown?" Alex raised himself up from his wife who was fingering the remote.

"Yeah, yeah, lavender, dilly, dilly. So, how many Cape Cods did you have? How many of your customers tickled your follicles under the table?" She continued with her fingering but now the skin on her face seemed to stretch as if she'd been put on a quick-acting steroid.

"Come on, Stephie, it's been a long one, don't start anything, okay? Did something happen with your mom?"

"Did something happen with my mom? Did something happen…Alex; have you seen how she has been behaving lately? Have you forgotten about the appointment tomorrow?"

"Jesus, keep your voice down; she's probably at her door listening." The old lady hardly said a word to him in the many months she'd been under his roof. Quiet types worried Alex; they often had hidden agendas. He was never sure what went on between his wife and her mother after he left the house. Underhanded dealings were commonplace on Wall Street, but home and hearth were safety zones, never to be tampered with.

"I will not keep my voice down; she has a…"

"All right, all right, don't get out of whack. Everything will be fine after we get her placed." Alex felt relieved when he raised the issue of moving her mother to an assisted living facility. To his delight, Stephanie had agreed with him. He'd be glad when the new living arrangements were settled for the secretive lady. Stephanie could be a pain in the ass, demanding and volatile, but at least you knew what you were dealing with. Alex switched his jacket to his other hand and started for the bedroom.

"I don't know if this is really going to happen; she's so weird now. Hey, King Rat, where are you going?

"I'm going to lie down and then take a shower." He put his pinky finger in his ear in a grinding motion. "Geez, now I have wax in my ears. First the eyes, now the ears; the only thing left is the goddamned throat."

"You're a real fuckhead; you waltz in, smell like a souse, barely say hello with not a word about tomorrow, and now you announce you want to lie down and shower?" Stephanie reached for a Capri. "I think you should come with us tomorrow; Ma doesn't talk back to you. She doesn't talk back to anybody but me."

"Honey, tomorrow is Expiration day—you know I can't leave the office on Expiration day." Alex saw the light dim underneath his mother-in-law's door. "Stephanie, why don't you give up those damn cigarettes?"

"I'll give up cigarettes when you give up drinking and supervising those girlie trainees at your office."

"For Christ sake, most of the trainees are men."

"Well, maybe you're switching gears, changing your luck," Stephanie said, throwing the remote at her husband who, despite the fire in his eyes, said nothing.

– 5 –

Oh no, here it comes, the dream that nudges me more nights than I care to remember. Cousin Alice says we dream every night and that dreams are spiritual messages from underwater parts of yourself. I don't know about that. Perhaps this time I'll be able to fashion a meaning to the images tampering with my sleep.

I am walking alone in a desert-like area. It must be some-where in the southwest because there are saguaros everywhere. The earth is baked by a golden sun. I see a mesa in the distance standing alone on the plain. When I move closer, I spot a steep trail leading to the mesa's highest point. I decide to take the trail. I am sweating and out of breath and the corn on my right foot is sore. On the flat top I see a single structure, a Swiss-style chalet with a broad roof of rough cut lumber. Green shutters highlight stained glass windows. Coats of arms and shields adorn the sides of the chalet. On the front of the house, above the open doorway, is a large rectangular piece of lacquered wood. Printed in bright yellow letters it says: 'PLOT A PHOTO PERFECT FAMILY PICTURE PUZZLE.'

I feel compelled to enter as if an invisible hand has placed itself on the small of my back and nudged me forward. I find myself in a great hall with a high ceiling. I feel like I am expected in this place and this helps to calm me. I scan the hall. There are card tables evenly spaced throughout. The tables are adorned with tribal, southwestern-style tablecloths with turquoise fringe. The motifs are primitive, idealized and spiritual, like maybe they had once been hung in caves or adobes. At each table an adult and child are seated on pillowed chairs. There is a large puzzle board fastened down at the center of every table. The children are smiling and sounds of contentment fill the hall. I walk to its center and find a table which has been kept unoccupied, as if it has been prepared for me.

It comes to me what the children are doing. They are making a photo picture puzzle of an imagined family. The children look to be between the ages of four and eight. The adults, who are dressed plainly in khakis and silk short sleeve shirts, are not the children's parents. I realize they are photo pictorial programmers. They carry black school bags and I can see photo puzzle pieces edging from the tops of the bags with more strewn about the tablecloths. The pieces are photos of human body parts. There are ones of half and full torsos, and smaller ones of noses, arms, chests with and without hair. Other pieces exhibit parts of a contented environment, like tots in a playpen, children hugging, or stuffed animals lying on a screened porch waiting to be held.

One pictorial programmer has a rolodex of puzzle pieces and is flipping them for a young girl who studies them pensively as she glances back at the puzzle board centered on her table. They are of eyes: blue, brown, and hazel, each suggesting a happy countenance.

I feel like I am in a laboratory, perhaps a fertility clinic where an ideal family can be hatched. Can a photograph capture the resilience of a family, its health and spirit? Can it be captured in the crease line on a crown, the sheen on a strand of hair, the shape of a breast, or the size of a nostril?

I turn back to the table at the center of the hall; the one I presume is for me. Standing before me is a pictorial coach. This man, however, is not like the other adults. He is older with graceful features. His hair has a touch of silver and is freshly washed and flows to his shoulders. He wears a black gabardine suit tapered to accent his well-sculptured body. A white handkerchief is neatly arranged in his left breast pocket and a green ringneck parrot sits on his shoulder. From behind his back with his right hand he produces a yellow bud-sized vase and places it on the tribal tablecloth that adorns the table. Now from the left side he pulls out a miniature sunflower and places it in the vase. It fits perfectly.

I feel my consciousness begin to dissolve, like my external body is but a suit of clothes to be shed, leaving my innards exposed and vulnerable. Still, I do not feel frightened because this man has a peaceful manner.

The man with grace looks at me and his lips begin to move, gently, "It's your turn, Miss," he said. "It is your turn, angel of the universe." He beckons me forward, his fingers resting in the air. I am not sure what it is he wants me to do.

"What do you mean it's my turn?" I ask.

There is the longest pause. There's always a pause. Though I see a smile which shows me a handsome set of teeth, teeth never darkened with age nor from food or drink, he does not answer. He only nods as his parrot nuzzles closer to him.

– 6 –

Mama, Stephanie's been touting Wellington Gardens like it's a mecca for elders like me. She tells me about the activities there, daily stretching and exercise, the art and bridge classes, knitting and crocheting, and the trips to cultural events. Why there is even a choral group for Sunday service; God spare me that. I know Wellington Gardens might be a good place for some, but it's not for me. I do want to change things, mind you, but I want to be in love with the changes and I want to choose them myself.

Yes Mama, I've had enough regrets, but I don't want to add another one. What's that football term Charlie used to refer to when he watched his games? "Hey, wife," he'd say, "Did you see that; they're piling on." Well, no more piling on, I say.

Since my Charlie died, I've been keeping company with Cousin Alice. Mama, you should see her loft on Rivington Street. You enter into a long, pencil-shaped space. At one end, she has Chinese screens that close off her living quarters. The loft is a great place for her to sculpt. She only does faces. She tries to capture the subject's spirit, not just replicate the face. I believe Rembrandt tried to do that in his paintings.

I take the bus a couple of times a week to visit her. We walk up Second Avenue to one of the Polish restaurants for golabki. I told her I walk slowly now, but Alice says when you walk slowly you see more. She wears sweatpants and never uses make-up of any kind. She's going to Paris soon where she has a place for a month. She doesn't care for the traditional tourist spots. She'd rather stroll the curved walkways of Parc Monceau where you only meet locals, or look for bargains at neighborhood flea markets, or wander Pere Lachaise cemetery to honor the famous writers and musicians laid to rest there. I like her sensibility about matters.

Mama, I feel agitated right now. I feel my body shifting and my arms moving from side to side. What's happening…? It must be time for me to wake up. Goodbye Mama, goodbye for now. You look so good in that lemon chiffon dress, like a genuine lady.

– 7 –

Stephanie Richards knocked and pushed open the door of the bedroom. Her mother was lying on her back with eyes wide open and with arms folded behind her head. Stephanie noticed the woman's elbows, edged and pointed, and ready for movement. A cluster of silver hair stood high on the top part of her crown.

The room looked sparse today. A Japanese lithograph, the one her mother bought at the Washington Square Art Show, had been removed from the wall behind the poster bed. It portrayed a Japanese traveler with life belongings navigating a wobbly bamboo bridge between two mountainous terrains. 'Crossing the Frontier' was its title. Three large shopping bags lay in front of the walk-in closet to the right of the poster bed, her mother's orange and white walking shoes popping up from one of them. Enough already, Stephanie thought to herself.

"Ma, would you get up already? It's past 10:30 am. Alex left for work more than two hours ago. You went back to sleep on purpose, I know you did that, Ma, just because of our interview at Wellington Gardens."

"What do you know, Missy? An interview? Ha, that's a laugh. It's a fait accompli, Missy, that's what it is." Her mother continued to stare at the ceiling.

"Come on, Ma. You make it sound like you're a victim here."

"Victim, puppet, guinea pig, draftee, you bet. Anyway, would you shut the door please; I'll be out in a few minutes."

– 8 –

"Ma, you are driving me crazy here. You're staring at your food like I laced it with arsenic. I made you eggs over easy and cinnamon toast with your brown sugar. Wait, I'll get you more." Stephanie rose from the marble breakfast table and headed toward the corner cupboard where the brown sugar was stored.

"Lace and arsenic? I know about that, too. Stephanie. You must think of me as an old piece of lace, that I can't cut it anymore, that I can't wash and dress myself without your assistance?"

"Stop it, Ma, you know I don't think that. You're so sensitive these days."

"I've had second-hand lace all my life. I want soft, fancy, first-class fabric now, and only from premium shops. No more irregulars, Missy; you're not going to stop me from making a life."

"Stop you? Stop you? Ma, I don't want to stop you from doing anything. I just want you to make sense. I love you but you can't stay here. It was only temporary, remember, until we figured out a plan for you." Stephanie grabbed her cigarettes which lay next to the box of brown sugar.

"Well maybe I want my own place. Would that be okay with you, Missy girl?"

"All I know, Ma, is that you couldn't stay in that walk-up no matter how many memories the place held. The uneven stairs would have crippled you, for Christ's sake. Your own place? Daddy was no millionaire. At least at Wellington everything is included and we can help out. You'll be a cab ride away." Her fingers fluttered as she fumbled removing a Capri. She finally lit it, and took a full drag.

"I'm not going." Her mother picked at the punctured eggs with her fork and pushed the plate to the far end of the breakfast table.

"What do you mean, to the appointment today? You still have an hour and a half to ready yourself, which is plenty of time."

"Time? Maybe you've got plenty of time, not me, girlie. Anyway, I'm not going to Wellington Gardens."

"What do you mean, Ma, we are going, I insist. Just let's go and take a look, you promised, remember? We agreed no contracts would be signed. This was just to take a tour of the place after the meeting with the administrator, Miss Julian. Nurse Foster will be there, as well. You know her from your book club, right?

"For your information girl, Julie Foster will not be there, because she knows exactly how I feel."

"What? You never told me that. I don't believe you. No more trouble, Ma, I did this for you, you know." Her fingers continued to tremble, even with the cigarette, so she placed her right hand back on the corner cupboard to steady herself. She sensed victory was being seized from her.

"I am not going Stephanie. No, I am not."

"You're putting me and Alex in a difficult situation, you know that don't you?"

"I don't know that at all."

"So, where do you think you are going to live, Ma? Tell me that, will you?"

"I am going to live with Cousin Alice."

"So that's what you've been planning, eh? Well that flat-breasted old witch down in drug city in that rat infested piece of shit loft; why, she'll eat you up before dinner. She's just sweet-talking you, that fake feminist weasel."

"Maybe so, maybe not, Stephanie, but she's not going to arrange intakes at institutions that will all but do me in."

"Alice will do you in first. How did that chicken-livered fraud get to you? Intakes? Give me a break, Ma."

"It's outtakes that I want, like the ones they show you at the ends of movies where you see the actors having fun on the set, dancing, just being themselves, and not living in the skins of their characters. Can you understand that?"

"Pardon me, but Alice is not going to give you outtakes. You'll be lucky to get wet clay for breakfast from that do-gooder. Right now at this very moment, Ma, I understand nothing, nothing, do you hear?" She hardly noticed the tears running down her mother's cheeks.

"There's another thing, Stephanie."

"What now, Ma? Don't tell me you're going to take fencing lessons and then, for kicks, run a marathon?" Stephanie moved back to the breakfast table. She crushed her cigarette in the brass ashtray near the plate of the dead looking eggs.

"I might be uh…I might be going to Paris."

"Paris? Paris, Texas? I saw that lousy movie ages ago. Wait a minute here. Just wait a minute here, Ma. You don't really mean…Paris, France?"

∞

Master Step

It was ten to eight in the morning and Ritchie had already slept through two alarms. He kept his room dark by pulling the grey flannel blanket up to the crest of his head. Still, fragmented rays of dust-filled sun staked a claim at the foot of his bed. He opened his eyes, poked his head out and checked the crack at the top of the Venetian blind. The clouds appeared thin, fast moving, like a kite flying wild through the sky. They would give way to crisp, bountiful air. Ritchie knew that meant it was going to be a clear day, and he could do nothing to stop it.

It was early fall, 1955. The Brooklyn Dodgers had claimed their place, a week ago, as world champions. His father, with spittle running from his parched lips, told him to give thanks to Johnny Podres, who pitched a masterpiece in the seventh game of the series. Ritchie put his left hand inside his blue plaid pajama bottom. He mirrored Podres' left-handed pitching motion under his grey flannel dome, the high leg kick and the overhead, downward movement. Woosh, the batter swung late, hitting nothing but air.

'Stee-rike three, you're out,' the imagined ump said taking off his mask and wiping the sweat from his brow. Ritchie reminded himself to get Podres' baseball card and paste it on the wall above his bed with the other Dodger players. If he was lucky, he might meet the great man on a Brooklyn street and ask for an autograph. Many of the Dodger regulars—Pee Wee Reese, Carl Furillo, and Duke Snider lived in the borough. He was not sure about Jackie Robinson.

Maybe he was the only person in the world who did not feel good today. For a week the neighborhood had gone wild with street partying and dancing in honor of the homegrown team. Small groups of men gathered on porches and building stoops to laugh, hand slap, and congratulate each other. Men Ritchie had known for half his eleven years stood straighter and taller. Even mothers were taking time off from their housework to join the men in celebration of the special time.

"Hey, kid, dem bums put it to those Yankee stuck-ups," said Oscar Ross last week, opening the gate of his barbershop on Flatbush Avenue. People were becoming weird, Richie thought, because smiling eyes were pointed in his direction, forcing him to make sure he had not stained his pants.

From the safety of his flannel cover, he noticed the shadow made by his terry cloth robe shifting as a brilliant ray from the sun broke through the top of the Venetian, covering the square-shaped window. It looked like a vampire bat flying around a deep cave. Uncle Stanley told him bats leave their caves at night to drink blood from farm animals, like pigs and cows, but they were scared of humans. Ritchie was not so sure.

The familiar footsteps nearing his room belonged to his mother.

"Honey, I don't know what you are doing in there, everybody is up but you. Are you okay? Your father is already staying home today. I hope this is not going to be sickbay, I've got stuff to take care of."

Ritchie's brother Kevin, older by four years, dressed in beige khakis and a navy blue sweatshirt pushed past his mother at the door.

"Hey Ma, Ritchie's going to do the box step at school today in the dance class. It's going to be a co-ed class."

Ritchie was now out of bed, flushed and red faced, moving to where his brother stood with his mocking smile.

"*Shut up, shut up,* I am not," he screamed, lunging at Kevin, fists clenched.

"Now stop that," said his mother. "Let him alone. Kevin, I mean it; let him be." Turning to Ritchie her expression softened. He could tell because the wrinkles and lifelines on her face seemed to even out and her skin looked like fresh white paint in a round open can before it went on the wall.

"What's Kevin talking about, Ritchie? Are you going to have some kind of presentation at school? Are the parents supposed to be there?"

"Ma, it's just gym class. Nothing's going to happen. They are making us take dancing as part of gym this year. I hate it." Ritchie glanced back at Kevin who was twirling his New York Giant cap. The rotten traitor rooted for Durocher's team at the Polo Grounds. The Duke was better than Willie Mays, Ritchie was sure of that. "You're a stinking liar, Kevin. I hope you fall through a pothole and get stuck for a hundred days."

"Now that's enough, both of you. Kevin, get your stuff and get going. And you, Ritchie, get dressed. I don't want you missing breakfast again. This is getting to be a habit. Move it, mister!" Her comforting expression of a moment ago was ancient history.

Ritchie felt his thin, slender, four-foot ten inch frame sink, like it had entered a marsh of quicksand. He checked his wrists. They were so thin you could see bone popping and that worried him, like maybe he was a walking skeleton. In baseball, power was in the wrists. He learned that from the radio announcers and the older kids. Phil Rizzuto, the pint-sized shortstop for the Yankees? Well, he'd hit a couple of home runs, so he must have strong wrists.

He thought about the upcoming day's activity at the school gym. He scratched his scalp. Crusty stuff moved through his fingers. It was not the same as the cotton balls and boogies that came out of his bellybutton. He didn't want to move but then his mother returned from the living room. She had a kind-eyed look again, like when she gave out fresh baked brownies. Damn, he said to himself, here comes the gooey lecture.

"Listen, Ritchie, if there are going to be girls in your dance class, well, it's a natural course of events. Try to make it a bit of fun."

"Aw, mom, please."

"The day will be over soon enough, besides; those girls might be making the same kind of fuss you're making now. Who says they are going to like dancing with the boys?"

Ritchie felt partly assuaged. His mother's calm helped, even if she overdid things. She had blue eyes that sparkled and brownish hair with fine strands which flew around her cheeks. When she cleaned the house, she would put her hair in a ponytail.

Ritchie got out of his pajamas and started getting dressed. In the background he saw Kevin move by quickly. He was holding his middle finger up, by the left side of his Giant cap, next to his ear. My brother needs a knuckle sandwich, Ritchie said to himself. He would get him back big-time, maybe spit in his food, or hide his YMCA swimming meet trophy.

His mind shifted to his father who was, no doubt, snoring down the hall. He laughed recalling his mother's stretched face when she told him his father was like a termite in the wall searching for food. Ritchie enjoyed his father's presence. He longed to have his father's large frame envelop him, hold him. He would smell the pungent odors of his sweat mixed with after-shave lotion.

"Where's Daddy?" Ritchie asked.

"He's pretending to be sick so he can take a day off from work," said Kevin, coming back in view to press the needle further into his brother. Strands of chest hair could be seen at the top of his brother's blue sweatshirt. He was showing his tufts off. Ritchie knew that girls liked that kind of stuff.

"Go away, you moron. You're going to get it," Ritchie said.

The news of his father huddling in the back chamber was troubling. He might just be on the telephone with one of his friends to arrange a golf date later. He could never quite understand if his mother was bothered by this. Sometimes her eyes lost that shine when she and his father talked. It usually was about money for the house, or their strange friends. It was never about what movie to go to or where the family might vacation. And there were occasions when they raised their voices to one another. Once he saw his father push his mother back on the blue sofa. More often, though, they kissed and touched each other with their hands.

Ritchie wished he could delay his own day. He had an impulse to run to the creaky door to his parent's bedroom, interrupt his father with a firm push and say…

"Daddy, what if…what if they have something in school that you don't want to do? Could you write me a note or something?" They could then watch the news events on TV and his father could explain things to him, things he would need to know later on in life.

* * *

The odor of body sweat, enhanced by nervous chatter, hung heavy in the rectangular shaped school gymnasium. The ceilings at Highland Middle School were high with military looking rows of patterned florescent lighting. There was a dark, stone structure descending from the ceiling center, held in place by four steel beams. Students had various names for the odd-looking fan that circulated stale air: The Black Fannie, Frankenstein's Bat, The Overhead Silencer, and Moon Beam. Four windows, up top and vertical in design, were encased in grey metal gating. Their height, which mirrored the fan, left little room for fantasies of escape and adventure.

Ritchie tucked his shirt into his pants. He stood next to his best friend, Wayne Nelson, who was dressed in a green plaid shirt, green pants and socks.

"You look like a green pea pod, no, like the Green Giant man on TV," Ritchie said, managing a smile. "Maybe you can pee on Ginny if you get her to dance with," he added, as an afterthought.

"Very funny, wisenheimer," Wayne responded with a measured look. "Maybe you can make number two on Miss Donahue and she could call this dance off because the smell would poison everybody."

Miss Donahue and Mr. Gilliam, the two teachers, were conferring at the center of the gym. Donawho, as she was called by the more enlightened students, was the pear-shaped middle-aged Dean of Girls and sometime assistant to the school Principal, Miss Adeline Katz. She was also in charge of the Glee Club and assisted in the production of school plays. She wore sandals that revealed yellow-stained, thick, fungus-ridden toes, and colored blouses—purples, reds and oranges mixed together with wide puffed shoulders. To Ritchie, she looked like an overweight majorette. Davey Richards once said he looked up her skirt and that her underpants were orange. The image gave Ritchie the creeps. Worst of all were her perfume smells that never left the closed, airless classrooms. Boys, especially, knew to steer clear of Donahue because of her temper.

Mr. Gilliam was the gym teacher for the boys. He was young, six-feet or more, and physically fit with brown curly hair. It was his first year at the school, a rookie. Ritchie thought about the rookie third baseman of the New York Yankees, Andy Carey, who he first saw play two years ago. It was at a night game at Yankee Stadium; the lighting was awesome as it turned evening into day. The grass was a perfect green, with a dirt infield swept so even a player could slide on it and not get a raspberry on his thigh. And kids, not much older than Kevin, were allowed to sell Ballantine beer.

"Let the kid go to the game, we'll leave after the seventh inning," his father had told his worried mother.

Andy Carey had made three errors at third, two in one inning which cost the Yanks four runs. He was booed by the crowd.

"Rookie mistakes," his father had said, "They all gotta go through that." Ritchie felt sorry for the player whose head was bowed so much Ritchie thought it might hit the ground. He'd read an article about Carey in the *Daily Mirror*. The third baseman was a self-made man, a photographer, who had built his own boat. He was studying to be a stockbroker and was engaged to an actress, Lucy Marlowe. Carey was one of the players Elston Howard, the first Negro Yankee player, credited with helping him to adjust in his rookie year. Carey must have put his arm around Howard, just the way Pee Wee Reese did with Jackie Robinson.

Ritchie shifted his eyes back to his gym teacher, Mr. Gilliam. He watched the veins in his thick, hairy arms as they curved downward. Gilliam's mood was usually cheerful; he could laugh with the boys if someone said or did something funny, like crack a fart. He was good in basketball, volleyball, and even punchball. Still, he seemed different today; he was letting Donahue take the lead in the dance class.

Twenty-eight girls were on one side, standing shyly, giggling, and occasionally glancing towards the other side where twenty-two boys were sitting with heads down on benches close to the wall. That meant six girls would either have to sit out a dance or foxtrot with each other.

Ritchie glanced at the clock above the entrance to the gym. Forty more minutes and he would be out of there. His body tightened while his legs trembled. And he felt a racing pulse at the bottom of his stomach. He stared down at his yellow shirt. It was moving in and out.

"Listen up, everybody. I promise you it is not going to be that bad," Miss Donahue announced. There was some tense laughter. Some girls giggled. Ritchie choked when he realized that he, too, might burst out. That was the last thing he wanted.

"We are going to make two large circles. Each will have twenty-two people. Six girls will sit out at a time. The boys will have four different partners and the girls, three. The outside circle will rotate clockwise four times, like musical chairs, and when I stop the music, the person opposite you will be your partner for that dance. If it is the same partner, we will move one person clockwise and he or she will be become your partner. Does everybody understand? Remember, we will move clockwise."

There was a hushed silence until Sarah Purcell shouted, "What if you can't stand who you've been matched with?" Now everybody roared and the noise shook through the gymnasium hall. Ritchie was relieved that he could let his laughter out. It made his chest feel better.

"What makes you so special, Sarah big mouth?' said Andy Preston, starting off another explosion. Ritchie was amazed at Andy's brave response. He had to try that one day.

Mr. Gilliam, after a brief laugh, held up his hands motioning for students to be quiet.

"All right. All right. Calm down. I am certain everybody can contain their feelings in the interest of practicing the foxtrot. Just concentrate on your feet and tune into the beat of the music. You've had enough practice. This is the only time in your life that you are likely to have your dance partner selected for you." The class hushed. Thirty more minutes to go and if this was to be the only time in his life that his dance partner would be selected for him, well, that wasn't too bad after all, Ritchie decided.

The music began. It was from an old Victrola brought to class by the aforementioned Sarah Purcell. The song playing was, "In the Still of the Night" sung by the Five Satins.

In the still of the night
I held you
Held you tight
'Cause I love
Love you so
Promise I'll never
Let you go
In the still of the night.

It was not a perfect circle. Ritchie stared at Wayne. They each realized the links forming its edges were dissolving. Ritchie saw the uncertain looks of the white-faced boys and the more excited, joyful step of the girls. What did that mean? His face felt hot.

"Stop, everybody stop," said Miss Donahue. "Now greet your partner and I will start the music over. Remember what you've learned."

Ritchie looked up and saw a tall, somewhat awkward, but smiling girl. It was Susan Pitts.

"Hi Ritchie, I'm glad it's you," she said.

Ritchie's face turned crimson. He managed to nod, but said nothing. Why did it have to be Susan Pitts, he asked himself, feeling punished? Every girl in the class was taller than him but Susan Pitts towered over him the most. Her blond hair was strange, curly on top, and propped up, making her appear even taller. He was sure she would grow to six-feet. And she also weighed more than him. The music began again.

I remember
That night in May
The stars were bright above
I'll hope and I'll pray
To keep your precious love
Well before the light
Hold me again
With all of your might
In the still of the night
(In the still of the night)

Susan moved a step closer, putting her arm in position to be taken. Ritchie took her right hand with his left and placed three fingers timidly around her waist. He gazed at the floor and, watching his feet, moved his left foot forward the way he did in practice sessions. He followed with his right foot moving close to where his left foot had journeyed, and then, doing a wide right to almost full extension, he planted his shoe firmly onto the floor. His left foot came over to cuddle with the right one before that one had to move downward. His hands were wet with perspiration so he removed two of his fingers from Susan's hand which, to his surprise, had remained warm to his touch. Her blond hair glistened and her cheeks had a pinkish hue.

Ritchie took a peek at his partner's frame. She looked like a cocker spaniel standing up. Her curly hair moved across her face, pushed by a humid wind. She smelled like a flower, a daffodil maybe. It was a gentle essence, not like the pungent stink of Donahue. His mother liked daffodils. He maintained his repetitive movement, looking to his feet, hoping to make the perfect square step…the perfectly square box step.

"That was fun, Ritchie," Susan said as the song ended. "I liked doing that. Too bad we have to have other partners."

Ritchie looked up knowing he had to say something. "It was okay," he mumbled, nervously. He spied a small yellow chain around Susan's neck.

"Nice necklace," he blurted out.

"Thanks, my mom promised to buy me a ruby red heart pendant for my birthday; three more weeks to go. Do you like heart-shaped stuff?"

"I dunno, I guess so." His eyes shifted to Miss Donahue who was motioning to set up the circles again.

Eddie Fisher could be heard singing, "Oh My Papa." Ritchie had once seen him on television in his Army uniform. People liked him and it was said he had a powerful voice. He had some other troubles, he heard, but wasn't sure what that was about. The song had a pleasant melody.

Oh, my pa-pa, to me he was so wonderful.
Oh, my pa-pa, to me he was so good.
No one could be, so gentle and so lovable.
Oh, my pa-pa, he always understood.

Gone are the days when he could take me on his knee.
And with a smile he'd change my tears to laughter.

Oh, my pa-pa, so funny so adorable.
Always the clown so funny in his way.
Oh, my pa-pa, to me he was so wonderful.
Deep in my heart I miss him so today.

The music stopped and in front of him stood Frances White, a shorter, heavyset girl with braided hair that looked more like brown rope. She wore a white cotton shirt, with starched collar and a grey poodle skirt. The rumble of Donahue's directions could be heard in the background. The pause seemed forever, like waiting for an elevator door to open. Ritchie looked up, nodded.

"Hello," Frances said. In class, she sat on the other side of the room. Ritchie had little contact with her except once when they were together on a science committee doing a term report on electricity. All that stuff about friction, induction, moving electrons, magnetic fields; it was intriguing. Mr. Fox, the science teacher, had everybody hold hands and shot a mild current through them with a generator to show how electricity was conducted. What a strange feeling, to have current running through you as lightening might or maybe a shot of penicillin in the butt would from Doctor Madison at the clinic. Frances was tight-lipped, and serious-minded.

He was doing the box step as well as he could. Frances was slow to follow him. He put his left foot forward with a more confident step. Then, it happened. He took a long left foot stride and…

"Ouch, ouch, stop…, you got me on my toes. That is the second time you did that, Ritchie." Frances dropped her hands and reached for the bottom of her right foot.

"I did not, you didn't pull back," Ritchie said, red-faced, again.

"You're such a liar, Ritchie. You…you are the worst dancer here. Now you ruined the day for me. You broke my toe."

"I did not. I did not. You're a big fat liar." He felt stuck because his words only half represented what he was feeling.

He wanted to strangle her for play acting the victim and blaming him, just when he was beginning to feel okay. It was like hitting a home run and then being called out by an umpire for not touching first base.

Frances White sat herself on the cold gymnasium floor, first clutching her right toe and then folding her arms around her middle.

"What in the world is going on?" Miss Donahue said, turning the music down. The crack lines on her forehead widened and the blue makeup around her eyes caked and rose. She was bothered that her dance recital was being interrupted.

"Miss Donahue, look what Ritchie did!" Frances said, holding her skirt down and removing her calf-length white cotton sock and black patent shoe. "He meant to do that; he thinks it's funny."

Ritchie yelled, "No I did not! Frances turned her toe or something. She stepped on me, also." He did not look up.

Miss Donahue looked at Gilliam, but either did not see, or dismissed his body language which seemed to indicate that he wanted to speak. A river of red and blue crossed Donahue's craggy, over made-up face.

"Out, out of my classroom, both of you, now. You will not, I repeat, you will not interrupt my dance class. Anyone else want to go?" She scanned the gym. The only sound was the rotating motor of The Black Fannie, overhead.

"But Miss Donahue," Frances pleaded. "I didn't do anything. I couldn't follow Ritchie's feet; he was all over the place."

"No way! I was not, you…," Ritchie responded. He eyed Donahue as she moved to face him. She smelled like a rotting chicken sandwich. He was on fire inside, but he knew Donahue was more dangerous than Frances White. She was like one of the boulders in the 3D movie, "It Came From Outer Space," crashing through the screen, and coming so hard at you that you ducked under your seat.

"I do not know what you did, Mr. Ritchie Lerner, but you can just take yourself out of here. Go to the exit on your right and wait. Frances, if you are in pain somebody will assist you upstairs and take you to Nurse Jensen."

"Hey kids," Mr. Gilliam said, moving forward. "Come on, get back to your positions, and let's see if we can make a real circle this time. Miss Donahue, can I see you for a moment after you start the music?"

The north end stairwell, with its black, pock-ridden banisters, and sullen grey concrete steps, matched Ritchie's mood. He turned away from the half-windowed swinging gymnasium door. His arms stretched downward, with his left fist cocked next to his thigh. Then the door opened and Mr. Gilliam approached him. The music, though muted, could be heard in the background. It was another slow song.

"Hey, Ritchie, you all right?"

There was a silence. Ritchie pushed up just enough to shift an eye right, to catch a glimpse of Gilliam. The rookie guy was kind-eyed, but even if he never "lost it" like Donawho, he could still be a disciplinarian. He dressed the same every day: blue chino pants and a wrinkled white shirt. The back of his pant was shiny, like a polished table. His shirts had food stains. Once, when he raised his arms, there was a hole in the armpit area.

"Well that certainly was not the Ritchie Lerner I know in there. Would you mind if I, ah…I want to help," Gilliam continued.

"You can't help. Miss Donahue didn't give me a chance. I didn't step on Frances' toe. That girl is a stinking liar."

"Hold on, Ritchie. It doesn't matter who was at fault. You both behaved badly. Look, we have one more song round to go. I spoke to Miss Donahue. We want you to come back for it. Frances does, also. She did not have to see the nurse."

"No way, I am never going back in there. I'm not going dancing anymore, ever. Miss Donahue hates my guts." There was a new pause, but this time Ritchie kept his eyes on Mr. Gilliam.

"Ritchie, Miss Donahue doesn't hate you. I'm going to go out on a limb here; I think Miss Donahue did react a little too quickly to what happened between you and Frances White, but…"

"She did. She did. She's nuts." Ritchie pushed so hard on the stairway railing that he almost fell over.

"Wait, Ritchie, would you let me finish? I am only saying this to you to tell you that teachers are not perfect. They feel frustrated by things too, or maybe they sometimes wake up on the wrong side of the bed. But, they are still teachers and want to help you grow up."

"Miss Donahue is one of the stupidest teachers that ever lived. She hasn't taught me anything."

"Ritchie, being right does not justify any action that you might take afterwards. Miss Donahue is the authority here and for what it's worth, you and Frances overreacted, even if Miss Donahue did as well."

"So, what am I suppose to do, go back in and make a fool of myself?"

"You would not be making a fool of yourself. No, what I want you to do is after the music stops, come join the circle for the fourth song, without a fuss. Hold your head high, that way you can look over everybody, even Miss Donahue, who I assure you has other things to think about besides you. Otherwise, there will be consequences brought to you…"

"Like what?"

"Well for starters, this could affect your gym grade. Then, you might have to take the dance section over again. If you continue to show a bad attitude, we might have to bring your parents in to discuss the matter further."

"My parents? What do they have to do with this?" Ritchie all of a sudden felt betrayed.

"Ritchie, Ritchie, is all this really worth the trouble? Hey, I am going back now. We are going to have a five-minute break after the third song finishes. I will then tell everybody to resume the circle. That is your cue, that is, if you haven't already returned by then."

Ritchie stared at him. Was the raggedy-dressed Gilliam his savior or his tormenter? He resolved not to look at Donahue if he did return. He would be cautious, as if watching an approaching ocean wave from the wet, suds-filled sand, one foot ready to embrace it, the other poised to return to the safety of the umbrella shading the powerful sun.

His final partner, Debra Spencer, took the lead putting Ritchie's hand around her waist. She had played Dorothy in the school production of "The Wizard of Oz." Attendance at one of the four performances was mandatory. Debra loved being on the stage. She sang and danced like a professional. She knew how to put lipstick on and to rub red stuff on her cheeks to make them look rosy. The stage lights for Oz had made her face shine, even if there was an arc to her backside. Everybody knew she was headed for Music and Art High School. Andy Preston said he was going to put his hand on the seat of her chair in homeroom just before she sat down. Today, Debra's hair was in brown pigtails and her skirt short, revealing her fleshy knees. It was her powerful voice that made Ritchie wary of Debra Spencer.

Ritchie's methodical, over-practiced dance step was no match for Debra's graceful movement. His stomach was pumping again; his nervousness had returned. Debra was enjoying the moment at hand and somehow that made things worse. The Victrola was playing, "Why Do Fools Fall in Love" by The Teenagers.

Ooh-wah ooh-wah
Ooh-wah ooh-wah
Ooh-wah ooh-wah
Why do fools fall in love?

Why do birds sing so gay
And lovers await the break of day?
Why do they fall in love?
Why does the rain fall from up above?
Why do fools fall in love?
Why do they fall in love?

"C'mon Ritchie, this is the last record. I know you got screwed by Donahue, but don't take it out on me," she said, midway into the dance exercise. After a long silence, her expression turned more serious. She was staring at him now, and not letting it go. "You know Ritchie, you are not that bad. You just need a little practice. Hey, I wanted you to come out for the school play, remember? You told me you would, but you never showed up for tryouts. What happened?"

Ritchie felt a rush to his brain. For an instant he recalled pulling the flannel blanket over his head in the morning but, no, Debra was not going to get away with this.

"I never said that, you're such a liar." They were dancing but he pushed his hands out, away from her waist, to widen the space between them.

"Yes, you did. Anyway, did you know there is going to be another play before the end of the term? Miss Donahue wants to do, 'Seven Brides for Seven Brothers.' Wasn't that a great movie, did you see it?"

"No, I did not. I hate musicals," he said.

"You would be great as one of the brothers. It should be a lot of fun. Cait Stirling must like you; she wants you to tryout, also. Come after school on Friday to Miss Donahue's room, okay? After what she did to you today, she has to give you a part."

Ritchie's shoulders tightened when he thought of the evil witch Donawho staring down at him, but then, just as fast, they softened like a balloon losing its strength. Cait Stirling, who sits next to him in homeroom, said she wants him to tryout for the play? She said that?

"Ouch. Ritchie, you just bumped my knee. You are a real killer. Did you do that to annoy me?"

"I'll think about the play," he responded. He ignored her question. A year seemed to pass until the music ended. He noticed she was wearing a purple charm bracelet that sparkled on her right arm.

"Nice bracelet," he said.

* * *

The boys turned the corner onto Church Ave. in East Flatbush, heading south. Familiar shops lined the route—Dobson's New and Used Furniture, Stella's Bakery, Eastside Luncheonette, and Anthony's Shoe Repair. School was done for the day and pedestrians tried to avoid the hordes of students enjoying their release from structure.

"I got Miss Pretzel Face, Laura Winston, did you see that?" Wayne said, loosening his green plaid shirt so it relaxed around his green pants. "I felt her bony ribs leading her."

"You should have moved further down, Green Giant man, you would've hit pay dirt," Davey Richard said, his nose reddening like a shiny McIntosh.

"Why, who did you have? Oh, I remember, it was the blond bombshell, Virginia Watts; she will take your thing off and eat it for breakfast." Wayne laughed.

"Kevin calls her Dagmar, because she looks like that crazy blond on television," Ritchie pitched in.

"Hey, Ritchie," Wayne said, turning to his friend. "You had a fart-filled day. You shoulda laid one on Donawho, she certainly laid one on you. What's she got against you?"

"Me? What about what she did to you last week when you walked in late, without your paper?" Ritchie said, "She hates boys. I feel sorry for her husband, if she has one."

"Yeah, he has to do the cooking, otherwise he gets swallowed up," Davey added, regaining his composure. For a half block no one said anything. Ritchie remembered his mother telling him not to think about painful feelings too much, that it takes room away from the pleasurable ones.

"Why'd you come back in for the last dance?" Wayne said. "We saw Gilliam go after you; we thought your goose was cooked. So, what did he say to you?"

"Gilliam's an asshole...he gives you lectures like you are a four-year-old, like he knows everything. I decided to come back on my own. I wanted to see my friends."

"Yeah, yeah, like you give a Howdy Doody crap about us," Wayne said.

"Debra Spencer had hot eyes winking at you in the last dance, eh, Ritchie? She was talking up a storm." Davey said, rolling his hazel eyes upward.

"She did not. She just wants me to be in the next play, 'Seven Brides for Seven Brothers.' Tryouts are coming up."

"Well your shape is too skinny for the lead; they're looking for a Buster Crabbe or Johnny Weismuller type. You can't even swim," Wayne said.

"Me brain man, like Charlie Chan. You two fat boys? You number thirteen and fourteen sons." Ritchie said, pushing out his middle to imitate Chan's bulging waistline. The boys laughed, and then at the corner they broke off to their respective streets.

His left toe was cramping as he neared the gray stone building where his family had the second story floor-thru over Fasano's Deli. He bent over to massage the top of it, but the edge of pain only widened. Gilliam said that pain puts the body under stress but that the human body needs to be stressed sometimes, so it can perform at a higher level. Ritchie was familiar with body stress, the jumping bean feeling in the pit of his stomach and the lightheadedness he experienced standing in front of his class giving a book report or showing his homework. How could that stress be good for him?

He caught sight of his father rushing past Samson's Pharmacy at the end of the block. His father was long-legged and had a distinctive appearance. He had run track and field in high school. Curly, grayish hair crept out from the sides of his blue Dodger cap. His dad had paid top price for the official merchandise. "Never crap on excellence" he had said. He was getting into a car. It looked like Ralph Watson's old Ford.

"Daddy, Daddy, wait" The car screeched forward and took off. Ritchie hurried home.

"Hey, Ma, did you see Daddy getting in the car? Where's he going?"

"He is driving with Ralph and a couple of other guys to a construction site. Wayne's dad hurt his left leg on the job. He was struck by a cement mixer."

"Huh. Geez, I hope Mr. Nelson is okay."

"I think he'll be fine. He's got some contusions, you know, bruises. I am sure having friends around him will help."

"Is Daddy coming back for dinner?"

"Not tonight, sweetie, they'll probably all go to the lodge," said his mother heading to the kitchen.

"Hey, sweetpea," she hollered from the kitchen door. "How did the dance class go?"

"Good."

Ritchie reached for the Wiffle bat and ball in back of the front door. He thought of Jackie Robinson, the black man who, it seemed, everybody hated. Vince Scully and Red Barber who did the Dodger games on radio told stories about letters Robinson received at each stadium he played at, threatening his life. The other team's infielders put a hard tag on Robinson when he slid into second base. Pitchers threw at his head, but Robinson was defiant, standing face-to-face with those who tried to put him down.

He recreated Robinson's batting stance, right hand back with a firm grip on the handle of the yellow bat while his left held the soft plastic Wiffle ball. He tossed the ball high, almost to the twelve foot high crack-lined ceiling. He saw it good, the puffed red and white tanned creases as it began its descent. The ball reached the center of his hitting zone. The bat thrust forward meeting the ball at the sweet spot.

The ball flew in a straight line, over the pitcher's head into a fantasized centerfield. Now the ball began to rise as if it had a second wind. The Yankee centerfielder, Mickey Mantle, went back, eyes wide, trying to locate the ball, calculating how far his feet and legs would need to carry him. He traced the majestic flight of the red and white dart as it continued its propulsion. Mantle reached high with his brown Rawlings leather glove, eyes filled with concentration, desperate to complete his mission. And then, his motion calmed, his facial contortions replaced by a smooth undertow, with nerves and tendons in place. Mantle watched the ball fly over the advertisements and past the centerfield wall at Ebbets Field.

"Yes, yes, that ball is going, going, gone goodbye," Ritchie said in calm, measured tone, just the way Vince Scully did on the radio.

"What did you say?" his mother said returning to the living room holding a celery stalk in her right hand.

"Nothing, Ma."

"How many times do I have to tell you about playing ball in the living room? Look what you did to the Venetian blinds; do you see the curve in the upper one? You don't know your own power. One day you are going to break a window. I'm going to get plastic covering for my furniture."

"Okay, Ma, okay."

"Anyway, you didn't answer my question about the dance class today. Did you make out okay?"

"Yeah, it was fine." What a stupid question, did he make out? Where was Kevin?

* * *

The family's eating space was spare. There was an oak table and four cane chairs. Two more chairs flanked a corner cupboard that was filled with blue and white Wedgewood ceramic ware. Some of the platters had dragon-like figures that first scared but now intrigued Ritchie. A tree of life tapestry was on the opposite wall. The images of fruits and trees on it were like paintings he had seen with his class on the museum trips.

Dinner was early tonight. He thought about Wayne, how scared he must have been when he heard his father was injured. Approaching the table, Ritchie noticed the stack of salmon croquettes and the supply of mashed potatoes. Jellied cranberry was also there, which he would put on top of the croquettes.

"Wow, Ma. You never make these on weekday nights. Yummy," he said with delight.

His mother smiled in acknowledgement. "Yes, I do. You just don't notice."

Kevin was staring at him with a devil-like grin.

"So, how did it go today, little brother? Did you pick up any beauties on the dance floor?" Ritchie overlooked the provocation. He knew his mother would be giving Kevin a look. He reached for the jellied cranberry. He wouldn't leave anything for Kevin, if he could help it.

The issue of the dance exercise at school did not come up any further during dinner. Even his mother had been unusually reserved and respectful. The croquettes were heavy and he wondered if he would pass gas. If he had to, it would be on the sly, and next to where Kevin was sitting. His brother was reading the sports page of the *Daily Mirror*, checking the weekend football games. He knew Kevin was betting, which accounted for his weird moods. Guys he had never seen before were coming over to the house. He didn't think his mom knew about it. Weren't mothers supposed to know everything?

"Yo, Ma, Ritchie said he loved doing the box step today. He wants to take dancing lessons at Arthur Murray's. I tell ya Ma, the kid's got a secret girlfriend."

"Kevin, leave your brother be. What if he does, it's no business of yours. Don't you have homework to do, the both of you? I have had enough for one day."

"Ritchie, give Ma a break, tell her what happened today. I got the word on you, buddy boy. Cait Stirling's got a crush on you. Or is it Debra, sweet ass, Spencer? I don't know what either of them sees in you. I'm gonna send them to the eye doctor."

Ritchie lunged at Kevin throwing his fist at his brother's chest, knocking the newspaper from his hands.

"I hated that class. I hate dancing. You just shut up. Debra Spencer is not my girlfriend; you don't know anything. I'm telling on you."

When the tears came, he bolted to his room. He failed to hear his mother's voice admonishing Kevin. He would get Kevin back, and take the cut-outs from the *Daily Mirror* with Kevin's football picks and place them on the oak table, near his mother's Singer sewing machine. There were fifty-cent and dollar signs at the sides of the listed teams. Somebody should put a frog down Kevin's back.

* * *

Ritchie sat curled at the edge of his Captain's bed in darkness, save for the light from the reading lamp at the head, bolted to the wall. It was past eleven o'clock. His father had come home about a half-hour earlier. He heard the refrigerator door open and close. Ritchie felt bad that there would be no more jellied cranberry for him. He heard the muted voices of his parents. He hoped they would not argue.

It was late. Ritchie changed into his pajamas, and propped his pillow and moved under the grey flannel. What was that, he said to himself, as his right leg hit something bulky in the middle of the bed? Maybe his mother left another sheet from the wash under the blanket by mistake. But it didn't feel like a sheet; it made the noise of paper. Ritchie reached in and pulled, from halfway down the bed, a soft package. What in the…?

He started to open it and saw a tan tissue holding something in place. If his mother bought him a shirt and tie, he would scream; she was always doing things like that. She just didn't get it about the way his friends dressed. He removed the tissue paper and there before him was not the feared shirt and tie, but rather an authentic Rawlings Brooklyn Dodger jersey.

"Wow." And it was the newest one because on the arm there was a patch that said 1955 World Champions. He wondered what player number she bought. Perhaps it was his father who purchased the jersey. Anyway, for the number, he turned it to the back. It was number 45. Holy Moses, that was Johnny Podres' number, just the one he wanted, well, maybe Robinson's number 42 as well. He stood up on his mattress, raised his hands high and jumped as high as he could. He imagined touching the net underneath a basketball rim. He felt tall and powerful. Soon he would be way past five-feet. He took off his pajama top and put the Rawlings beauty on. Number 45 would be his pajama top until it started to smell.

It was after midnight now. He was under the cover of darkness. True, his body still had that electric feeling when his fingers felt the major league quality of his brand new jersey. But now his mind shifted to the day's events and other matters. He hated Debra Spencer for putting his hand on her waist and leading him in the dance exercise. He heard older guys describe certain girls as being ball-busters. He hated Miss Donahue because she'd embarrassed him in front of the class. He hated his father, sometimes, because he promised lots of things to him and then never delivered them. While he respected his mother, she was too protective and babied him. And then there was Kevin.

Ritchie repeated to himself what he had said to his brother. "I hated that class. I hate dancing." The air became still. He thought of Cait Stirling and her interest in, "Seven Brides for Seven Brothers." Oh my God, Lucy Marlowe, Andy Carey's wife, was in that movie; he remembered from the article in the *Mirror*. Marlowe played one of the brides, so she must be pretty. Maybe he would be in that stupid musical after all.

Cait Stirling was short with reddish, curly hair. She was freckled-faced, with dimples on each side of her face. Her parents were from Scotland. His ma had told him that Scottish lassies often had reddish/orange hair and were cute as buttons.

There were no shadows on the wall, now. His mind quieted and, in the calm, he recalled his father's spontaneous laughter as he read the fortune cookie that Friday night at Bill Lee's China Palace restaurant: *"You will never receive everything you wish for…but then again, maybe you will."*

His eyelids were heavy, but not like the waterlogged sponge feeling he'd had in his head at morning's light. It was more like the way his eyelids felt when he was resting after a warm bath.

৪০

Shep's Block

Medford Village, an eight block complex of high-rise cooperative apartments, has a population of five thousand. Its families are working-and middle-class, struggling to maintain that status. Federal subsidies ended in the last fiscal year and, as a result, amenities diminished for residents. Tenant committees formed to replace the twenty-four hour private security guards whose contracts were not renewed. Each residential unit was asked to provide a volunteer to serve four-hour, bi-weekly shifts with five others to guard entrances and report suspicious activities.

"Harvey, tell me you didn't ask Shep Stone to sit in for you tonight downstairs? The guy did it for you two weeks ago, and you didn't even reciprocate." Anne placed the last roller in her orange-tinged hair and turned on the super airflow dryer. She was a tall, plain woman with freckled arms. She eyed her husband of thirty-seven years posturing in his sleeveless undershirt that made an arc around his middle. He was unshaven and his white hair was wild.

"First of all, it's been four weeks, not two. I just spoke to him and he agreed to do it. I'm not going downstairs if Stan is there; that moron hogs the space and barks out orders like he's Dirty Harry."

"Would you just stop that? You guys with your egos. So take a chair and sit at the back entrance, what does it matter? I never understood what you had against Stan. Anyway, why take it out on Shep, after what he's been through."

"You want to know what I have against that bozo? First of all…"

"I can't hear you, Harvey."

"Could you please turn off that contraption? No, I mean it. You asked me a question. I'm going to give you the answer. TURN OFF THAT GODDAMN MACHINE!"

"What's gotten into you?" Anne's face flushed as she shut the dryer and eyed her husband. "Okay, you've got two minutes, and then I'm finishing my hair, if that's all right with you, my King."

"Very funny. You just don't care about these things. I'm trying to educate you; don't you see what's happening around here?"

"What I see is your supposed friend, Shep Stone, going through the motions. Have you seen his face? Sally Langer says he has the shingles and can't sleep at night."

"What are you talking about? He looks fine to me."

"If you'd stop yapping about nonsense, maybe you could find out if the blisters hurt and tell him to use Calamine lotion. Anyway, Stan Franklin, what's wrong with him? Enlighten me." She learned to go straight at her husband even if his brown eyes looked as if they would burst out of their sockets.

"Did you see that fuck in the hallway? I never saw anyone take in and put out so much garbage. He's polluting the trash area. The man goes around the neighborhood collecting things people leave outside: newspapers, clothes, boxes, small pieces of god-awful furniture that even a thrift shop wouldn't take."

"Big deal. Each to his own crappola."

"Maybe it's his wife who makes him do it. Boy that must be some marriage. In bed there must be a lot of 'trash' talk, heh heh. How'd you like that one, love?"

"That's awful. What do you care about his collecting habits? Somebody should look at your piles." She put her hand back on the dryer's power button, glaring at her husband.

"The guy's a pack rat, Anne, admit it. Isn't that a mental disease or something? Did you see the notes he leaves: 'Keep the compactor room door closed, contain your pets, carpet living room and bedroom floors.' Check out the suggestion box downstairs with the list of complaint numbers on top of it; that was his doing, right? I can't stand that phony. I'm going to put in an anonymous…hey, are you listening to me?"

"You know, I think you're losing your mind. So, what are you going to do about Shep?" Anne reached for the Kleenex box next to her to wipe the moisture from her nose.

"What do you mean?"

"Because of this, you had to ask Shep to take your shift tonight? Harvey, the man lost his wife. I think he's got trouble with his daughter as well. The guy's a sweetheart; he never says no to you. Invite him to dinner; he probably hasn't had a home cooked meal in months."

"What are you, his guardian angel? Look, it's good for Shep to do things, even the extra duty. Maybe he'll meet a lady from another building."

"Let the man grieve; he'll find a companion when he's ready. He's so thin and undernourished; I just wonder what's going on with him."

"Well, I'm trying to help him, too."

"Spare me. Listen, if you want me to be beautiful for tomorrow, let me finish my hair." She picked up a magazine as the super flow air dryer resumed its work.

— EVEN EARLIER —

Downstate Budget and Credit Counseling Service is in its fortieth year of operation but the counseling of credit rights and debt management has become a mainstream community service. Now several agencies have incorporated and vied for public and corporate support to offer services.

David Mitchell, Downstate's Executive Director, placed the phone down and folded his hands on his mahogany desk. He stared at the two Cezanne still life reproductions of fruit baskets and wine bottles to his left. Mitchell was clean shaven with smooth, alabaster cheeks. He prided himself on being exact in business and his wool worsted suits and wide ties added a dimension to his six-foot, lean frame. His black wing tips were buffed this morning at Buster's Shoe Cave in Grand Central.

Sitting on a green sofa opposite the desk was Rich Levitt, the agency's Associate Director. He noted his mentor's stiffening body language when he placed the receiver down.

"That was Livingstone; the news is bad. Government subsidies were down thirteen percent last quarter. The board wants me to come up with a plan to cut staff by eight, including a supervisor in the next thirty days. Rich, my boy, you can forget about bonuses at Christmas this year."

"You've got to be kidding, eight people? How the hell are we going to keep up with new referrals and our pilot programs?"

Levitt tried to dismiss any thought that he, too, might be in job jeopardy. He was aware of a moist sensation on the top of his forehead. His face flushed as fear rifled through him like buckshot.

"It's a buyer's paradise out there, Rich. It's a fucking irony that if you go broke in this life you'll have the pick of the litter as to who will keep the creditors off your back. And the customer is always right even if he's an arrogant, impulsive son of a bitch."

"Jesus, David, this is the worst I've ever seen it. So which supervisor do we drop, Shep Stone or John Thomas?"

"Aw, hell, man, we've got no choice now. Shep's got the most experience; he's loyal and takes on extra work without complaint and does the odds and ends that make life bearable here. But John has the law degree and the updated courses in accountancy. He's better at networking and his banking connections have brought in more clients. What do you think?"

"I agree, even if Shep's better with the clientele. He's folksy and personable with them; he doesn't lose cases once he gets their trust. He's been a little distracted since losing his wife. I think he may have money issues." Levitt uncrossed his legs, trying not to think of his own overspending habits.

"Welcome to the modern corporate world of greed and blood and guts, Rich. I never thought it would get to us. It's all about market share and how you look to the consumer. We've got to better our bottom line or we're history. John can get us new business; Shep is out."

– EARLIEST –

The Wrecking Station Bar is in the oldest part of the
Jersey Township, near the docks and commercial piers.
Two-story row houses line most blocks but there are others
that house rectangular shaped warehouses. There is Standard
Marble and Ceramic Tile, where countertops are custom cut,
Danny's Detailing and Tires, with stock for any car or van, and
Leonard's Public Storage Facility, holding wishes and lost
dreams. A large kennel with indoor and outdoor habitats sits
dockside.

The tavern's name originates from the auto salvage
business that operated fifty years ago at Bailey's Field, now
the Bailey Street Apartments. There have only been three
owners in the bar's existence, with Eddie George being the
present owner and manager.

Inside, Mickey Testa emptied his stein and placed it next
to the empty one on the uneven table. His fingertips pressed
on a dent he'd found in the middle of the oak wood. He was
not one to think about matters and today he'd spent too
much time thinking. It made his head ache and kept him in
an agitated mood. He knew he was impulsive, not caring a
whit about consequences. And he hated rules, as if they were
contrivances shaped against him. Three years in an adolescent
residence had only reinforced this view of the world. Family
Court remanded him to the residence. He was called a PINS
kid, a "Person In Need of Supervision." At more than six-feet,
square-shouldered with fully exercised biceps, firm waist, and
shaven head, he could stand up to anybody. He carried his
cigarettes under a tightly fitted green polo.

Testa watched Julie Stone, his girlfriend of ten months, as she moved toward him, head down, failing to respond to Eddie George's wave. She was five-foot on the nose. Not bad thought Testa, considering her pop, Shepherd Stone, was dwarf-like. She wore a pleated green skirt with a loose peach-colored blouse. Her golden brown hair glistened even in the depths of the dimly lit bar. She changed hairstyles often and the thought that she did it just for him turned him on. If she was a touch pale today maybe there had been a problem with her boss. Still, there was the outline of her luscious nipples as she took a breath and straightened when she saw him in the booth.

"Hello Mickey," she said in formal tone. "Get me a Genesee will ya? I see you had a couple already."

"Hey babycakes. I've been waiting for you the last hour. I got us your favorite booth; I'm gonna etch your name on it. Didn't you see Eddie waving at you?" Testa rose and with a swift movement cupped his girlfriend's face with his rough hands, knowing how women responded to them. He went for a kiss but she pushed him away with a 'not now' gesture. Why did women pull shit like that? To maintain his cool, he sauntered to the packed bar, waving his left hand to catch George's eye.

"Here's your Genesee, baby. They got it on tap tonight. I got us a pitcher."

"Mickey…Mickey, I…don't want a pitcher. I haven't eaten since breakfast. The meeting with Mr. Clayton's sales force went over and he wanted me to organize the inventory and shipping orders right away." Julie squeezed her hands together as if weaning perspiration from them. She took a swig of the beer.

"I ordered us a pizza, with sausage and peppers." Testa reached for the pitcher to replenish his mug. "Okay, Julie baby, I'm gonna ask you. Did you speak to your Pops last night?" Testa reached for her hand, which she allowed. He knew she needed a few more minutes to chill but he couldn't help himself.

"Honey, I thought about it a long time. I was too scared. I just couldn't do it. I'm sorry. I will tomorrow."

"Yeah, I know it's hard to do but my man's got to know by Friday. If I can't come up with the four thousand by then, the truck's gone. I told you I've already got five orders in the fall to deliver cords of wood in the Poconos."

"How do you know they won't change their minds? I mean, only five orders..."

"Look, I know every inch of land there; it's my home turf and I know these guys. I got big plans for this truck. I'm not gonna hang around here much longer. You know I'll pay your Pop back every red cent, you know that, don't you?"

"I know you would, honey. I do love you Mickey," Julie said in a softer tone, touching his left earlobe, caressing it. "Maybe we should just wait and keep saving. There'll be other trucks. What about your brother, can't he help you out? Cops make a good living now."

"My brother's an asshole. I'm the one that gets sent away while he continues the good life. He's a goody two-shoes, thinks he's Frank Serpico. The guy won't even take a free meal when it's offered. Julie, you gotta know this is a great deal. Don't take this away. I'll never get a deal like this again. Trust me on this."

"Suppose my father won't loan me the money? What would you do Mickey; would you still go to Pennsylvania?"

Julie stared straight at her lover's face, at the crisp lines that spread wide above his eyelashes.

"You would see a man reduced to a shell. I would be the lowest human being on earth. But, baby, I wouldn't go to Pennsylvania. I'd stay here with you. Your name ain't Stone for nothing; you're my rock."

"Aw, Mickey, what a sweet thing to say. I hope you mean that," Julie said, shifting her fingers from his earlobe to his craggy cheek. "Honey, would you do something else for me?"

"I would do anything for you, anything."

"Would you, ah, bring me flowers, sometime? I want red roses because they symbolize deep love. Don't ever get me yellow roses, because they mean jealousy; I don't want to ever feel that."

"You like flowers, baby? I'll get you truckloads with that moneymaker once we get on the move. Let's drink to our future."

She slid into his arms, kissing him, tasting his moist lips, experiencing in that moment a blissful surrender. Despite her fatigue, she danced the dance of secure presence. She would have his baby.

"Where's the pizza, I'm suddenly hungry. I'll speak to my father, tonight. There's just one thing I'm still scared of, Mickey. Remember, I told you that my Dad bailed me out when I wrote a bad check? What if he brings that up in my face?"

"Honey, he ain't gonna torture you about that no more."

"I don't think he has a lot of money. There was only a ten thousand dollar life insurance policy on my mother." Testa pulled Julie closer, stroking her golden brown hair.

"Babycakes, your Daddy could never refuse his one and only daughter. You're trying to make your life better, and

I'm here to make sure it happens. You just tell that Daddy of yours to keep a watch. In a year he'll have his money back, with interest. Little one, don't you take no for an answer." He reached for the pack of cigarettes held by the green polo.

— SOMEWHERE IN THE HERE AND NOW WITH A GLIMPSE OF THE FUTURE—

"Sheppie, honey, how can a round jelly apple head contain such a pin of a brain?," his wife used to remark before she passed a year ago. Shepherd J. Stone's head was, indeed, oversized and it was reddish with broken capillaries from too many ales. At five-foot three and a half, balding in the middle of his crown and with a stiff upper body, he might have gone eyeball to eyeball with Napoleon. His friends told him his hands were large, too large to stuff in his or anyone else's pockets. And his beautiful but problem-ridden daughter, Julie, would make matters worse when she'd call him "jelly apple dead" if he didn't respond to her.

Shepherd saw himself as grounded except when he went to purchase shoes, his left foot being a half-size larger than his right. He recalled the childhood game of Hop, Skip and Jump on the cracked pavements of Hoboken, when that foot landed just ahead of the right one on the pebbled stone. He could still hop and skip, but he knew he could no longer jump and that made him sad and grumpy.

It was a fall day, humid, with a threatening sky. Shepherd turned onto West Carson Place. The block looked the same today. Its most distinctive feature was at the far end, a copper beech with purple leaves. On the left were eleven brownstones, and a twelfth that was gray. All had cathedral windows and lined flower beds on their ledges. A rust-colored drain at mid-block was clogged today with fallen leaves, rendering the street vulnerable to overflow from a swift moving storm. The drain looked more like a beaver's canopy than a duct.

At eyes right were three stone-faced buildings, the eastern sun glancing off their metal sidings. There was St. Catherine's Elementary School, six stories high with rectangular windows. A year ago a mourning dove had made its nest on the fire escape, outside Room 424, near a heating pipe. Students checked the fire escape hoping for the mother dove's return.

Shepherd knew the nuns were in charge; he'd witnessed their stern routine many times. They would not tolerate any departure from the regimen of self-control required of students. Lunch recess was coming and the street's ordered space would lift like a majestic theatre curtain to bring forth the sights and sounds of children set free to play. Boys in dark rumpled pants and green St. Catherine polo shirts would gather to trade the latest gossip and to make after-school plans. Girls in green plaid skirts and crisp, starched white shirts with the school logo, a green salamander on the front collar, had their own meeting. They moved with a sprightly gait, being much more at ease than the boys, even as they shot furtive looks at them. All of this would make for a joyous interlude until the school bell rang and the nuns reappeared.

The other two structures were remarkable for their juxtaposition. Next to St. Catherine's was a red inlaid firehouse with sturdy occupants going about their drills. And next to this, at the end of the long block, opposite the copper beech, was the local police precinct. It was the only place in the city where the two uniformed departments, so often competitive, had the challenge of architecting a co-existence. Political commentary trumpeted it as a successful experiment in unity. Area residents knew there had been flare-ups, fisticuffs and drunken brawls that had gone unreported. The firehouse was large, domiciled in what had been an earlier era neighborhood center with a bathhouse. It held a ladder truck and a Big Red Fire Truck Slide which children could climb and slide down.

The police station was less impressive, a Victorian structure that retained the heat in summer despite the recent installation of ceiling fans in rooms. An assortment of petty thieves could be seen being brought in by overweight, sweaty officers, pushing them handcuffed down a side ramp to avoid the "civilian" population hovering at the main entrance. Shepherd was curious as to the happenings in the dungeon area. Was there a monastic cell at its core of the kind that the Count of Monte Cristo endured for many years? Was there a torture room? Were prisoners deprived of water, sleep, food, and toilet? Rumor had it that the dark shaded areas near the garage door were really the dried blood stains of Big Frank Lazarus, the only criminal to have escaped from the station.

Shepherd obsessed about all sorts of matters local, financial, and political; but it was ones of history that most fascinated him. How did Captain Edward Smith die as his ship, RMS Titanic, foundered off the Grand Banks of Newfoundland? Did he place a revolver in his mouth and fire or was he pushed into a life raft only to leap then into an ice-glazed sea? Was his act driven by unimaginable despair or of a fear of being charged with improper conduct? (Another ocean liner he commanded, RMS Olympic, had collided with a British warship, HMS Hawke, less than a year prior.) What if Pickett hadn't charged; would Gettysburg have had a different outcome? What if Alexander the Great had permitted his men to return home after two years of military campaigning to honor their wives with lapis beads and to be feted with succulent game flanked by wild pears, beechnuts, and dried figs? Would Alexander have been able to re-constitute his army and advance more successfully through India? And Tutankhamun, the boy king, may not have had a head injury after all. What killed him might have been nothing more than a virulent flu that compromised his youthful system.

Shepherd pulled his baseball cap down on his uneven crown. He'd resolved to wait as long as necessary for his opportunity. He was approaching his fifty-fourth birthday. His shoulders were beginning to round. Dark lines gave a ridge to his lower eyelashes. His nose was reddened from years of sun damage and his fingertips were puffed from inflammation. He pulled his black corduroy pants to his waist hoping to blend his shape to those around him. His maroon oxford shirt was poorly pressed and his sleeves were rolled to mid-arm. He looked up hoping to feel a faint sun but a nimbus blocked any potential warmth.

He reached into his pant pocket and felt the cold metal casing of the weapon that would serve his present need. He removed the prescription sun glasses from the breast pocket of the oxford and put them on making sure to maintain vigilance of the block's activity. Finally, he observed the man moving to the parked vehicles in front of the police stationhouse. Shepherd crouched and moved cautiously toward him. His movement was steady, forward, and without the possibility of reversal.

It was here at this personal passageway that Shepherd J. Stone stabbed Mickey Testa in the back of his left shoulder. He felt the knife breaking through the protective barrier of skin. He saw the young man's contorted and terror-stricken face. There was no time for Testa to turn his shock into a defensive response. And then Shepherd heard his own voice rise up from its prison of sand to shout to all who could hear: "fornicator, liar, cheater, manipulator, abuser, scum of the earth."

It was here, within steps of the police and fire stations, within steps of St. Catherine's, and by the watchful foliage of the copper beech with its purple leaves, that Shepherd J. Stone lost his freedom for one hundred and seventy-three days and one hundred and seventy-two nights.

Shepherd will learn later that Big Frank Lazarus was not the first to have escaped the police house, and that the dark brown stains near the garage door were not Big Frank's or anyone else's blood; they were discolorations made by a delivery truck that had misjudged the width of the entrance. He will learn that the dungeon at the bottom of the precinct was an invention in his mind. There would be no monastic cell, and no evidence that a Monte Cristo type had ever been shackled for years there. The interrogation room would be antiquated, crumbling, and malodorous, but he will be allowed the use of the toilet. A police sergeant will help Shepherd obtain legal counsel.

Even later, Shepherd will understand that drains, like the humans who built them, will get rusty and blocked from overuse and lack of proper maintenance. He will affirm that purple is his favorite color, the gift of the copper beech. He will search for African violets to adorn his bedroom. He will wait in line for seats in the Family Circle at the Metropolitan Opera. He will take a painting class for beginners at the Art Student's League. He will work again at Downstate Credit because John Thomas would suffer a massive heart attack. He will be informed that he can never again sit on the Tenant's Committee at Medford Village and he won't give a shit. But in the Tenant's Garden at Medford he will sit with his daughter Julie, who will visit weekly. She will listen to his revisionist history, but Shepherd will pause long enough to hear her takes on life. His lasting comfort will come when he remembers that an hour after his wife told him his brain was the size of a pin, she'd come up to him to tweak his bulbous, sun damaged nose with both her dimples showing.

None of this had given birth in the cerebral cortex of Shepherd J. Stone as he put the knife to the left shoulder of Mickey Testa. Finality came when Testa's brother, the rookie patrolman, who was just steps behind the two, wrestled the weapon from his brother's attacker, cutting the man's arm and hand in the process.

Now, as blood dripped from Shepherd's limb, he felt alive. He felt all there was to feel, the wetness under his armpits and the bunion on his left foot pressing against his black Florsheim shoe. He felt pubic hairs rubbing up against his abdomen. He felt his heart chamber pounding and he imagined blood percolating against its arterial walls. He noticed the key access to both sides of the handcuffs and felt the cold of the stainless steel.

Shepherd knew he would be cared for and that soothed him. Spittle formed at the side of his lip, and a tear hung on a lash, replacing the mask of nothingness that had stretched his skin. And with the soothing that opened each capillary to a gentle wind, came the realization that he no longer had to accede to the wishes of others. He no longer had to provide for his children, his neighbors, his colleagues. The aches of dismissal and disregard would be remembered but, for now, all his pain was on the outside instead of the inside. It was here that he lost his freedom but gained a measure of control.

⁊

Power Walk

have been power walking in the morning on the Central Park reservoir path a month now after deciding that the love handles puffing out of my middle aren't all they're cracked up to be. Used to be my ex would grab hold with her silky fingers, and fondle them like leftover down from an abandoned pillow factory. Her sweet ministrations turned nasty pretty quick. She ditched me for a doctor who practiced alternative medicine and had young hands that seared her core. The Zen bastard; let him take her to Tibet where she can have dirty water and the mountain cold. My doc, Winfield's his name, suggested the power walking. He's a skinny guy, even in his lab coat. He's an empiricist, who tells me of the latest health studies in the *Harvard Newsletter* and what I need to do to improve fitness. He maintains he is just following the red flags in my body chemistry, even if he seems more interested in managing his one-man professional corporation on Fifth Avenue.

"Jeremiah," he says to me, "you're approaching sixty, your body mass index is over the norm, you're on a statin, and you have muscle tension and headaches. You have a choice now: combine exercise with stillness or you are headed for a pill for hypertension, and maybe one for depression. Is that what you want?" He has a clear-eyed, neutral expression like he is God's scientific angel, not giving a flying fuck that I feel like a dog.

The stillness thing I didn't get. "Speed up and then slow down," he says, "that way your body can regulate itself. Remember 'homeostasis,' from your biology class?"

All I can think of is going to a health food store and buying a Caramel Nut Blast Balance Gold bar. Winfield wants me to change my routines, maybe do something unplanned, something I might look back on as a serendipitous experience. And at work he says I should take a period of quiet time in the afternoon.

"Close the door of your office; avoid taking messages for twenty minutes, and see what happens." I would lose my bonus, that's what would happen.

I settled on the power walking, doing twenty or thirty minutes at a shot every other day. I kept my mind on the promised prizes: fat loss, increased energy and endurance, and improved heart health. I imagined a calorie burning ceremony inside me, shirtless laborers gleefully heaving fat globules into a blazing flame.

If only I hadn't taken notice two weeks into my new wellness routine of the old, disheveled looking man at the entrance to the park. Doc Winfield would probably have said it was a good sign that I was distinguishing the environment around me, that it's the regulation of inner and outer vision that results in a harmonious state of being. Still, I wished I hadn't spotted the odd looking fellow who was there each morning I walked.

This morning the grey-haired geezer, in a stained sleeveless T-shirt, stands on a self-appointed patch of grass, stretching his hairy arms upward with thumbs clasped together. His blue sweatpants stop at mid-calf. His lips are cracked and curled with a scornful grin. He is broad-shouldered and looks to be in his late sixties. He wears old style black and white low-top sneakers. I can see varicose veins, ugly purple black rivers rising up above his ankles, as he wears no socks. There is a half-circle scar on his left cheekbone. He's known for bothering the runners and walkers, following them for a time, talking drivel to them and asking for change. Once I saw him trip a short, fat guy and then move away with the ease of a floating gazelle whose backward pointing horns cut a path in the breeze.

Holy Jesus Christ, today the old devil is eyeing me. Please, not now I say to the unfeeling God who is arranging this trial for me. I try to look away but before I know it, the man with the half-inch scar that looks like a sickle is next to me.

"Do you have a quarter, love bubbles?'

"Go to hell," I reply with all the bravado I can muster.

"Hey, moose man, run your own errands. How about a ten cent piece, then?" I say nothing. I know my face is flushing. I quicken my pace and roll my hands into fists, but he keeps up with me. I realize I'm rushing like I do at the office, but I want to stay on top here. I dismiss the idea of telling him to beat it again because even with my overstocked middle area and six foot height, I feel small next to this man. He is more stocky than tall and makes me think of James Cagney when he played Cody Jarrett in "White Heat." Jarrett was pint-sized, but a volatile and eccentric criminal who loved his mother.

"Well Dr. Strangelove, won't you give me a centavo, then? I need to buy groceries." He laughs mockingly as if I'm a source of amusement to him, yet he increases his speed as I do and stretches his stride when I stretch mine.

* * *

The grey-haired, semi-hermit man, Fenton Smith, lives under the 79th Street Boat Basin in Riverside Park aside the tracks where freight cars from the Hudson line creep up from Grand Central Terminal. The entry points to the Riverside Park tunnel are well known. Underground people seeking shelter had fashioned crawl spaces and loosened the bars on stone framed windows to slither through and form make-shift, earth-raked domiciles. Residents found ways to suck down electricity from up top park fixtures and retrieve water from leaky steam pipes. The cops are tolerant because of the squatters' nocturnal lifestyle.

Fenton Smith has lived the life of an invisible man there for three years. He places himself far away from the other troubled souls, particularly the addicts and crazies. His only companion is a sewer rat he keeps in a barren cage near his makeshift bunk. Other mole people were rumored to trap rodents, rabbits, and raccoons roasting them on a gridiron over a steady flame.

"The rat is the most affectionate of all the rodents," he often mutters to himself while holding his little consort and caressing its pale underside. "Yes sir…ee, it is a scientific fact they recognize you by the smell, that's why I keep Mr. Ratchet close to my follicles. The rat is a loyal being for life once they feel a hand warming em."

Nobody bothers Fenton, not even the younger transients, because he's quite unpredictable in his behavior—agitated, often waking others when he's startled or yelling and slapping at imaginary foes in his sleep. Added to this Fenton, although short, is wide-framed with an imperious chest and elephantine hands that once crushed an enemy's four fingers.

Every morning at exactly 8 o'clock, Fenton Smith walks to the West 90th Street park entrance and the 1.58 miles running track circumscribing the park's reservoir. The adjacent horse path is also paced by a myriad of would-be athletes and runners. Careful mothers push strollers housing buckled infants on both paths, with short bursts of speed. Other women, young professional types, run in small groups laughing contentedly. Fenton has noticed they do not check their timepieces as much as the men runners. The men, some bare-chested, run solo searching for admirers as they look to chart a personal best time.

"Them measly male berrypeckers are running marathons in their mind. Ha, ha, the Trojan boys ain't never gonna make it to the first water station."

Fenton Smith does not respect the young adults with their Ivy League educations, inherited money, and new-fangled machines. "Those goddamned computers, cell phones, and fancy organizers should be rounded up and pitched into a shallow grave. No radioactive rays, no brain cancer for me!"

Fenton is closing in on seventy years of age and though fortune hasn't shot a rainbow his way, he has pride. He was a linotype machine operator years ago in Wheeling, West Virginia but he had difficulty adapting to electronic typesetting that made the linotype machine into a museum piece.

"The boss people was spying on us with hidden cameras, thinking we was drinking," he tells others at the Boat Basin when he is of a mind to talk. "Fuck them capitalist cronies. I'll meet the cowards on their way to Satan's nest and break their bones one by one." A vein still thickens and pulsates on the right side of his forehead when he speaks of his old job.

Fenton lives now for the mornings to annoy and provoke the overseers of city life. He delights in stepping in front of their path, pushing them off-stride, engaging in menacing looks and asking them for bits of change. It doesn't matter that he'd have more luck finding coins in the telephone booths near the park. With sweet-assed women, it is shock and awe, taking out his rat from inside his top and feigning hurling it to them.

"Meet Mr. Ratchet, here. Ain't he cute, with his bumpy brown fur balls and tail?" The rat, having lost its warm cubbyhole and its host's fragrance, squeals like a shot pig.

Having been a runner it is easy, even at his age, for Fenton to keep up with the wannabe track and field champions. He sees how his antics, his quick step, body jerking, and shadowing raise his mark's anxiety. He relishes watching the quivering lips, fluttering eyelashes, and the beads of sweat that glisten on their creased cheeks in the cool of a spring morning.

* * *

The old guy, matching my speeding up and slowing down, feels like my Siamese twin. I feel my breath being stolen from me, and that my wits will soon follow. His hovering reminds me of the late night times when my ex would stare at me, her silk robe breaking at the middle, questioning an action of mine. Her eyebrows would raise and point to the heights and the moments of silence that followed felt like an eternity.

"Jeremiah, what did you do now?," she'd finally say, as if she was reading my mind like it was a tea leaf, and could taste with the tip of her tongue all my unpleasant notions. I would drop my head and admit to everything, and entreat her forgiveness.

So, as I continue my full-tilt power walking around the reservoir, I shift my stance when the grey-haired geezer repeats his request.

"C'mon sport, spot me a centavo. You look like a big spender." I just listen to his malicious laugh and note how he still keeps up with me, matching me stride for stride.

"Fella, you are one hell of a walker," I say. "Where'd you learn your technique?" I have no idea where this comes from, but when I ease my pace, my breath moderates.

A sweet sensation fills my nostrils and moves up through my head, almost lifting it from its base. I feel airborne, weightless, in a self-directed flight. I move past him and glance back to where the old geezer has stopped, glued to the ground with bent knees and a puzzled expression on his face.

* * *

The soft crusted, pear-shaped, power walking man had told him to go to hell when he asked for a quarter. Another swelled head, another fat baboon, thought Fenton. He'd seen the man's face redden and his footstep quicken, if ever so slightly. He saw how the man clenched his fingers into a fist and then, after a moment of hesitation, open them, dismissing the idea of becoming physical. He saw how the man's right knee had almost buckled as if his heart had missed a beat, but then saw his gait calming and the shoulders lower to reveal a gentle parallel between them, and the man turned and complimented him.

He started to reach for Mr. Ratchet from inside his blue sweatshirt where he huddled in a coarse gunny sack under his owner's armpit. Fenton was caught speechless, like a porcupine shorn of its quills. He stopped and soon the man was far ahead, his body moving in purposeful alignment. Beyond were Central Park South and the city skyline, the brick and glass structures vaulting majestically toward a full-bodied sun.

Fenton remained freeze-framed on the fertile track. The soft mud, shaped from the midnight drizzle and the morning mist, snaked its way up past his bare ankles while his mind raced for an explanation as to what had just occurred. Mr. Ratchet's squeal had a sinking quality. He flapped his eight inch tail, fidgeted and tried to use his forepaws and sixteen teeth to cut through the coarse hemp of the bag.

∞

The Garment Bag

figure I'm at the end of a dream because my bladder is full.
I'm sure to awaken soon so I can shower and get warm. It's
happened before, waking up from a forbidden place in an
ancient land and being pursued by someone out to do me in.
What the...my bladder is emptying. I move my left index finger
down the ruffled sheet. Strange, I don't feel wet. I imagine a
frown on my face and one of the nurses where I work staring
at me. "What's with you Andrew, are ya sick or something?"

Now I'm running fast like a sprinter. I know my nature is
to move fast but this feels different, like my mutton-sized legs
are encased in armor and being run by an unknown force.
There is no road beneath me, just wide plains without mesas,
and with only a few shrubs sprouting from the ground. The
wind is pushing me. I feel a tickling sensation from the patch
alopecia on my scalp. There is no soccer-shaped sun; someone
has taken the bulb from its socket and spread its glow over the
horizon. I need it turned back on me because a chill is creeping
down the small of my back.

I see movement in the distance, a low-flying shape skim-
ming the barren landscape pushing the wind aside. I pull to
a stop as the structure lands on the soft earth as a gull might
on a calm sea. I suppress a laugh because what's in front of
me looks like a rectangular shaped garment bag, perhaps the
size of a football field. Its frame is yellow velvet. It has no
engine and no arms or legs. Still, it advances towards me in

a steady manner. I can see its container is full because of the slow weaving motion of the yellow velvet. I wonder if there are people inside, carrying their belongings, their yens and hurts. I look for glass windows or air pockets; there are none.

I know I'm going to meet someone. I have no idea how I know this. "C'mon Andrew, stay alert here," I say out loud, snapping my thumb and middle finger.

I have a crazy idea. Maybe I should look for sheep grazing on the plains and count them. Mother said counting sheep will put you into restful slumber. Mother's been dead twenty years; a heart attack took her. I wish she was here to deal with the garment bag. I run left to its end and scan the plains; there are no sheep, no animals of any kind on them. I walk back and cross my legs and sit on a patch of earth with a few blades of grass pointing up. I'm thirsty, desperate for liquid to calm me. Crossing my large, leaden thighs is no easy task. I wonder how long I can remain in this position. I wait, shifting when I need to.

"What circumstances brought you here?" It is a familiar voice—deep, resolute, but tender in tone. It fills the air, like surround sound does in a movie theatre.

"Who me? Are you talking to me?" I realize how stupid this sounds. I pull myself up feeling a cramp in a calf muscle.

"What circumstances brought you here?" It feels like I'm in the exact middle of this surround sound.

"I don't understand. What do you mean circumstances?"

"It is not for you to understand. It will come to you. Breathe into your solar plexus and let it rise--through the back, neck, and crown."

I have it, now. I'm in a yoga class. I must be dreaming I am in a yoga class. Soon I'll be asked to do the Plow, the Cat, the

Stork and Bent Knee Bridge. But what did the voice mean when it said it is not for me to understand?

"There, I did a deep breath. So what comes next?"

"What comes next is irrelevant. You must recall the steps that brought you here."

"Do you want to hear my life story? Is that what you are asking for?" There's no answer. "Did I say something wrong?", I mutter in a low tone.

"A life can be told in hours, minutes, even seconds. It can be recalled in the journey here."

I'm quiet; the words have a philosophy I can't tune into. The chill in the small of my back is intensifying like a spreading body rash. I wonder what it's like to sit in front of the Dalai Lama in Lhasa, Tibet. Is his breath warm? Does he have a prayer rug pointing north? And does his voice envelop you like a heating pad?

"I can remember what happened yesterday. I could do that," I offer.

"Are those the circumstances that brought you here?"

"As a matter of fact, they are," I say, wanting now to contribute to the dialogue.

So, I take another full breath and I remember yesterday.

* * *

"Hey, Andrew," Nurse Jackson said. "The patient in 406A is being transferred to hospice care at St. Mary's. I want you to help with the driving; the hospice can't send an ambulet right now. The patient needs to be moved so we can open up the bed."

"Yes ma'am, I'll be right over," I said. "Will there be an ambulance available downstairs?"

"Yeah, it's a quiet day, except at the hospice. It's a slow day for healing, but a fit one for dying." That was the start of it, bossy Jackson, the cannon-breasted hussy telling me what to do like she always does.

I've been at Plymouth Community Hospital six years. I started as an aide, transporting patients and equipment, like blood pressure kits and EKG machines to different wards and pavilions. I pushed towels, linens, sterile gloves, and stethoscopes. I handed out satisfaction surveys to be completed by near comatose patients so the hospital could rate well. I fed the sickest and helped the docs restrain the most agitated, the ones remanded by the courts for psychiatric evaluation. I even took the patients who succumbed to the morgue in the basement of the hospital. I never liked the fixed stare of the dead. I kept thinking their eyeballs would fasten on me. And the smell was awful. One time, as I was about to shift a patient to a body bag, a doc ran up to me with panic in his eyes.

"Hold on, Andrew, let me take another look," placing his stethoscope on the man's chest. The doc's cheeks flushed, to the deep red of an apple. "Holy Jesus Christ. This man is not deceased. Wheel him back into ICU." Hey, that actually happened, made the front page of the town newspaper because the man's wife had been informed that her husband was dead. I felt bad for Doc Palmer. He was a good guy.

I went to Miss Sheri Lynn Anderson, who was a big shot counselor in the Human Resources Department, and told her I wanted to be an Emergency Medical Assistant. She arranged schooling for me; the hospital paid for most of it.

Miss Anderson is a brown-haired beauty, a single lady with gray eyes and a sheepish smile. She had a crush on me, thought I was some kind of a gentle giant.

I am big, maybe a touch heavy in the middle, but despite being forty-two years old, I'm still muscular in my six-foot-five-inch frame. I have the largest sized lab coat in the hospital. Three years ago I received my certification. I could now assist with triage of patients and transport them to facilities for further care. I had static strength, as my supervisor liked to say. I could use full force to lift, push, and pull. Loading stretchers in ambulances was easy for me, and I could tolerate the screams and protests from the patients. I always did my best to soothe them.

So I went down to the loading area on the ground floor near the emergency room entrance. Sure enough, there was an ambulance waiting for me. Short distance transfers were commonplace in the community. I called the fourth floor medical-surgical ward and told them I was ready to go.

"Is there anything I need to know about the patient?" I asked the voice on the phone.

"Not really. Patient's name is Emma Lincoln. She's eighty-seven years old and has been here twelve days. She was brought in with bedsores and went into septic shock. Her systems are shutting down. The social worker arranged the transfer to the hospice," said the voice. It was a soft voice I'd heard before, but I couldn't put a name to it.

"Does she have any family meeting us down here?"

"No, her only visitor here has been the home attendant. The old lady must have outlived everybody, poor thing. The attendant is a real sweetheart, very attached to the lady. She'd been on vacation for a month and the relief aides must've been negligent, keeping her in bed and not turning her; the whole thing is enough for a lawsuit, if you ask me."

"Is the lady still conscious?"

"In and out. She's a tough one, can't weigh much more than eighty pounds. She can really stare you down, though, and doesn't like anyone doing stuff for her. 'I will do for my own self,' she keeps saying when we attend to her."

"Sounds like you took a fancy to her. Who am I talking to?"

"This is Gillian Rose. I've seen you around, Andrew. I just started on med-surg; I was doing private duty before. Come, I'll do your job for a week and you do mine for one, that way we can refresh ourselves. God knows we need a break here."

I'm telling you this part because I made a note to go back and meet Gillian Rose.

I checked the ambulance the way a pilot would fine-tune his cockpit. There was a trauma kit, an oxysaver, cardiac monitor defibrillator, airway management and IV kit, suction unit, sphygmomanometer, and a radio. The scoop stretcher was intact. Most likely we wouldn't need that, because that was for a heavy load, like a patient more my size. I put my medical gloves on, as attendants were subject to asthma-like illnesses and skin breakouts.

I was trying to decide whether the twenty-minute trip to the hospice would require using the siren and the flashing red, blue, and white strobe lights. I sometimes broke protocol on that depending on the situation and the patient. I fancied myself a tailor doing only what the garment needed.

The service elevator opened and out came my load on a hospital stretcher, attended by Alvin, an aide I knew well. I'd taken the wheelchair out from the left rear of the ambulance so we would have more room to place the patient comfortably inside, on the ambulance stretcher. It worked well. Other than a nodding grunt from Alvin, and a knowing look to each other, nothing was said.

Miss Emma Lincoln was on IV and oxygen. The docs knew how to keep the patients level; at least that's how they looked on the outside. Hell, last time I went to my dentist for a cleaning, the hygienist wanted to smear novocaine on my gums so I wouldn't feel anything. I looked at her as if she was nuts.

Miss Lincoln was as described: small, thin-boned, and with a pigeon chest. Her cheeks, what were left of them, were red. Alvin saw me staring at her pink-hued face. "The home attendant put make-up on the woman. Weird, huh, going to a hospice with blush-on," he said.

I wanted to get a closer look at the woman who required a face of dignity as she prepared to meet her maker. I noticed pine needles of grayish hair sprouting on her upper lip. Spittle stains were on the linen sheet that covered her bottom half. Her breasts were flat and withered, and her Adam's apple above it, jutted out like a poniard. The home attendant must've tried to comb the lady's fine-strand white hair because it was neatly arranged in front. I could tell the woman had been bedridden for a long time. Her ankles and calves were so thinned they could pass for chicken bones.

What struck me most, just like Gillian Rose said, were the old lady's eyes. The lids were soft, cream colored, and even though she was semi-comatose, her eyes were half-opened and had a piercing quality. In the middle of placing her onto the stretcher in the ambulance they opened wider, and she looked directly at me. They were hazel colored and their balls moved, imperceptibly, as if she was trying to ask me what was happening to her. I understood she wanted to be an active participant in the events that were unfolding.

"Are you okay, Miss Lincoln?" I asked her. I was glad I used her name rather than calling her sweetie or dear. She said nothing. She just stared ahead, but the slight movement of the eyes to the right told me she'd heard my words. I signed the discharge papers, closed the back door and told Alvin I'd be back in under an hour.

* * *

I knew it could not be too comfortable for anyone confined to such a narrow stretcher, but for a dying patient likely in pain, well, it was beyond my ability to imagine. I decided to use the siren and the strobe lights. Make it quick I said to myself. It was late afternoon and traffic was sure to get heavy. I headed down Security Blvd. I didn't take the usual shortcuts to save time; I knew sharp turns would cause Miss Lincoln to shift, even if she was fastened tight. Still, it was a bumpy ride. The cars moved aside to let me through. A piece of cake, I thought.

"Turn that siren off. Turn it off." I thought it was a recorded voice, as crazy as that sounds. I took a quick look back.

"Was that you, Miss Lincoln?" I said. There was no response. Maybe the lady had taken a last gasp and kicked off. I turned the siren and the flashing lights off and pulled into a bus stop.

What happened next was so strange I'm afraid to tell you. At the bus stop everything around me stopped moving as if a movie projector had jammed. The steering wheel started to come out of its casing and my body rose up from the driver's seat, enough that I thought my head would hit the roof of the ambulance. I hung on, powerless to stop the shifting movement. I was midway between the driver and passenger seats. There was no support, not a handle of any kind to grab hold of. As if on a magician's prompt, I began to move back into the ambulance cabin. I was weightless. I was too afraid to turn around to see if Miss Lincoln was there or if she was still breathing.

The backward advance continued. Soon I was next to my patient who was to the left of me and in the low berth. When I was parallel to Miss Lincoln, her stretcher rose and widened like a hi-riser to make room for a mate. Finally, the movement ceased. I could see the traffic light out the front window had turned red. I thought about that fifties movie, *Invasion of the Body Snatchers*. Yes, that explained everything, an osmosis was occurring.

Miss Lincoln was lying beside me. She turned toward me. Her eyes were now full open. The first thing I noticed was her smell. It was a light scent, not the one of waste or decay. The red traffic light turned green and the cars and trucks moved ahead.

* * *

"I'm so glad you are next to me, mister. Could you come closer? I would really appreciate that."

I rolled my eyes. I felt a cracking sound in the back of my neck. The lady, the living corpse, was speaking to me in a clear and firm tone. My arched knees were shaking.

"Miss Lincoln, you just take it easy, I'm going to take care of everything," I said in a halting voice.

"I don't need you to take care of everything. I will take care of my own self. Come closer, I want to talk." Another woman wanting to talk, I mused, just when I needed to hide.

"Okay, Miss Lincoln. I'll move a little left, here." I grazed her right side. I could feel her hipbone. "Is this close enough, ma'am?"

"If that's the best you can do, that will be okay. You've got the leg of a primate, you know that?"

"Aw, Miss Lincoln, you must be feeling my thigh. That's where I get my strength from to lift people like you. Remember Lou Gehrig, the famous New York Yankee first baseman? He had huge thighs."

"Is he the one that died of that disease where your body caves in but you still have your mind?"

"Yes ma'am, until that disease came, he was called the Iron Man. He was just thirty-nine years old when he passed."

"What a shame. He never got to the heart of it all, except for baseball. I heard he was a momma's boy."

"I don't know about that, Miss Lincoln."

"Well, if he was, that's something he would've had to break."

"Miss Lincoln, my job is to get you over to St. Mary's. Are you hurting in any way?"

"What's the rush, I've got some more I want to do. Any pain I have is thanks to your driving. Did you hit every pothole on purpose to annoy me? And don't you give me any painkillers. I'll spit them out and anything else you try to give me, except maybe water."

"Hey, I'm not going to do that to you. I have water right here, though. And if you need more oxygen, I can…"

"Give me *more* oxygen? Haven't you got me on enough? Isn't that what they do in gambling places to keep you alive so you can lose more of your money, and humiliate you in the process? Maybe I will take a drink of water, my mouth is so dry. Are we in a sunny spot, here?

"Why there is some sun poking through, yes ma'am. Hold on tight, now." I noticed three women waiting for signs of their bus. I knew from their flapping arms and menacing eyes that they were spouting venom about the ambulance being parked at their bus shelter.

I found the bottle of water and poured some into a foam cup. I put my hand under the lady's neck, and propped her so she could meet the water moving toward her parched lips. I expected her to brush the cup from my hand telling me she'd do it herself but she must've made a deal that for the flow of nature's purest she'd accept a helping hand.

"Thank you, Andrew. Your name is Andrew, right?

"Yes ma'am, that's correct. How did you know that?" I replied.

"I can read, you know. I know lots of things. Have you a family, Andrew?"

"Ah, no ma'am, I've never been married. I have no family in the area."

"Are your parents alive?" I began to feel uneasy, like I was facing a supervisor.

"My father died when I was fifteen years old. He was a long haul truck driver. He fell asleep at the wheel and crashed into a gully."

"Oh, I am sorry. So, you were raised by…"

"I was raised by my mother. She died twenty years ago from heart disease."

"I see. You are a loner type, then."

"I've been told that before."

"There is nothing wrong with that if it is your true nature. It's wonderful to sense your nature, Andrew."

"I imagine it is, like knowing what seedlings are going to sprout even if you don't know what's in the package of seed when you spread them on the earth." I said.

"It might not be as difficult as that."

"Have you been married, Miss Lincoln, if I might ask?" A bus pulled wide of us and picked up the three busybodies.

"The nurses probably told you I had no visitors, except for Victoria, my home attendant. She's a Christian woman from Nigeria who lived in England before coming to America six years ago. I traveled many times to Great Britain on business. There is an English dessert fruit called the Victoria plum, which I love."

"I never heard of that one," I said.

"Oh my goodness, you have missed something sweet and juicy. Maybe you had it in a jam or a wine. Anyways, Victoria and I have an understanding. I call her a 'plum' when I like something she does. Mind you, I tested that woman and gave her a touch of Lucifer for a good year. But she sensed my nature and never did anything for me that I couldn't do for myself. Oh pardon me, you asked if I had ever been married?"

"I did, Miss Lincoln, but you don't have to talk about that if it causes you any discomfort."

"I bet you think I never had a holy matrimony. Most of the nurses were surprised to learn that I danced at the altar with a good man."

She was staring straight at me with rounded globe eyes that reminded me of marbles you collected as a kid. I took the lady for a loner, for sure. I couldn't imagine where the strength came from for her to talk like this.

"How long were you married, Miss Lincoln?"

"Well, Andrew, I married Mr. Courtney Lincoln when I was thirty-two years old, after I'd established my business."

"What kind of work did you do, ma'am,"

"Hats, ladies hats. I was a milliner. I designed hats for all occasions. I did church hats, rain hats, and dressy pillboxes. I wanted my ladies to walk with a confident step, proud to show themselves to the world."

"Did you design hats for big occasions like the Easter Parade or the Kentucky Derby?"

"Oh, absolutely, but I never cared much about those highfalutin functions. I liked it more when ladies wore my hats to celebrations for their achievements. I helped them to become full-bloomed, that's all that mattered to me."

"You have a good attitude about that, ma'am. Have you been a widow long?" Now her breathing appeared shallow, even if her conversation remained serious minded.

"Oh, I didn't finish about my marriage. Mr. Courtney Lincoln died twelve years ago from an aneurysm. We were married forty-three years. We were readying ourselves for a summer weekend in the Green Mountains of Vermont. We went to the same inn every year for the better part of twenty years. Last thing Mr. Lincoln said to me was 'Global warming is pushing more birds north. It's going to be a birdwatcher's field day up there, honey.' Then he went into our bedroom to finish his packing and keeled over."

"I'm sorry, Miss Lincoln." I started to reach over and cradle her face with my right hand, but I pulled back.

"Why be sorry, that's a wasted emotion. I had a chance to live with someone for forty-three years. We didn't always get along, but we were together through many difficult times. Everyone says the honeymoon is the sweetest time. I liked the other times, when you had to deal with money stuff, job layoffs, sickness, family squabbles, retirement, and then our aging when we both slowed down. Those tugs of war were the sweetest because there were hugs and rainbows waiting at the end of each of them."

"If you say so, Miss Lincoln. I know it's an awesome feeling when you see the arc of a rainbow after a rainstorm." I was sweating because of the humidity in the cabin. Miss Lincoln had a droplet of perspiration above her lip. I took a Kleenex and reached to wipe it off.

"Stop that," she said, pushing my hand away with a gathering force. Then, she looked wide-eyed at me for what seemed like two full minutes.

"Andrew, you were going to touch me before, weren't you?"

"Well, I don't know ma'am," I said.

"I want to touch you, Andrew. Can I do that? How about if I design a cap for you, maybe a Torero? I can mix the colors and make it unique."

"Miss Lincoln, maybe we should think about moving on now. Do you want some more water?"

"Men are in such a rush."

"It's just that we're expected at St. Mary's about now. I want to get you there so you can be more comfortable. I can't imagine it is agreeable for you here."

"There's nothing to do at St. Mary's but linger and wait. I need to smell the roses as long as I can, even if I have to smell the stink as well. I told you about one's nature, didn't I?"

"You did and I've been thinking about that, and how I run sometimes. The problem is I never know if it's toward something or away from it."

"Best to find that out, young man."

"How do you find out about stuff like that, Miss Lincoln?"

"Why you go into the core of the matter, Andrew, into the pus, into the stained liquid of the infected tissue. You set up a tent and live in the realm of the senses."

"You mean you have to live with things for a time?"

"Yes, until everything settles to where it's supposed to be. With enough practice you can learn to thrive in any temperature."

After a time, Miss Emma Lincoln said she was ready to resume the trip, admitting she was growing tired. It was strange, because I was the one that did not want to leave, like maybe our roles had reversed. She lifted the frailest hand I'd ever seen, beckoning for me to take it. I held the stained, sun-spotted, aged hand whose depleted fat cushion exposed the unsightly veins covering her fingers. But it was in our merged fingers that she conveyed a pathway to a shared hope. I hadn't had a feeling like that since I was five years old, opening my Christmas presents under a dressed-up tree at early dawn.

And then everything stopped again, everything but me that is. From the side view mirror I spotted a sparrow stuck in midair. The light at the intersection of Security Blvd. and Crossland Ave. was red again and pedestrians held stiff body postures crossing the avenue. My body began to shift, edging up from the hi-riser. The steering column came into view and

I grabbed hold of it. Once more I felt powerless, like a living puppet whose movements were being crafted by a hidden overseer. I managed to check my patient; her eyes were closed with hands clasped over her heart.

The slow, shifting movement continued. I was turning, and heading back to the driver's seat. I spotted my extra large white hospital coat on the passenger side. The steering column swung back as it veered left and then moved forward to merge into its casing. The seat belt was engaging and when I heard the metal click certifying my safety, my senses were restored.

When the light turned to green I began to drive again, pulling out of the bus stop. The sounds and sights of Security Blvd. in late afternoon came alive. A driver behind me honked his horn twice. Pretty gutsy to do that to an ambulance, but it got me going. I kept the sirens off. A dozen more blocks and we would be at the driveway of St. Mary's. I was sure there'd be a medical team waiting for us.

At the last light, an old station wagon was next to me with a female driver. In the backseat an infant secured in a car seat turned and with the fingers of his left hand pointed sideways at the ambulance as if asking his mother 'what's that?' An inquisitive little fellow, I thought to myself.

I made a final pass to check on my patient. I knew her work on Earth was finished. She couldn't control her passing though she was being active in her surrender. I wondered if there was a joy to that; I mean, was there bliss to be had in surrender?

I pulled the ambulance into the receiving end of the hospice where we were met by a doc and a nursing supervisor. Aides took care of the transfer to the hospital stretcher. I didn't have to do much, but I told them to be gentle.

I took hold of her hand again, not knowing what to expect. Her eyes were shut. The tops of her fingers were wrinkled, with tiny crevices. There must've been a lifetime in each crevice. Nonetheless, there was a return squeeze and it was a firm one. Was she saying farewell to me or conveying her fear of the journey ahead? I got an odd look from the nurse. I didn't care a whit about that.

I watched as the aides prepared to move her. I was parallel to her like I'd been in the ambulance cabin. A flake of caked-up rouge flew off her cheek. She must've been a good-looking woman in her time. Her foot had been briefly exposed during the transfer to what I knew would be her next to last bed. What a rounded arch it still had, like a crescent moon. I wondered if she might've been a dancer in her youth. If she was, she'd have to pick out the tune and her partner before gracing the dance floor. I burst out laughing. And then I laughed, again, for good measure.

* * *

I took Security Blvd. back uptown. I was late, so I put the siren and strobe lights back on. I found myself thinking about the hospice. I'd never actually seen the inside of the place. How many beds did it have? What did the rooms look like? Was there religious stuff on the walls? Did any of the patients rouse themselves and have a miracle recovery the docs couldn't explain?

I sped uptown, weaving through the thickening traffic. There was a yellow caution light at the intersection of Crossland Ave.; yes, it was there on the other side that I'd parked at the bus stop. I felt a little uneasy. The congestion looked heavy just ahead.

I gunned the accelerator just to be sure to get across. I wondered what Nurse Jackson would have me doing next when I reported in. If you asked me, with my new attitude, was I worried about that hussy who liked to control the world? Well, I would say to you everybody has to be worried about a person like that. I was halfway through the intersection when I saw the eighteen-wheeler on my left. It looked like half a football field. I imagined the truck's handsome engine with its twelve gears, the five axles, and the double wheels on each side. I checked the driver; he was pulling himself up from his seat and had a crazed expression on his face. And he was bearded. Jesus, God in heaven, the length of time to stop an eighteen wheeler is way greater than that to stop an automobile.

Darkness hovered like theatre lights just before being dimmed for the night. I heard the feint sound of an ambulance. The guys would need the scoop stretcher to get a safe fit because of my size. I was pierced bad…the levees on the islets of Langerhans ruptured. Everything was rupturing. Male menstrual blood…flowing everywhere, seeking fertile resting places. And then the darkness was complete.

* * *

"There they are; my circumstances you wanted to know about. Hey, were you responsible for removing the sun from its socket? I'm looking for light to warm me." One time I was on a tour of a dried-up coal mine outside Pittsburgh. The guide was an ex-miner. To show us what it was like to be in the dark, he had the wattage turned off in the dank cavern. It was a freaky feeling, like being in midair without a brace around you and none in view you could go to. "Do you know where the sun is hiding?" I say, with an edge.

There is no further surround sound. I decide not to put myself into a pleading position anymore. So I cross my arms around my belly. I am gaining confidence. I figure the more I go through here the easier it will be to adjust. I wait, but this time it feels like an active maneuver.

"Suppose your life is like being on a bridge." I feel powerful because I've made the voice that feels so familiar speak. "Suppose you find yourself standing mid-span on one. The banks on either side of the river are hidden by two great walls that rise a hundred feet. You look out over the water and in the distance you see a gentle waterfall and above it, a village. You can make out people moving about and appearing content. Luscious scents float over the river and reach your nostrils. The waterfall and village are in the exact mid-point of the bridge and of your vision. Which way do you move to travel there?"

"What do you mean?" I say.

"Well, do you exit the bridge right, or left? Forward or back? Do you even know which way is forward and which way is back? The water is rough and the distance to the waterfall and village is far."

"What is this, a riddle? A brainteaser? Hey, I'd look for signs of life, maybe footprints on the bridge." I like what I say.

"See, you have a possible answer right there. But what if it was a newly paved bridge that offered no such hints at all?"

"You know what? I'd run to one of the walls, doesn't matter which one, and I would look for grooves to climb it. I could make a hundred feet easy if I could find grooves."

"Now that is an interesting idea. You have more answers than you think. But what if the two walls were shiny, like a newly minted coin or a buffed floor?"

"You are putting roadblocks no matter what I come up with. There has to be a way." I'm not ready to be checkmated just yet I say to myself. I start to imagine timber guys in Oregon as they shimmy up trees.

"Well, you appear to have drive and resilience."

"You make up the all the questions and then play with my answers. That's not exactly a level playing field, you know."

"Who said life is fair? So, tell us what would you do on the bridge as the sweet scents of the good life pass over?"

"If all else fails, I'd jump from mid-span into the water, no matter the current. I would swim towards the village and use whatever the strength I have to reach the garden of the contented peoples. I would do my best and let the chips fall where they may."

There is a long period of silence. Then the monolith starts to rise like a majestic curtain might at an opera house. I try and protest the sudden departure but the only voice I hear is mine, as if it's the center of the world. I let my arms drop to my side. I do a quick stretch to open up my back. I look away from the rising garment bag and begin to run to the original point of my entry into this plain of nothingness. I notice the sun has been placed back into its socket. Its rays provide a path for me to follow.

I'm running fast, but not like a hundred-yard sprinter. It's a slower pace, better for me. I no longer feel encased in armor. My body is responding, lengthening, widening, growing, and opening. I know there's still danger around me but not enough to undermine the building strength I feel. I believe I'll be able to make it back, back to where I belong.

ॐ